A DEEPER SLEEP

ALSO BY DANA STABENOW

Blindfold Game

THE KATE SHUGAK SERIES

A Taint in the Blood

A Grave Denied

A Fine and Bitter Snow

The Singing of the Dead

Midnight Come Again

Hunter's Moon

Killing Grounds

Breakup

Blood Will Tell

Play with Fire

A Cold Blooded Business

Dead in the Water

A Fatal Thaw

A Cold Day for Murder

THE LIAM CAMPBELL SERIES

Better to Rest

Nothing Gold Can Stay

So Sure of Death

Fire and Ice

THE STAR SVENSDOTTER SERIES

Red Planet Sun

A Handful of Stars

Second Star

ANTHOLOGIES

Powers of Detection

Wild Crimes

Alaska Women Write

The Mysterious North

A DEEPER SLEEP

DANA STABENOW

ST. MARTIN'S MINOTAUR

NEW YORK

This is a work of fiction. All of the characters, organizations, and events portrayed in this novel are either products of the author's imagination or are used fictitiously.

www.minotaurbooks.com

Library of Congress Cataloging-in-Publication Data

Stabenow, Dana.

A deeper sleep : a Kate Shugak novel / Dana Stabenow.—1st ed.

p. cm.

ISBN-13: 978-0-312-34322-4

ISBN-10: 0-312-34322-1

1. Shugak, Kate (Fictitious character)—Fiction. 2. Women private investigators—Alaska—Fiction. 3. Alaska—Fiction.

PS3569.T1249 D44 2007

813'.54—dc22 2006052221

First Edition: January 2007

10 9 8 7 6 5 4 3 2 1

For
Gary and Jeanne Porter,
with thanks for the summer lease
so I could finish this book

ACKNOWLEDGMENTS

My thanks to Colonel Tom Anderson, retired, of the Alaska State Troopers and the Alaska State Trooper Museum, for letting me run barefoot through his files and back issues of the *Banner,* greatly aiding the plot of this novel.

My thanks to Rob Rosenwald, who taught Kate how to make French onion soup, even if she won't put the cognac in.

A wink and a nudge to Barbara Peters, who will remember a conversation we had concerning the story arc of the Kate Shugak series. I would like to point out that this book was written before that conversation, so there.

If you want to know what the Ahtna courthouse looks like, book a room at the Talkeetna Alaskan Lodge, from which I borrowed the decorating scheme.

And whether he likes it or not, my thanks to Captain Donal J. Ryan for helping me byzantine up the plot.

Death is a deeper sleep,
And I delight in sleep.
—Theodore Roethke, "Plaint"

Sec. 11.41.100. Murder in the First Degree

(a) A person commits the crime of murder in the first degree if

(1) with intent to cause the death of another person, the person

(A) causes the death of any person . . .

—Alaska statutes

She'd had to spell the word *weary* in a spelling bee in grade school. She'd spelled it correctly, but she'd never really understood what it meant, until now. It sounded like what it meant—there was a word for that, too, but she couldn't remember it—and she was weary, weary from the marrow of her bones out. If he would just let her sleep one night all the way through, if he would just let the old bruises heal before he gave her new ones, if she could just have one single moment in the day to think, to rest, to be.

At first his roughness had been exciting, from the very first time when his hands shackled her wrists over her head, his knees forcing hers wide, the foreign invasion so shocking, his eyes narrowed and intent, and then the rush of feeling that spread out and up in a searing flush that seemed to melt down to the base of her brain. He enjoyed making her body rise to his, she could see it in the triumph in his face. In those early days—how many months was it now?—when she had said no, he had always been able to seduce her into a yes, always.

Now he didn't even seem to hear the no.

She wondered when Ekaterina would come out to visit again. In spite of the old woman's obvious disapproval of her marriage, of her husband, which always provoked retaliation after she left, her visits offered a respite. He couldn't hit her when Ekaterina was there.

She'd been coming out more often lately. Maybe she'd come tomorrow.

Next to her the bed heaved and feet hit the floor. She lay unmoving, willing herself to disappear beneath the covers.

Maybe Ekaterina would come today.

He stripped the covers back. "You aren't asleep. Get up and get down to the creek."

When she didn't move as fast as he thought she ought to, he kicked her off the bed.

She thumped onto the floor and scrambled to her feet and scurried to the door. She reached for her parka.

"You don't need that," he said, handing her a bucket. "Get going. I want my coffee."

She slid into boots barefoot and opened the door of the cabin. She gasped when the bitter February air hit her lungs, and shivered in her nightgown.

A hard hand shoved her off the step. "Get a move on, you lazy bitch!"

She stumbled down the path to the creek. It was frozen over. She took the axe leaning against a nearby spruce and chopped a hole. She squatted over it, dipping the bucket into the clear, cold water beneath.

A sound made her look up, but she wasn't quick enough. Something hit the back of her head. In the seconds she had left, she felt a starburst of pain, and knew only an astonished relief that it was finally over.

A quick hand moved the bucket out of the way so that her head dropped through the hole she had chopped in the ice.

The soft splash when her face hit the water was the gentlest kiss she would ever receive.

ONE

JANUARY

Niniltna

This is just wrong, on so many levels, Jim thought.

For one thing, he was freezing his butt off. Even if the front of him was plenty warm.

For another, his boss might legitimately qualify his current activity as a colossal waste of Jim's time, not to mention the taxpayer's dollar. Crime had yet to be committed anywhere near or about his person.

If you didn't count the one he was about to commit if Kate kept rubbing up against him like that.

Her head was a very nice fit beneath his chin, even if her hair did tickle. She shifted again, and when he spoke, his voice was a little hoarse. "Are you sure you didn't get me out here under false pretenses, Shugak?"

He heard the smile in her voice when she replied, felt the warmth of her breath on his throat. "Well, since it seems crime is the only thing that makes my company tolerable to you, I figured I'd find some."

He disregarded what she said for what she meant. "I'm not afraid of you."

She tilted her head to meet his eyes. "I make you want to run away like a little girl."

"You do not." It sounded weak, even to him.

She leaned back against him, warm and firm from chest to knee, and dropped her voice to a whisper roughened by the scar that bisected her throat. "Say it again. And make me believe it."

He could have told her to step away. He could have pushed her away. He did not do either of those things, and the sound of the truck coming down the trail was the only thing that saved him.

And, sadly, Jim wasn't one bit happy when Kate's focus shifted, too.

It was an elderly blue Ford pickup minus tailgate and rear bumper, its passenger-side window replaced with an interwoven layer of duct tape, the body rusting out from the tires up. The engine, however, maintained a steady, confident rumble that indicated more beneath the peeling hood than met the eye.

The homeowner had dutifully cleared the requisite thirty feet of defensible space around her house in case of forest fires, which in this era of dramatic climatic change were inclined to hit interior Alaska early and often each spring. This and the winter's meager snowfall made it easy for the pickup to crunch through the thin layer of snow on the driveway and pull around to the back of the house, where half a dozen fifty-five-gallon drums rested in an upside-down pyramid on a solidly constructed two-by-four stand, connected to each other so that the fuel from the top drums ran down into the lower drums, with the bottom drum connected to the furnace in the house by an insulated length of copper tubing.

Kate and Jim had positioned themselves in a convenient stand of alders at the edge of the clearing, so they had a clear view of Willard Shugak as he got out of his truck, disconnected the copper tubing, connected a hose to the spigot, and began to siphon off the fuel in the drums on the stand to the black barrel tank in the back of his pickup.

Kate swore beneath her breath. Jim kept his arms around her so she'd shut up and stay put. When he judged that enough fuel had been transferred from the drums to the truck's tank to merit, at the $3.41 per gallon for diesel fuel he had last seen on an Ahtna pump, the definition of theft as provided for in the Alaska statutes, specifically 11.46.100, he said, "Shall we?" and turned her loose.

Willard looked up when they emerged from the alders. When he saw Kate, he went white and then red and then white again. "Oh shit," he said, his voice an insubstantial adolescent squeal that sounded odd coming out of the mouth of a forty-year-old man.

"At least," Kate said, boiling forward.

Willard Shugak was all of six feet tall, but he dodged around Jim, keeping the trooper between him and Kate. His voice went high enough to wake up bats. "No, Kate, wait, I—"

"You moron," Kate said, forgetting for the moment that Willard was almost exactly that, "what if Auntie Balasha came home to a cold house, her pipes all froze up?"

She reached for him and Willard backpedaled, stumbling and almost losing his balance, both hands up, palms out, in a placating gesture totally lost on its intended recipient. Jim watched, delaying official law enforcement action, mostly because he was enjoying the show.

"I wasn't going to take it all, honest I wasn't."

"You're not even out of oil," Kate said, cutting back around Jim and catching the cuff of Willard's jacket. "I went out to your place this morning and checked. You were going to sell it, weren't you, Willard?"

Willard yanked his arm free and darted back around Jim. "I would have paid Auntie back, honest I would!"

"Sure you would, you little weasel. Howie put you up to this because you were behind on the rent?" Kate feinted a move, Willard dodged back out of the way, and the Darth Vader action figure peeping out of his shirt pocket fell out and vanished into the churned-up snow.

Willard let out a cry of dismay. "Anakin!" He lumbered forward, his hands pawing wildly at the snow. Kate took advantage of his distraction and grabbed a handful of Willard's dirty blond hair to haul him upright.

"Ow! Kate! That hurts! Jim! Help!"

Jim had less than a second to revel in the sight of a man the size of Willard terrified by a woman the size of Kate before Mutt burst out of the undergrowth, mistook the attempted homicide for a game and romped around the three of them, barking madly while trying to catch the first available hem in her teeth.

At this point Jim, tired of feeling like base in a game of kick-the-can, grabbed Kate and Willard by the scruffs of their necks and held them apart as far as his arms would stretch. If he'd been an inch shorter, he wouldn't have been able to pull it off with near as much aplomb. "All right, you two, knock it off."

Kate kicked out with her right foot in reply, which would have connected in a meaningful way with Jim's left knee had he not moved it smartly out of range just in time. It threw him off balance, though, and Kate wriggled free and was on Willard before Jim could recover. She had Willard flat on the ground, her hands at Willard's throat and a knee in Willard's balls. Mutt divined that this was not a game after all and added her two cents' worth with snaps and snarls that came entirely too close to Willard's left ear for anyone's comfort. Willard was bawling, eyes squeezed shut, mouth wide open, face wet with a river of tears, shoulders shaking with big sloppy sobs. "I confess, I confess! Jesus, Jim, couldja please just arrest me? Please?"

"Oh, for God's sake." Kate let him go in disgust and rose to her feet, brushing snow from her pants. "Get up, you big baby. I didn't hurt you."

His eyes rolled toward Mutt, whose head was sunk beneath her shoulder blades, her impressive canines bared in a manner that could only be described as distinctly unfriendly. It was a sight made even scarier by the bloodstains and the ptarmigan feathers adhering to her muzzle, remnants of the lunch she had just finished in the next spruce copse over.

Kate made an impatient sound. "Mutt," she said.

"Graar," Mutt said to Willard, conveying a wealth of meaning in one syllable, and trotted more or less obediently to Kate's side, where she received a compensatory scratch behind her ears in lieu of bloodshed, always Mutt's preference.

Jim stretched out a hand to haul Willard to his feet for what they both sincerely hoped was the last time. Willard gulped down a sob, smeared tears and snot across his face with his shirtsleeve, and said in a plaintive voice, "Couldja guys help me find Anakin before we go to jail? Please?"

The state trooper building in Niniltna was so new, it squeaked. In a rare decision of foresight and wisdom, the state had built it on a five-acre lot next to the Niniltna Native Association building, whose authority rolled downhill to embrace the post and whose chairman, Billy Mike, was known to Park rats as a law-and-order kind of guy. The post was a solid structure, an unthreateningly bland beige square divided into fourths, a front office, Jim's office, an interview room, and the jail, two cells big enough for a bunk and a toilet each.

Willard, Anakin tucked safely back in his shirt pocket, scooted inside and turned to watch closely as Jim locked the cell door behind him. He wrapped his meaty hands around the bars and gave them a shake. The door trembled but held. He appeared reassured, and looked at Jim, his dark brown eyes still wide. They were set far apart, giving him a fey, elfin look. It was a look seen all too often in Bush Alaska. "Kate's crazy, Jim," he said.

"Tell me about it," Jim said.

"Yeah, I heard you got a thing going with her." Willard's expression approached something like awe. "Man. You must have some kinda death wish."

"Ain't got no thing," Jim said, and he might have closed the door to the cells a little more firmly than absolutely necessary.

Kate was pacing his office, fuming. Mutt had wedged herself into a corner, her tail tucked safely behind her and her front paws as far back as she could get them.

Kate rounded on Jim as he came in. "You're going to throw the book at him this time, Chopin."

Jim sat behind his desk, shoulders very square and correct. He turned on his computer and clicked on the icon that brought up the right form. "I'm going to charge him with theft in the third degree—"

He waited out the expected eruption and continued unhurriedly. "Theft in the third degree if the value of property is between fifty and five hundred dollars. Even at third degree I'm pushing the envelope here. I know Mac Devlin's charging three seventy-five a gallon for fuel oil, but I doubt if Willard was able to pump fifty gallons before you mugged him."

Kate called Willard's legitimacy into serious question and then started in on his friends.

Again, Jim waited her out. He was prepared to be patient, for two reasons. One, there was no Alaska statute for Crimes Against Auntie, which was what Kate really wanted Willard charged with.

Two, it had never done anyone a bit of good to try to match Kate Shugak in either volume or vituperation. The wisest course—he winced when she kicked one of the visitors' chairs across the room—was to wait her out.

The arm of the chair thudded into the wall. Kate glared at the resulting chip in the brand-new Sheetrock as if it were to blame. Into the gift of silence Jim said, "You know she won't press charges."

"She can decide that for herself when she gets back," Kate said with a snap.

Mutt decided that a mediating influence was called for and, albeit with some trepidation, positioned herself between the two combatants. She followed the conversation with her head, her tail wagging vigorously, as if this display of goodwill would put out the fire blazing up between her personal human and Mutt's favorite man.

"You know she won't, Kate," Jim said. "She'll shake her head and look like her heart is broken, and I'll feel like six different kinds of slime for delivering the bad news. Then she'll make me a cup of tea, and she won't forget I like honey in it, and then she'll sit down across from me and reminisce about how she babysat Willard's dad when he was little, and got a great set of pink-and-purple towels at Willard's paternal grandmother's potlatch, pink and purple, her favorite colors, and she's still using them, they're such good-quality towels, and what a lousy boat Willard crewed on last summer and how Alvin Kvasnikof never does pay off his crews at anything like what they're worth, and then she'll remember that bad girl Priscilla Ollestad, who broke Willard's heart when she married Cliff Moonin, and then—"

He could hear the rising exasperation in his voice and broke off. "She won't press charges."

Kate fetched the chair she had kicked across the room and sat down in it. She folded her arms and scowled. "And it's only a class A misdemeanor."

"That's all it is," he said. "And if all of that doesn't work, she'll say it was all her fault anyway because she couldn't get her daughter to stop drinking while she was carrying Willard."

Gloom settled in heavily over the room. Mutt's tail slowed. Comfort was needed. Jim was the love of her life, in spite of that human male thing he had going on, but Kate had time served. She laid her chin on Kate's knee and blinked up at her with a sympathetic expression, or as much sympathy as predatory yellow eyes could exude.

The phone rang, and it was a toss-up as to which of the three was more relieved. "Yeah?" Jim said into the receiver. His face hardened. "Thanks."

"What?"

He put the phone down. "Jury's come back, but it's so late, Singh is delaying hearing the verdict until the morning." He hesitated, but she'd been helpful to the investigation, with an eidetic memory of Deem's past offenses. Plus she was related to the victim somehow. She usually was. "I'll fly to Ahtna tomorrow morning. Wanna come?"

"Are you kidding?"

"Hey?" Willard's mournful howl was muffled by the intervening walls but perfectly understandable. "Um, I hate to bother you guys, but Anakin and me, we're kinda hungry?" A pause. "Maybe we could have a coupla those cookies I saw next to the coffeepot on the way in? And maybe we could have some coffee with them? Maybe with cream? And a couple three sugars? Anakin really likes his coffee sweet."

Jim closed his eyes and shook his head. "Willard Shugak could smell the filling on an Oreo cookie at a hundred yards." He got up, and Kate followed him to the outer office.

"Maggie, I'm outta here, and I won't be in tomorrow until late. Get Laurel to bring Willard some dinner, would you, please? He'll be staying with us for a few days."

Kate growled, mostly for show, and because she knew Willard was listening.

"Protective custody," Jim said.

Maggie gave Kate a wary look. "Got it, boss."

As Jim turned the Blazer around to head back to Kate's homestead, she said, "What's your prediction? On the verdict?"

The road was mostly bare, frozen gravel. "I heart global warming," Jim said, and eased up the Blazer to a steady forty miles an hour. "I stopped guessing jury verdicts after my first case, Kate."

"What happened on your first case?"

"First case that came to trial, I should have said." A bull moose sauntered out from the undergrowth and paused in the middle of the road, looking around with a distracted air, as if he were trying to remember where he had mislaid his rack. Jim tapped the brakes and flicked the headlights on bright and back again. The moose blinked at them bemusedly and then galumphed back into the undergrowth, embarrassed by his naked head.

Jim stepped cautiously on the gas, goosing her back up to speed. The Blazer rattled over the gravel base, and he had to raise his voice to be heard. "Perp and his best buddy pick up the victim on the road, try to get him to perform oral sex on them. When he won't, they shoot him nine times with a twenty-two. And then cut his throat just to be sure. Tossed the body in the city dump and hot-wired the dozer to run it over him a few times to mash him into the garbage.

"Vic was missing for four days before anyone noticed it, but amazingly enough, we had a witness who saw him get into the perp's truck, and at lineup could ID the driver and the passenger." He shrugged. "Eyewitnesses, you know . . ."

"Yeah. I know." In five and a half years as an investigator for the Anchorage district attorney's office, Kate knew that you could have five witnesses to a crime and come up with five different descriptions of the perp.

"But we found blood and hair matching the vic in the truck's cab."

"Excellent. And the gun?"

"No such luck, and of course the perp and his best bud denied everything. And then we caught a break, a bear rooting around in the dump uncovered what was left of the body when some guy was pitching out his old dishwasher. Plus, the best bud's girlfriend was mightily pissed off that we were suspecting her bright angel of anything as heinous as murder. It was all the perp's fault, she said, why were we even looking at his best bud, as the best bud got out of the car after the perp picked up the vic."

Kate silence was eloquent.

"Yeah, I know," Jim said, "nobody ever said jails are filled with smart people, and why should anybody they hang out with be any smarter? I—persuaded—the best bud to turn state's evidence."

"Excellent," Kate said again.

"Yeah."

"But."

"But." Jim sighed. "He wasn't real convincing, and he had a rap sheet it took a whole ream of paper to print out. Jury didn't believe a word he said. Hell, I didn't believe a word he said, and I knew it was all true. Well. Mostly true."

"And the perp?"

"The perp says he was out of town at the time. Real sincere on the stand, as I recall, young and clean-cut and all his family in the courtroom, including his Miss Alaska fiancée."

"Please tell me you're kidding."

"I would if I could. She spent the whole trial trying to hold hands with him over the divider."

"What happened?"

"The third time the judge told her to stop holding hands with the defendant, he raised his voice, and she burst into tears. You should have seen the jury, you'd have thought he'd just shot their pet cat."

"Not guilty?"

"Not guilty." He sighed again. "The case was mostly circumstantial anyway. As I recall it, Brendan—"

"Brendan McCord was prosecuting?"

"Yeah. One of his first cases. He was good, even fresh out of law school. Brendan said a member of the jury came up to him after the verdict and scolded him for harassing that nice young man and putting his fiancée through such a terrible ordeal."

Kate had also seen the inside of her share of courtrooms, and she had very few illusions left about the wheels of justice. "What happened to the perp?"

Jim brightened a little. "Six months later, he accompanied his fiancée to the Miss America pageant in Dallas and shot a cabdriver during a robbery. He is currently enjoying the hospitality of the state of Texas at Huntsville. One of four hundred and ten on death row, last time I checked."

Kate wondered what had happened to the fiancée, and the perp's family. She always wondered what happened to the rest of the victims. It was one of the reasons she'd left the DA's office.

"So," Jim said, "I don't predict verdicts. The game is rigged, all right, but in this case the house doesn't win often enough. It's discouraging enough without letting your hopes ride on it, too."

What little snow had fallen that winter had melted off in a four-day chinook that was the lump of coal in the Park's stocking the week of Christmas. At five thirty in the afternoon, it had already been dark for an hour and a half and with nothing to reflect what light there was, anything beyond the reach of the Blazer's headlights looked like a black hole. The good news was that the road was drivable at all. It wasn't maintained in winter and normally became a snow machine track from October to May, but not this year.

Kate peered up at the sky. "Lights'll be out tonight, I bet."

"Yeah." He didn't bother looking at the stars; he was watching for the next moose. "Ever thought about getting a telescope?"

"Binoculars work."

"Yeah." He was silent for a moment. "In high school my junior class drove to Tucson and visited the planetarium at the University of Arizona. They had it pointed right at the Orion nebula. It was amazing, like this huge pink and purple star had exploded right across the sky."

She checked the exterior temperature readout. Thirteen below. The red digital three changed to a four as she watched. "Couldn't stay out very long to look, it'd be too cold."

"That's why God invented Carhartts."

She laughed, a low husk of sound that transported him instantly back to the moments in the clearing that afternoon, waiting without enthusiasm for Willard to show.

Fortunately, Mutt was sitting between them. And if Mutt failed, there was always the shotgun bolted to the dash. Although Jim wasn't entirely sure shotguns worked on witches.

They passed a Suburban going in the opposite direction. It was easily identified, bright orange with the left front fender missing and the right front fender caved into the wheel well, hanging on through sheer force of will.

"Howie Katelnikof, headed to Bernie's," Jim said.

"Probably thinking he's going to find Willard there," Kate said, not without satisfaction. "And probably got a customer waiting for Auntie Balasha's fuel oil."

Jim thought she was probably right about that. "Howie should choose his roommates more carefully."

They thought about Howie's other roommate, which naturally led them to think about the murder trial under way in Ahtna, now before the jury. "All of the evidence was circumstantial." She remembered the story about Jim's first trial. "Again."

He turned to look at her but Mutt was in the way, and it was too dark to see her expression anyway. "Louis Deem's a wrong guy, Kate."

"You haven't been around the Park long enough to know how wrong," Kate said. "Louis Deem was broken before he was born."

"Why didn't you do something?" Because as had every practicing police officer who had ever served the cause of justice in the Park, he knew doing something was what Kate did best.

Kate remembered the time she had tried to. "You assume it was up to me."

Jim thought this over. It didn't take him long. "Ekaterina?"

"Emaa was his godmother."

Jim snorted. Half his time on the job was spent disentangling the lies one Park rat told to alibi another because they were second cousins twice removed.

"Yeah, I know," she said, not very apologetically, "but it mostly works for us."

"Not this time."

She shifted in her seat and craned her head to peer through the window, still looking for the northern lights. "No. Not this time."

"So your grandmother ran interference whenever Louis got in trouble?"

Kate had heard all the stories from her aunties about Emaa and

Louis Deem's first two wives. Ekaterina Shugak had made a point of, at minimum, weekly post-marriage visits to both Jessie and Ruthie. If Kate knew her grandmother, those visits had included the offer (when Louis was out of the room, of course) of a spare room in Emaa's tumbledown, riverside house in Niniltna the moment either one of them wanted to pack it in.

One day in the Park during an August vacation from her job in Anchorage, Kate had driven out with her grandmother to see Ruthie. Ruthie, not yet out of her teens, moved like she was twenty years older than Ekaterina.

Jim took Kate's silence as assent. "When did that start? When he got caught running for that bootlegger, what was his name?"

"Sandy Halvorsen, and I think it started when Louis was in grade school and he used to beat up the other kids and steal their lunches. The teachers learned that the best they could do was give him detention, and even then I remember one time he talked Robby Kanaback into bringing him a candy bar into the detention room and then he beat him up for the hell of it. He was a miserable little shit then and he's a miserable little shit now."

"I hear his parents sucked."

"They were drunks and dopers, and Louis was an accident Daisy couldn't get rid of, although the story is she tried hard enough. Wesley drowned in the Cordova small-boat harbor the year Louis was fifteen. Louis pretty much raised himself."

"And I bet Mary Waterbury's parents think he did a hell of a job."

There was no answer to that and Kate attempted none.

Little Mary Waterbury, brown as a nut and round as a ball. Homely, cheerful, kind to children and animals, born to be a mother, and so very young. Twenty-one years younger than Louis Deem, her first boyfriend.

And her last. *Why didn't you do something?* Jim had asked. She had tried. She thought again of Mary Waterbury, that young hopeful life brought to a sudden and violent halt at the hands of a man who had pretty much perfected the art of ridding himself of unwanted wives.

Yes, she had tried, Kate thought now, but she hadn't tried hard enough.

The rest of the journey was accomplished in silence. Twenty-five miles from Niniltna, they turned down the narrow rutted track that led to Kate's homestead. Jim stopped the Blazer in the center of the flood of light pouring out of the tall windows that ran across the prow front of Kate's house.

Her house. It still seemed so odd to come home to a whole house, all two floors and two bedrooms and two bathrooms and hand-carved pine dining set of it. To have so much room, to have hot running water instead of hand-pumped cold, to take a hot shower instead of a snowmelt bath in a galvanized round steel tub, to be able to keep half and half in the refrigerator instead of it freezing up in a cooler on the porch, and most miraculous of all, to be able to get up in the middle of the night to use a real live flush toilet ten steps from her bed instead of fumbling around in the dark for her boots and parka and traipsing outside to the outhouse—it still seemed too much, and she still felt unworthy of the gift the Park had so generously given her.

She had learned the hard way not to say so, however.

She opened the door of the truck, and Mutt leapt over her in a graceful gray arc. She landed easily and loped into the brush at the edge of the clearing and to all intents and purposes vanished. Kate looked at Jim. "Want to stay for dinner?"

He was tempted, as he'd missed dinner at Auntie Vi's, where he was renting a room until he found a place of his own—which in Niniltna wasn't going to be easy, inexpensive, or any time soon.

On the other hand, he knew there was a better-than-even

chance that dinner wasn't the only thing on offer in this invitation. At least the lights on inside the house meant that Johnny was home, so he would be chaperoned. He ought to be safe.

"Sure."

He followed her inside, where they shed their coats and boots at the door and padded forward on stocking feet. Johnny was stretched out on the couch, so engrossed in a book that he didn't hear them come in. Jim walked over and pushed the book up so he could read the title. "*Reflex*," he said. "Any good?"

Two years into adolescence, Johnny's towhead had turned a rich mink brown, over a face growing into strong, blunt features, including a formidable chin. He blinked up at Jim with a dazed expression. When Johnny read, he read. It was on such occasions difficult to remember that Kate really wasn't Johnny's mother. "Huh? Oh. Hi, Jim." He sat up. "Kate," he said, surprised. "You're home."

"That I am." She nodded at Jim. "Company for dinner."

Johnny shrugged. "Cool."

Jim tapped the book. "Any good?" he said again.

"Huh? Oh. Yeah, real good. Science fiction. Sequel to *Jumper*?"

"I read that," Jim said. "Good book."

He sat down and they plunged into an animated debate on the desirability of teleportation as a human skill. Johnny, of that generation of instant gratification which ipso facto believed going anywhere took longer than they thought it ought to, took the pro, and Jim, as a practicing law enforcement professional with a lively sense of self-preservation, took the con.

Kate put John Hiatt on the boom box and got out the stock she'd made from moose marrow bones, onions, and carrots two days before. She sliced more onions into olive oil and butter and let them cook down while she sliced French bread she'd baked that weekend, brushed it with olive oil, and browned it in the oven on both sides. When the onions were ready, she poured in the stock, brought it to a boil, and let it simmer while she brought out three large bowls. She put the soup in the bowls, floated the bread on the soup, and grated Swiss and Parmesan cheese on the bread. She slid it into the oven to bake and brown, and set out spoons and knives and paper towels for napkins and more French bread and butter. "Soup's on."

They came to the table, noses twitching. Johnny dug in with the finicky appetite of any normal fourteen-year-old vacuum cleaner. Jim tasted and considered. "Be better if you added a little cognac," he said.

Johnny paused between one inhalation and the next, spoon suspended in midair.

Kate gave Jim a long, steady, fairly expressionless look.

"Not," said Jim very carefully indeed, "that it isn't absolutely perfect just as it is." He slurped up some more, with sound effects. "Yessiree bob, the best French onion soup I've ever had in my life."

Johnny sneezed something that sounded an awful lot like "suck up" into his paper towel.

Kate took firm control of the conversation and asked him how school had gone that day, and Johnny told them about the field trip his class had made to the dump to watch the eagles roosting there, not neglecting to include a vivid description of the projectile pooping incident. Jim retaliated with a description of the apprehension of that dastardly villain, Willard Shugak. Kate contributed a little Park gossip, including the Niniltna postmistress's recent dalliance with the traveling dentist, ending unhappily with the appearance of a representative of the Alaska Division of Occupational Licensing, who informed everyone waiting in line in the makeshift clinic in the gym that not only was the traveling dentist not licensed to practice in the state of Alaska, but he appeared not to have attended medical school at all, anywhere. This came as something of a shock to the five patients he'd already treated that morning (one cleaning, three fillings, and a root canal) and who at last report were still investigating the teeth he'd worked on with cautious tongues. Bonnie Jeppsen, the postmistress, was heard to be mending her broken heart by beading everything that didn't move out of the way first in bright primary colors, including a rock the size of a small suitcase.

It wasn't until he was helping with the dishes that Jim realized how very domestic it all felt. A frisson of fear ran up his spine.

Kate smiled sweetly at her two men, or would have if she'd known how. "Would you like to spend the night, Jim?"

Johnny tossed down the dish towel and wagged a monitory finger. "I don't want to hear any noises, is that clear?" He snatched up his book and shot down the hall, his bedroom door closing with unnecessary firmness behind him.

Kate laughed. It was the sexiest sound Jim had ever heard coming out of a woman's mouth. It was also the most frightening sound he'd ever heard coming out of a woman's mouth. "No, thanks," he said through suddenly dry lips.

She sauntered around the kitchen island and backed him into a corner, there to run a delicate finger down his shirtfront. "Whatever can I do to change your mind?"

He knew this was a bad idea and he tried desperately to remember why, but his brains had relocated somewhere south of his belt buckle.

He thought, ruefully, that this was his own damn fault. He'd been chasing after her for years, even before Jack Morgan died. Now he had a tiger by the tail and he didn't know what to do with her.

Wait a minute. Really, when he thought about it, it was all Kate's fault. She was the one who had lulled him into a false sense of security, fooled him into thinking he could chase her forever with impunity because she had made it manifestly clear that there wasn't a hope in hell he was ever going to catch her.

The pattern was set, he thought indignantly. He chased. She ran. Then, last year, something had changed. It was hard with that finger fiddling with the buttons of his shirt to focus on exactly what had, and how, but there was a fuzzy memory somewhere in the back of his mind of him trying to do the right thing, of telling her that he was calling off his pursuit, that she was a one-man woman and he was neither capable of being nor willing to be a one-woman man and that—oh hell. Now she was tracing the brass bear on his belt buckle.

Somehow him telling her it was over had been the beginning of her chasing him, and while he hated to admit it, she had been far more successful at it than he had. The last time she had managed to seduce him had been two weeks before at the New Year's potlatch, when she'd lured him out of the school gym and taken him standing up in a corner he fervently hoped had been too dark to see into because there sure as hell had been a lot of foot traffic on the sidewalk not twenty feet away. He had held out for a nice long time before that regrettable if thoroughly enjoyable incident, which he assured himself was the only reason he'd been such an easy target.

There was no such excuse this evening. He had a perfectly serviceable vehicle parked right out front, too, providentially positioned for a quick getaway.

"What the hell did you put in that soup?" he heard himself say as she led him up the narrow wooden stairs to the giant sleigh bed in the loft.

"Not cognac," she said.

TWO

JANUARY

Ahtna

They took off from the Niniltna airstrip before dawn. The sun was taking its own sweet time climbing up over the mountains, grudging every ray as it spilled over peak and crag to wake up the Park, all twenty million acres of it. It was home to six thousand people living in two towns, a dozen villages, and on hundreds of homesteads, traplines, and mining claims.

And that was only if you didn't count the squatters, Kate thought, more of whom seemed to arrive every day. Most of them had roseate expectations of a life at one with nature, and nature was reliably and enthusiastically prompt in disillusioning them. One guy pitched a tent on a bear track, and the bears, delighted by this change of diet, obligingly ate him and his girlfriend. Another guy hiked out to a broken-down bus and sat there until he starved to death, having neglected to study the part of the noble savage lifestyle about learning how to hunt. A team of Korean climbers went up Denali and got stuck in a storm without a radio. Rescued by a passing Italian climber, they were back the following year, this time with a radio with which they got stuck in another storm and used it to yell for help. Unfortunately, they hadn't bothered to learn English.

"Suicide by Alaska," Kate called it, and everyone within hearing at Bernie's snickered and repeated it to the first six people they met. As any Park rat could tell you, there was far more truth than hyperbole in her gibe.

Most of those who survived were on the first available plane south. A hardy few stuck it out to take up residence. Now and then George Perry, owner and operator of Chugach Air Taxi Service, would spot a roof he hadn't seen before tucked into a stand of trees. He never reported it. If he had, Dan O'Brien would have had to try to run them off, to which they might not have taken kindly, like with maybe a .30-06. Dan was a friend of George's. Not to mention, the Park Service was a good client whose checks always cleared the bank.

It wasn't like the Park couldn't absorb them all, Kate thought, riding shotgun in Jim's Cessna at a thousand feet. Four times the size of Denali National Park to the west, the Park's north and east boundaries were the Quilak Mountains, which included Angqak, or Big Bump, a sixteen-thousand-foot peak that straddled the Canadian border and provided a rite of passage for many a climber longing to see the view from the top. A hundred glaciers wrapped icy arms around the Quilaks. Some of those arms were three thousand feet thick and thirty miles long.

Others hung from the sheer sides of cliffs or inched their way to the coast and calved into the Gulf of Alaska, which formed the Park's southern border. Also known as the Mother of Storms, the gulf was half a hemisphere of water congenitally prone to every kind of meteorological mischief, to be approached with prudence and vigilance by any seaman of sense.

The Park's western edge boasted its only man-made boundary, but more than made up for it by boasting of three, the Trans-Alaska Pipeline, the Glenn Highway, and the Alaska Railroad.

As the Cessna droned westward, the mountains gave way to foothills, the foothills to a broad valley. The sun summited Big Bump and turned the frozen surface of the Kanuyaq River into the Yellow Brick Road. A 250-mile serpentine strip of water, the Kanuyaq rose in the Kanuyaq Glacier and wound its tortuous way around mountain and foothill, over fall and through canyon, gathering to itself the runoff from a thousand creeks and streams and rills and becks and depositing them into the gulf through a vast delta that spanned fifty miles of coastline and was home to a thousand species of shorebirds, including many that were of a size to fill a pot, and very tasty. The river was navigable in summer only as far as Niniltna, Kate's village. In winter, when it froze over, it became a Bush highway, an ice road for anyone with a snow machine.

What wasn't Park was wilderness, and what wasn't wilderness was wildlife refuge. Less than 1 percent of it was privately owned, that tiny portion shoehorned in by sourdoughs and stampeders who came north during the gold rush in 1898, who saw to it that their property rights were grandfathered in when the Park was created around them. Another, larger fraction belonged to the resident Alaska Natives, some Eyak, some Athabascan, a few Tlingit, and a lot of Aleuts transplanted there by World War II. They'd come into the land in 1971 with the enactment of the Alaska Native Claims Settlement Act, when they traded the federal government an oil pipeline right of way over aboriginal grounds in exchange for money and land.

They called themselves Park rats. Some of them did a little farming for barter, many of them trapped, and all of them hunted and fished. Salmon ran up every stream, mountain goats and Dall sheep made a good living off the mountain kinnikinnick, and two different caribou herds disregarded the Alaska–Canada border on their migratory routes. Moose were plentiful. So were the wolves, the black bears, the grizzly bears, the wolverines, and all the other smaller fur-bearing mammals.

Kate had watched a lot of people come into the Park. She had watched even more of them go, traveling the only road in, the surprisingly solid remains of a gravel roadbed laid down nearly a hundred years before for a railroad from Cordova on the coast to what had then been the richest copper mine in North America in the interior. After forty years, the ore got harder to get at, and war came, and the copper company turned off the lights in Kanuyaq and pulled up the tracks behind them as they left. The ties were immediately scavenged by those who stayed behind. Once every spring or so, the state road grader would scrape off a layer of frozen dirt to reveal a rusted spike and the grader operator would carry it into Niniltna and hand it over to the school, where the teachers would pass it around their classes, a useful aide-mémoire in underlining the boom-and-bust nature of Alaskan history.

There was only the downriver road from Niniltna to Bernie's Roadhouse, the up-the-mountain road from Niniltna to the Step and Park headquarters, and the fifty miles of road from Niniltna to Ahtna, which connected the Park to the Glenn Highway, or it did when it was navigable, which it wasn't most of the time. Which helped explain why flying was the number one means of transportation. One in seven Park rats had a pilot's license, and every family owned to at least one pilot, most of them private but some commercial. There were dozens of airstrips. Two were paved, Ahtna and Cordova, and the rest were gravel, including Niniltna's

4,800-foot strip, courtesy of a USGS survey forty-odd years before. Most were narrow strips carved out of the forest or riverbanks or lakeshores or the one mostly level spot on the side of a hill, access for fishing lodges and gold mines and hunting parties, plus the occasional airstrip for companies exploring for oil or minerals. Those were always the best airstrips, because they'd had the most money spent on them, but almost every homestead had a mowed strip of grass out back long enough to get a Piper Super Cub into the air with a haunch of moose loaded in the back.

Which reminded Kate. "Who did you say got a moose?"

"Eknaty Kvasnikof." Jim leveled off at a thousand feet and adjusted the prop pitch. The engine smoothed out. "He was coming home from Betty Moonin's late. He said he didn't see the moose until he hit it. His bumper caught the ass end of the moose, which then slid over the top of his hood and busted out his window. The moose then took a dump in Eknaty's lap."

He grinned when Kate laughed. "Both the moose's back legs were broken, so Eknaty shot it and butchered it out before it froze solid. He loaded it in the back of his pickup, which actually still runs even though the front end is totally trashed, and brought it to me." He added parenthetically, "We really could use a brown shirt in the Park. I don't have time to be screwing around with critter problems."

Brown shirts were Alaska State Troopers who enforced those wildlife regulations with regard to animals. Blue shirts were Alaska State Troopers who enforced those wildlife regulations with regard to humans. "Tell your boss, not me," Kate said. "What'd you do with the meat?"

"I told him to have Billy Mike distribute it to elders."

"You didn't keep the liver?"

"Was I supposed to?"

"You were supposed to keep it and give it to me."

"Oh. I didn't know that. Next time."

Kate subsided, mollified. "I love a moose liver."

"Tasty?"

"And huge. You can get half a dozen meals out of one moose liver. Remind me to make you my moose liver pâté one day."

"I like mine fried with bacon and onions."

She gave him an approving smile and he felt his heart turn over, before he remembered his heart had no business doing any such thing.

Kenny Hazen, Ahtna's chief of police, was waiting for them at the airport. Mutt, who woke up from her comfortable snooze on the backseat as they landed, greeted him with her usual excessive enthusiasm for the male of the species. "You are such a slut," Kate told her.

Kenny jerked his head. "Come on. Robbie hates people coming in late to her courtroom."

"Any word?" Kate said as she climbed in.

Kenny put his truck in gear and the wheels spun a little on the ice of the apron before taking hold. "They were out for four days."

Kate looked over her shoulder at Jim, with Mutt in the backseat. "Doesn't mean anything," he said.

They all knew different.

Ahtna, a bustling community of around five thousand, was the market town and transportation hub for the region. Safeway, Costco, and Home Depot had all opened stores there in the past ten years, and Fred Meyer was rumored to be scouting for a location. The University of Alaska Ahtna held down one end of Mountain View, Ahtna's main street, and Ahtna's brand-new courthouse the other. Ahtna was also the seat of Alaska's fifth judicial district.

The Sadie Neakok Courthouse in Ahtna had been open for

business for less than a month when the *State of Alaska v. Louis Deem* landed on its one bench with a thud heard round the Park. Funded by a federal grant, it was part of a pilot program to conduct the state's judicial business in the smaller communities in the more inaccessible parts of the state. Climbing the front stairs, Kate suffered the same shock of surprise she had the first time she'd seen the building, as it was remarkably handsome, an infrequent occurrence with public buildings in the Bush, or anywhere in Alaska for that matter.

The curve of the sides reflected the curve of the river it was built on. Surrounded by a small park, the courthouse was two stories high. Inside were two courtrooms: a small one for arraignments and a big one for trials. There were administrative offices and judge's chambers on the second floor. The lobby and the courtrooms were paneled with spruce harvested from the spruce bark beetle kill from the Chugach National Forest and wainscoted with river rock from the Kanuyaq River. The windows were many and large, and they actually opened.

The massive wooden doors at the entrance bore a cedar carving of Raven, great black wings outstretched across both of them, memorialized in the act of bringing the sun, the moon, and the stars to the People. The sun, moon, and stars were inlaid with hematite and steel and dazzled in any light. There had been some discussion among the architects, the citizen's advisory committee, and the Alaska Department of Law as to whether the first thing Park rats saw as they entered the halls of justice should be the very first grand theft. In the end, since it was such a cross-cultural legend and as such immediately recognizable, and since, all appearances to the contrary, their collective sense of the ridiculous was strong, they went with it.

The courtroom was packed. Kate, Kenny, and Jim leaned

against the back wall. Mutt touched noses with a handsome husky, whose ears flattened ingratiatingly and whose tail began a rapid whappety-whap against his master's leg, after which his knees gave out and he slid to the floor, rolled to his back, and waved his paws in the air. Jim knew just how he felt. Mutt trotted back to Kate's side, looking insufferably smug.

The prosecuting attorney and his assistant, neither of whom Kate knew, sat side by side, staring straight ahead with their hands folded on the table in front of them. The rigidity with which they were holding their heads erect told its own tale. "Oh yeah," she said under her breath, "this'll end well."

"What?" Jim said, and she shook her head.

By contrast, defense attorney Frank "Tex" Rickard and defendant Louis Deem were displaying an almost boisterous enjoyment in each other's company. The conversation—Kate strained to hear—appeared to concern recipes for the best Super Bowl snacks. Hot wings, she thought. Or maybe blackened wings. Blackened something.

Louis turned suddenly and looked straight at her. She forced herself not to jerk away, meeting his eyes steadily, hoping her color hadn't risen.

At first glance, Louis Deem was a very handsome man. Certainly enough women had thought so. He was almost six feet tall, with broad shoulders, a narrow waist, and long, strong bones clad in a smooth layer of muscle. His hair was thick and dark blond and always cut in the latest style. It was just beginning to recede, but only enough to create a broad brow that gave him an air of intelligence barely contained.

Well, that was true enough, Kate thought, still holding his gaze.

His cheekbones and jawline were bold slashes of bone clothed in healthy skin with a faint brown tint, the only indication of his

Aleut grandmother, something he shared with his many Park cousins. He had dark brown bedroom eyes, thickly lashed, seductive, and completely without soul.

Louis smiled. It was a good smile with good teeth, except for the cap on the left front incisor from which Kate was pleased to see the gum had begun to recede, leaving a black line between tooth and gum. Perhaps no one but Kate might have noticed it. Perhaps no one but Kate would have reason to.

"All rise." Rickard's hand was on Louis's shoulder. He knew Kate and he winked at her. She remained impassive. She would have ripped off her own face before she let Tex Rickard see how angry she was.

Everyone stood and the judge came in. She was tall with enormous dark eyes, a high-bridged nose with a hint of a downward curl at the end, translucent olive skin, and salt-and-pepper hair whose natural wave had been severely restrained in a tight roll caught low on the back of her neck.

She was also so thin, her cheekbones looked as if they'd been sharpened on a whetstone. "Has she been ill?" Jim said in a low voice, too low for Kenny to catch.

Kate replied at the same volume. "Breast cancer."

Jim looked at Kenny. Kenny nodded once, his mouth a tight line.

The Honorable Roberta Singh dealt her bench a sharp rap with a gavel that belied any hint of weakness and got right to business. "Madam Foreperson, has the jury reached a verdict?"

A woman rose to her feet and replied, "We have, Your Honor." She handed the bailiff a piece of paper. The bailiff carried it to the judge, who read it and then set it to one side. "The defendant will please rise. Madam Foreperson, in the case of the state of Alaska versus Louis Deem on the count of murder in the first degree, how do you find?"

The foreperson swallowed hard and lowered her eyes. "We find the defendant not guilty."

There was an immediate and vocal stir in the courtroom, which Judge Singh quelled with the immediate rap of her gavel. "There will be order in my court," she said in an austere voice, and such was the force of her character that no one doubted her. It didn't stop Mary Waterbury's mother from weeping softly into Mary Waterbury's father's shoulder, nor did it stop the rumble of discontent from assorted Waterbury family and friends, which included, Kate saw when the crowd shifted, Auntie Vi, who was sitting with her arms around Mary Waterbury's two surviving sisters, Alice, eighteen, and Martha, sixteen. Children naturally gravitated to Auntie Vi; she was like the Pied Piper. Billy Mike sat on the other side of Mary's father. Billy and Auntie Vi wore similar expressions, in which could be read anger but no surprise.

The district attorney rose to his feet. "Your Honor, the state asks that the jury be polled," he said, which was the least that he could do.

One by one the jury said not guilty. None of them spoke much above a whisper. Few of them were capable of meeting the district attorney's eye, or anyone else's, for that matter. When the twelfth gave his verdict, Louis Deem turned to Howie Katelnikof, sitting directly behind him, and slapped him a high five. Howie, Louis's other roommate and sworn vassal, grinned widely and clasped his hands together over his head in a victory shake. Kate noticed several members of the jury, their attention drawn by the sound, avert their eyes from the spectacle. Mr. and Mrs. Waterbury wept on.

"Members of the jury, I thank you for your service," Judge Singh said. "You are dismissed."

There was a distinct sense that the words *Go and sin no more* were hovering on the tip of the judge's tongue, but she managed to restrain herself. She didn't bother to hide her contempt when she looked at Louis Deem. "Mr. Deem, you are free to go."

"Thank you, Your Honor," Rickard said, and was wise enough not to extend any of the usual fulsome pleasantries he was known for upon victory. Her Honor was definitely not in the mood.

And Louis Deem? Louis Deem turned, found Kate in the milling crowd, and smiled.

And what the fuck was all that business with the fucking truck tires? Jesus Christ, it was O.J. and the fucking glove all over again!"

Kenny Hazen had the district attorney backed into a corner of the courthouse's first-floor conference room.

"What the hell are they teaching you morons in law school these days, to on purpose ask the fucking questions you don't know the fucking answers to?"

The district attorney, who Kate saw now was very slight, very short, and very young, looked very frightened, too. A cowering sinner.

By comparison, the Ahtna police chief looked like the wrath of God made manifest. "I told you, you fucking moron, I told you and I told you that manslaughter was a lock, that murder two was a stretch, and to give the fucking jurors an easy out. Deem has fucking terrorized people in this fucking Park for years, I told you—"

The door opened. "We know you told him, Chief," Judge Singh's voice said. "Pretty much everyone in the building heard you tell him." She put a hand on Kenny's arm, thin, long-fingered, and elegant. Under the robe she'd been wearing an embroidered Russian jacket, black palazzo pants, and step-in black shoes with thick rubber soles. She looked like she'd just waltzed in from a hard day at Nordstrom.

The fury in Chief Hazen's tank-sized body diminished but did not entirely dissipate. The little ADA demonstrated his gratitude for the rescue by tugging at his wispy goatee, evidently a nervous habit. His wiser associate had previously demonstrated his instinct for survival by his rapid exit from the building and was probably already on a plane back to Anchorage, leaving his hapless superior to try to talk his way out of what Kate thought was most likely his own ineptitude. "I'm sorry, Chief," the little ADA said in a voice perilously close to a whine, "I tried—"

"Yeah, you tried all right," Kenny said in a growl that had the ADA trying to back through the wall again. "It's the best case we've ever had on Deem, and you blew it. Right now he's down at the Seven Come Eleven, knocking 'em back and bragging on how he got away with murder. Again. And probably picking his next victim out of the adoring crowd. You little shyster, I oughtta—"

The judge caught Kenny's elbow in a firm grip and said to the ADA, "Mr. Carter, you should leave. Now."

The ADA didn't need telling twice; he ducked between judge and police chief and scuttled out the door. Mutt sent him on his way with a passing nip to his calf, which startled a scream out of him and left a hole in his double-knit pants.

"Good girl," the judge said in a much warmer voice, snapping her fingers. Exhibiting a rarely seen streak of diplomacy, Mutt trotted over, sniffed the judge's extended hand, and endured having her ears scratched by an unknown female.

"What happened?" Jim said. "I would have bet—" He caught Kate's eye and changed that to "I thought you had it all sewn up. What went wrong?"

"It was the fucking tire tracks," Kenny said, still steaming. "I took impressions of tire tracks found at the scene. There were three clear sets, more than what you might expect at Heartbreak Point, given all the juvies rodding in and out of there with their girlfriends. I traced one to Deem's truck, which put him where we found Mary." He jerked his head at Kate. "She found the other two drivers for me. One was there before Deem and one was there after, and this firms up the time frame nicely, and I'm thinking this prick has finally done something that's going to stick to him."

"And?"

Hazen snorted. "First Rickard put the other two drivers up on the stand and cross-questioned them about how many times they'd driven out there to make out with which girlfriend and got them all confused about the timeline, which got the jury all confused about the timeline, which that little prick"—a hooked thumb indicated the direction of the fleeing ADA—"doesn't do anything to clear up. Then Rickard puts up a truck tire expert who contradicted all the crime lab's findings, and then to top it off, there was a long-haul trucker on the goddamn jury!" The judge winced, and Kenny moderated his tone. "What the hell do we have discovery for if not so we don't have jurors standing up in the fucking jury box their own fucking selves contradicting fucking sworn testimony!"

"I've got some Scotch in my chambers," the judge said.

It was probably the only thing that could have stemmed the flow, and it did the trick. They adjourned to the judge's chambers. Kenny knocked back a double in one long swallow and held out his glass for a refill.

"We'll get him next time, Kenny," the judge said.

"That'd be fine, Robbie, except by next time another girl will be dead."

The door to the judge's chambers opened without invitation, and Auntie Vi marched into the charged silence following this incontrovertible statement. She looked around and found Kate. "You come," she said flatly. She marched out again.

Kate hesitated, and then rose and followed, Mutt at her heels.

It was enough to startle everyone into silence. After a moment

Kenny Hazen said respectfully, "A heretofore immovable object manipulated by an irresistible force."

"A violation of all the known laws of physics," the judge said, nodding.

Jim didn't say anything at all.

Auntie Vi led Kate into the now empty courtroom and closed the door behind them. She glared at Kate. "What you do about this?"

"There's nothing I can do, Auntie," Kate said. "You heard the jury."

Auntie Vi, not given to profanity, made a few choice observations on the intelligence of the jury, individually and collectively.

"It's not their fault, Auntie," Kate said. "You know Louis must have sicced Howie on them. They're afraid for their families. And they're right to be."

Auntie Vi, who did not enjoy being interrupted, turned a cold eye on Kate, who braced herself. "That girl dead."

Every Park rat below the age of fifty was a child to the aunties, but Auntie Vi was well known as the guardian angel of every Park female under the age of twenty-one. "Yes."

"That boy kill her."

"Yes."

"No one blame that boy."

"Everyone blames him, Auntie," Kate said. "Everyone knows he killed her. Even the people on the jury know it."

Auntie Vi brooded on this. "He scare them."

Kate nodded. "It's the only reason they wouldn't convict. They were afraid of what he'd do to them. And he would do something. Louis will never be convicted of anything by a jury made up of Park rats. The state should have petitioned for a change of venue."

Auntie Vi poked Kate in the chest with a force strong enough to push Kate back a step. "What you do?"

"There is nothing I can do."

"Bullshit!"

Kate didn't know what was more shocking, that Auntie Vi would speak such a word or that she'd say it in front of one of the children.

Auntie Vi poked her again. "We give you time, Katya." She pointed at the scar on Kate's throat. "You almost get killed when you stop bad man from hurting baby girl. You come home to heal. Okay, we let you heal." She pointed a stern finger at Mutt. Mutt's tail gave an ingratiating wag, but Auntie Vi wasn't having any. "We even give you the puppy to help you heal. Instead you fight with your emaa. Okay, we let you fight. Ekaterina die. Okay, we let you mourn. Your man die. Okay, we let you mourn some more. Your house burn down. We build you another. The whole Park, we build you another!" She poked Kate a third time. "How much longer, Katya?"

"How much longer for what, Auntie?" Kate looked at the door for rescue, but the cavalry was late.

"How much longer we wait?" Auntie Vi said, her voice rising. "We give you life, we send you to school—"

"I didn't want to go to school, Auntie. Emaa made me."

"Ekaterina make that decision for all of us! And then instead of coming home like you should have, working for your people, you take job in Anchorage!" Auntie Vi struck her breast fiercely with one fist. "What about us! Your people!"

Forgetting for a moment that she was speaking to her elder, Kate raised her own voice. "What have I been doing for the past seven years but work for my people! Who's the first person Billy Mike comes running to when the Bingleys start fighting or the Jeppsens and the Kreugers start shooting? Somebody burned down my cabin, my parents' cabin, the cabin I was born in and lived in my whole life. It's gone because I was working for my people, looking for a killer!" With an effort, she brought her voice back under control. "And if the price of my new house is me taking a seat on the board of the Niniltna Native Association, I would never have let you build it for me."

Kate watched with mean satisfaction as a vivid flush washed up over Auntie Vi's face, but she, too, struggled for control. "You need to be on the board, Katya."

"Like hell I do, Auntie. I don't know the first thing about how to run a corporation."

"You can learn!" Abruptly, Auntie's voice gentled. "Billy not young anymore."

"He's not old, either, Auntie."

"He sixty-three, Katya, and not healthy. Annie says his heart goes funny sometime. Old Sam older than his name. Joyce, Demetri, Harvey—all old enough to be your parents." She looked, if it were possible, pleading. "Where you lead, others will follow. Since you are a child, always this has been so. All know it. You smart, you strong, you young." She added, unfortunately, "You chosen by Ekaterina."

"Yeah, that shows you how smart Emaa was, Auntie. Abel would still be alive if I hadn't come home."

Auntie Vi shook her head, refusing to be drawn, and waved at the courthouse they were standing in. "That boy kill that girl," she said, "and get away with it."

"Getting myself elected to the board wouldn't have changed that, Auntie."

Auntie Vi opened the door. "A hundred and seventy-three shareholders, Katya. When something bad like this happen, they want answer. Who here to give them one?"

• • •

Jim took one look at Kate when she got back to the judge's chambers and rose swiftly to his feet. "Lunch, anyone?"

They adjourned to the Ahtna Lodge where, Jim hoped, exchanging gossip with Tony and eating one of his partner Stanislav's famous steak sandwiches would soothe Kate's savage breast.

How bad an idea that was was immediately obvious when they walked into the restaurant and saw that instead of heading for the Seven Come Eleven as was his usual MO following an acquittal, Louis Deem had for reasons best known to himself decided to park an elbow on the Ahtna Lodge bar, long known to be the hangout of Kate Shugak when she was in town. He was surrounded by the usual suspects and appeared to be having a high old time of it.

"Let's go," Jim said.

"Oh, let's not," Hazen said, and thwarted Tony's attempts to seat them as far away from the bar as he could get without actually putting them at a table in the river.

Jim looked at the judge, who shrugged and sat down in the chair Hazen had pulled out for her.

Such provocation did not go unnoticed. "Oh man," someone said in a not very low voice, "that's just a nine-one-one call waiting to happen."

"No point," someone else said. "Everyone who would answer it is right here."

There was a nervous titter, quickly squelched. Kate and company gave a jittery Tony their orders, and he fled their table as if pursued by demons. Everyone was watching out of the corner of their eyes, and those eyes got sharper when after a fraught ten minutes Louis Deem strolled over to their table. "Nice to see a man pull a chair out for a woman anymore, Kenny," he said, and looked down at Robbie Singh. "Gotta love the manners on that good ol' boy, dontcha, Judge." He gave her a slow once-over. "Gotta say also that you're looking mighty good. Glad to see getting the tit cut off didn't slow you down."

Hazen was up and out of his chair and Jim was right behind him, only he was grabbing hold of Hazen and hanging on. Jim Chopin was not a small man, but next to Kenny Hazen in a rage Paul Bunyan would have looked frail. "Kenny. Don't. You know it's what he wants."

The judge said coolly, "Thank you, Mr. Deem. I appreciate your good wishes, given the antagonistic state of our professional relationship." She even smiled at him. "Which I do assure you is far from over."

Louis was wise enough to let this pass. He took a long pull at the draft beer he was holding and looked at Kenny, who shrugged off Jim's hands and restrained himself to a killing glare. "Man, that's good. The one thing I've missed most inside." He grinned. "Well. Maybe not the thing I've missed most."

Kate thought of Eve Waterbury weeping into Nick Waterbury's shoulder in the courtroom. Next to her Mutt showed her teeth, a growl rumbling out of her throat.

Louis looked at Mutt. "Hey, Mutt," he said softly.

The growl, if anything, increased in volume.

"Fuck off, Louis," Kate said, just as softly.

His gaze shifted to her for the first time, and while no one saw the "target acquired" sign flashing over his head, no one who was watching in the Ahtna Lodge Bar that day could mistake the hostility that sizzled between the two of them. "Hey, Kate," he said in what could be described as an almost caressing tone. "I hear somebody burned down your cabin."

"Pity you were in jail at the time," Kate said. "Arson, attempted murder. Right up your alley."

His smile widened. He even turned his head a little so the dead tooth faced her straight on. "I also hear you got a brand-new house. And a brand-new son."

There was a moment of silence.

"Kate," Jim said on a warning note. He felt like he needed a striped shirt and a whistle. And body armor.

Slowly and with a certain ceremony, Kate rose to her feet.

The room was absolutely silent.

Kate leaned forward with her hands flat on the table and met Louis's eyes. "Buzz off now, Louis," she said softly, "like the little gnat you are, before someone slaps you down." She smiled, a wide, warm smile that terrified everyone who saw it, and dropped her gaze to his teeth. "Again."

The hair standing up all over his head, Jim said, long after he should have, "You have no business here, Deem. Go on back to the bar."

Deem ignored him, raising his glass to Kate. "Be seeing you."

"Be careful what you wish for," Kate said. "Little boy."

Tony, frozen two tables away in the act of taking someone else's order, greeted Stan's call of "Order up!" with the demeanor of someone reprieved from the gas chamber thirty seconds before the balls dropped, and bustled over with their steak sandwiches, full of false good cheer.

"You okay?" Jim said to Kate in a low voice as they sat down again.

"I'm fine," she said. She even ate all of her sandwich, although he noticed she didn't appear to taste any of it. He noticed also that Mutt eschewed the plate of chopped meat Tony set before her in the manner of one setting an offering before a god, instead positioning herself between Kate and the bar, her considering yellow gaze fixed on Louis Deem's back.

"Stay away from Deem," Jim said after they were in the air.

"Tell him to stay away from me," Kate said.

To his surprise, she didn't sound angry, or even threatening. On the contrary, she sounded calm, almost matter-of-fact. As if, Jim thought with a sudden chill, as if the gauntlet had been thrown down, and the challenge accepted. He concentrated on getting them to cruising altitude before speaking again, more cautiously this time. "You and Deem appear to have something of a history."

Kate stared through the windshield with a face devoid of all expression.

He tried again. "It wasn't—"

"Personal?" She looked at him, her mouth a straight uncompromising line. "Is that what you're trying to find out, Jim? If Louis and I got it on?"

He was honestly appalled. "No! Jesus! No way, Kate. No way would you ever have anything to do with that lowlife." He examined the dials on the control panel and then the horizon, hoping for a loss of oil pressure or the onset of clear air turbulence as a way out of this conversation. No such luck. "Let's just drop it, okay? Sorry I said anything."

They flew on for a few minutes. To Jim it felt more like a few hours.

"I saw the results of him doing something he shouldn't have been doing," Kate said. "Which is pretty much the story of Louis's life."

Jim maintained a hopeful silence.

"I . . ." Kate hesitated. "I instructed him as to the error of his ways."

Jim thought about it for another twenty-five miles. "The cap," he said. "You knocked his tooth out."

Kate said nothing.

"But he keeps smiling at you with it."

Silence.

Jim sighed. "So he didn't stay instructed."

A great snowy owl was startled awake by their passing over his roost and exploded into flight, a vast sail of pure white feathers and matchless grace. Kate turned her head to watch it out of sight.

"He beat the rap," Jim said. "Again. Still."

The back of Kate's head was unresponsive. Mutt stuck her head in between them and touched her nose to Kate's neck. Kate didn't even jump.

"Shit," Jim said.

They were silent the rest of the way home.

It took Jim a while to figure out why the encounter between Kate and Deem bothered him so much.

Louis Deem might be the only Park rat Jim Chopin had ever met who wasn't afraid of Kate Shugak.

THREE

The Park

But January passed into February, and Louis Deem made no noticeable ripples in the peaceful winter surface of the Park. It stayed cold enough long enough for the school to build and maintain an ice-skating rink on the baseball field behind the gymnasium. Everyone pulled their skates out of the crawl space, dusted off the dead spiders, and met on the ice, where someone set up a bonfire every night, next to which Auntie Vi sold hot chocolate topped with whipped cream that froze into mustaches on everyone's upper lips. Word was at least two children were fathered just beyond the glow of the fire that winter, but word also was that many more had been attempted, so the fallout wasn't as bad as it might have been.

As expected and in spite of strenuous arguments by Jim, Auntie Balasha refused to file charges against Willard for stealing her fuel oil. She told Jim she was sure the poor boy was driven by hunger, as nothing would convince her that her grandson harbored a larcenous bone in his body. He'd fallen into bad company, although she did think that perhaps Howie wasn't quite so black as Park rumor had him painted. He was misunderstood, that was all, and she was sure—

Jim tuned out the rest of her apologia, finished his tea with honey, accepted a dozen freshly baked oatmeal raisin cookies, the ones she had gotten up at five A.M. to bake because she knew he was coming out that morning and because she knew they were his favorites, and left.

On the way back into town, Jim drove past the little grocery store that the Bingleys had just opened. Several men were loitering with what to Jim looked like intent near the door, including Martin Shugak, Howie Katelnikof, and, yes, there was Willard.

For the hell of it, he pulled to the side of the road and got out. "Hey, guys."

Howie and Martin eyed him warily, but Willard broke into a big smile. "Hey, Jim."

Jim stamped his feet and blew into his gloves. "Damn, it's cold. I sure could go for a hot toddy about now."

"Me, too," Willard said with feeling.

"Know anywhere I could buy a bottle?" He made a show of getting out his wallet. "I've got cash."

Martin and Howie both made convulsive moves for Willard, but they were too late. "Why, sure, Jim," Willard said happily. "I can get you a bottle," and he ducked in back of a snow berm to come up beaming with a plastic pint of Windsor Canadian. He handed it over in exchange for a wad of money.

Martin sighed heavily. Howie said with resignation, "Willard, you dumb fuck."

"What?" Willard was bewildered. "What'd I do?"

"What you did was sell me liquor without a license, in a damp town," Jim said. Damp today, anyway. Tomorrow, depending on the mood of the voting citizenry and the fishing season, it could be wet or even dry. "You're under arrest. You have the right to remain silent. . . ."

Willard went without question, by now well versed in the form. As Jim held the cell door open for him, Willard was patting Darth Vader's head, whose shiny black helmet as usual peeped from the top of Willard's shirt pocket. "It's okay, Anakin. The evil Sith Lord has us trapped again, but you know we always escape."

In fact, Jim felt a little ashamed of himself, but at least Willard got to spend the night in a nice warm jail, with three hot meals hand-delivered by Laurel Meganack. He spent it there alone, though, because he refused to implicate either Howie or Marty in the bootlegging. Jim hadn't expected much else, and he let Willard off the next morning with a warning, which he estimated Willard retained for possibly as long as thirty seconds. Jim had confiscated and poured out the rest of the booze, which had been his target all along, and an added bonus was that Auntie Balasha gave him a little less hell than he was expecting when she heard of the incident.

Martin vanished into the woodwork, probably fearing what would happen when Kate heard. Howie remained distressingly visible. Howie Katelnikof, Louis Deem's boon companion, Willard Shugak's in loco parentis, and Jim Chopin's ever-present thorn in his side.

Louis Deem was bad because he was good at it and because he enjoyed it. Willard was bad because he was FAS and incapable of making even one good decision unless it was by accident. Howie was bad because he was lazy, because it paid better than straight work, and because somebody had once told him that girls went for bad boys. He was similar enough to Louis that the girls were initially interested, but that interest always wore off fast. One of life's losers, that was Howie Katelnikof, and the sad thing about Howie was that he knew it. It was one of the reasons he'd hooked up with

Louis Deem, his cousin, his idol, his mentor, and his meal ticket, from whom he'd absorbed just enough gray matter wherewithal to make beer money screwing over everyone who didn't get out of the way first. The bootlegging operation was a classic example of Howie's entrepreneurial skills. He had just enough brains to acquire product and hire staff, but then he parked the operation on a road providing direct access to a trooper post, and the staff he hired had shoe sizes bigger than their IQs. Jim suspected that Louis Deem's delusions of invulnerability were starting to rub off on his henchman.

Not that Deem was looking all that deluded lately.

In February, two snow machiners were stranded on one of the Quilaks' minor peaks in the middle of a raging storm. They had no survival gear and no radio and it was only a miracle that another snow machiner in the area had seen them and reported their location to Dan. Dan called Jim, and together they called out the Llama high-altitude rescue helicopter, which swooped in to pluck up the morons during a momentary lull.

Their chief concern, they explained earnestly to Jim, was the recovery of their snow machines. "Jesus Christ," Dan said when Jim reported this, "they were highmarking in a place we told them not to go, right when a ballbuster of a storm was coming in off Prince William Sound, which we also told them. You'd think they'd be happy just to be alive."

When the storm blew itself out, Jim had to fly to Chistona on one of a wearying number of domestic assault cases that winter, all of them involving alcohol, and he did a flyby of the area in question. "Not much point in it," Dan said when Jim told him what he was going to do, and Dan was right. Even in the aftermath of the storm, the vultures had managed to strip both machines of anything of value. The tracks were gone, the cowling with the instrument panels gone, the engines, the seats, the shocks, the skis, the treads, all gone. One of them looked like someone had tried to tow it behind another snow machine. It was lying in a narrow canyon in a heap of broken metal. The other sat where it had been abandoned, minus even its gas tank.

"What's left isn't worth fifty bucks," Jim told Dan when he got back to the Park. Dan relayed the news to the owners, who weren't happy, but as they were home in Anchorage by that time Dan didn't really care, and truth to tell neither did Jim. Dan was right. The snow machiners were lucky to be alive. Still, Jim harbored no doubt that they'd both be back in the Park the following winter pursuing their death-defying hobby of extreme snow machining. With any luck, they'd get themselves killed before they had a chance to procreate. The gene pool needed all the help it could get.

As for where the parts had wound up, Jim had a mild hunch that a search of the Deem homestead would provide a few leads. If only a hunch was sufficient cause for Judge Singh to issue him a search warrant.

In March, Kate—in the employ of the state Department of Revenue—concluded a ten-week investigation which broke up a ring of grifters who had been filing applications for the state's annual permanent fund dividend in the names of forty-three children, all of whom had died five years or more earlier. The last five dividends totaled $6,264.20, which times forty-three brought the amount embezzled to well over a quarter of a million dollars, which qualified for grand theft, while if not quite on a scale of Raven stealing the sun, moon, and stars, certainly bumped up the charging documents to a felony.

Jim and Kenny were called in to make the arrests, warrants in hand that Judge Singh had been delighted to issue. "You have the right to remain silent," Kenny said, and was interrupted when Margaret Kvasnikof spat at Kate.

"Nice to see you again, too, Mags," she said as Kenny cuffed her third cousin once removed and led her out.

"Hey, a fan," Jim said. "You okay?"

"It's a living," Kate said, and suffered no qualms of conscience three weeks later when her fee arrived in the mail with three lovely zeroes on the end of it. She didn't enjoy being spit at, but Mags was no longer the girl who had played kick-the-can with the gang on the riverbanks when they were all kids together. Of course, she thought, it helped that Mags's branch of Kvasnikofs came from Ouzinkie instead of Nanwalek, and as such was an extremely distant relative. If she'd been yet another of Auntie Balasha's three hundred nieces, Kate would have cashed the check anyway but would have braced herself for an onslaught of reproachful glances and baked goods.

"Wow," Johnny said, reading the zeroes over her shoulder, "let's go to Disneyland."

"Hell with that," Jim said, "let's go to Vegas."

Instead, she sent 30 percent to the IRS, put 20 percent into Johnny's college fund, dropped $1,200 at Costco on essentials like bread flour, kept a thousand in a roll of fives, tens, and twenties for walking-around money, and banked the rest.

"My snowgo's falling apart," Johnny said.

"Snow's almost gone," Kate said.

"Yeah, but my four-wheeler is in even worse shape."

"Cannibalize mine for parts."

"Couldn't we at least get satellite television?"

"Over my dead body."

Johnny, who obviously still had a lot of work ahead of him before he could start violating all the known laws of physics, gave up and trudged mournfully to his bedroom. Not neglecting to take the copy of the latest Harry Dresden novel with him, even though Kate's bookmark was prominently clasped at the halfway mark.

During these months Louis Deem remained snugged down on his homestead, drinking beer and watching WWE *SmackDown*. He did have satellite television. Naturally.

In fact, Jim's usual winter workload was down considerably, which didn't hurt his feelings any but which left him a lot more time to brood over Kate Shugak. He haunted the Riverside Café, flirting desperately with Laurel Meganack, a very easy on the eyes twenty-something who had indicated her interest on more than one occasion but who had now totally backed off. He feared that she knew he and Kate were an item, which of course they weren't, but he couldn't seem to muster up the strength of character to out and out say so.

And more and more often at the end of the day his vehicle seemed to head up the road to Kate's house, where more and more often he seemed somehow to spend the night. True, six months into this, he still didn't know what to call it, this whatever it was he had going on with Kate, the frantic, almost ferocious sexual need that marked the beginning of all his best affairs had settled into a slumberous ardor. But that ardor had the damnedest way of flaring up and leaving nothing but scorched earth behind it, all the more enjoyable—and unsettling—because he wasn't expecting it. Usually by this point in Jim's relationships boredom had set in and he was looking for a way out with the least amount of damage to everyone involved, especially him.

And then he would look down at Kate, her face flushed and glowing, a smile curling the corners of her lips, her legs still tight around his waist, and feel complete, whole, all his empty spaces filled up.

Like he was home.

When he realized this, he waited for the panic to set in. Hell, he would have welcomed it.

It just wasn't there.

One evening he was helping Johnny with his algebra. "Man, I hate this stuff," Johnny said, grumbling. "It was a lot easier when *X* was just a letter in the alphabet." He looked up from where he was torturing a page of his textbook. "You're really good at it, though. How come?"

"I don't know. Probably because I had a really good teacher." They were seated at the dining room table. Kate was curled up on the sofa, her nose in a book. Typical. It would be easier to get over her if she were a little more labor intensive. Jim shifted in his chair, ostensibly to stretch but really to get a look at the title. *Pride and Prejudice.* Jane Austen. Bleah.

He looked back at Johnny. "I never went as far with it as I wanted to. Someday I'm going to go back to school and take bonehead math right on up to trig and calc."

"Why the he—?" Johnny looked over his shoulder at Kate, who he knew from personal experience was never so oblivious to her surroundings as one might like. "Why would you want to do that?"

"I always wanted to take astronomy. You need calc to take astronomy."

"Oh. You gonna buy a telescope?"

"That's my plan."

Johnny considered, and then jerked his head toward the front windows. "We got a deck."

"Yeah," Jim said, "I noticed."

"All I'm saying is it'd be a good place to put a telescope."

"Yeah," Jim said. "About that *X*—"

He felt reasonably confident that the implication of that conversation was going to jerk him out of a sound sleep at three A.M., sweating bullets. Instead he was woken at three A.M. in the middle of being taken thorough advantage of by Kate.

Well. It wasn't like he could resist. Male anatomy being what it was.

The next morning he woke up before she did and looked over to see that she was still asleep. It didn't happen often. He lay very still.

She was curled on her right side facing him, close enough that he could feel her breath on his cheek, although he couldn't hear it. She was the quietest sleeper he'd ever shared a bed with, to the point that sometimes he'd nudge her to get a grunt or a moan, just to prove that she was still alive. With her eyes closed you could see the Aleut in her even more than when they were open, the slight upward tilt of the eyelids, the high, flat cheekbones, the wide mouth, the strong, stubborn chin. Her skin was a warm olive tint, her hair black and straight and very short. It had fallen to her waist at one time, usually bound back in a thick braid, and then for reasons she had never explained to anyone, she had cut it all off. He'd wondered if it was in reaction to Jack Morgan's death, some kind of cultural custom to express grief, but of course he had never asked.

Jim knew women, knew a lot of them and knew them well. Jack Morgan had known just one woman, and known her very well indeed. This woman, this five-foot, 120-pound package of strength and courage and intelligence and humor. Her grandmother had for many years led Kate's small band of transplanted Aleuts and consanguinated Athabascans and adopted Eyaks and conscripted Tlingits, and it had been obvious what Emaa had wanted when she died. She had wanted Kate to step into her shoes.

Thus far, Kate hadn't. She was too blunt for the diplomacy required to shepherd a tribe between the Scylla of government funding and the Charybdis of intertribal warfare, and she had too little patience with human foible to be able to turn a blind eye. Both qualities had made her an excellent if intimidating investigator for the Anchorage district attorney, and they made her an even better private detective now. Other skills were called for when shepherding the lives and fortunes of 173 shareholders who tended to be fiercely independent, suspicious of authority, and united as one in their determination to retain their cultural identity. They were also to a man, woman, and child completely divided in opinion as to how to go about it. He'd seen an article in *Alaska* magazine a while back that had reminded him forcibly of life in the Park, something about putting four Alaskans in a room and getting five marriages, six divorces, and seven political parties. Tip O'Neill had it wrong: All politics was personal. All Niniltna shareholders were related by birth or marriage, and nobody fought harder or meaner than family. Jim had had a front-row seat at a few NNA examples of the internecine warfare that rose periodically among the shareholders, and every time he'd come away thankful to be white.

And then there was the almighty dividend, a sum representing a percentage of the association's previous year's annual earnings, which amount was set by the board of directors to be paid out quarterly to shareholders and which was always subject to being second-guessed by even the best-natured among them. If the fishing had been bad, if gas prices started rising, if the state's annual permanent fund dividend dropped, the nastier the fight over the dividends was. There was currently a controversy brewing over quarterly payments versus one annual payment, with a critical minority in favor of liquidating all the association's assets and making one lump sum payment and walking away. Billy Mike, the Association's chairman, had been looking more than usually strained this winter. Jim put that down to Billy losing his son, Dandy, the year before, but the Association's internal conflicts couldn't be helping.

And Jim had a shrewd suspicion that Auntie Vi had addressed this very topic in her conversation with Kate following Louis Deem's acquittal. Clearly it had been gnawing at Kate ever since. She hadn't said anything, but Jim had been an eyewitness to her running Billy Mike off the property twice now in the interim, and

Johnny had told him that the four aunties had spent an hour at Kate's table one morning the week before, sipping coffee and tearing into fresh-baked bread with nothing other than "please" and "thank you" being spoken out loud. "Enough to freeze the blood in your veins," was the way Johnny had put it, not without relish.

Jim noticed that Kate had been baking a lot of bread, too, her preferred method for expiating rage, sin, sorrow, and pretty much any emotion that might be alleviated by beating the hell out of flour and water.

Like maybe guilt.

Kate's eyes opened, and Jim promptly forgot about the trials and tribulations of the Niniltna Native Association.

As always she opened her eyes completely awake, aware of who and where she was. And who she was with. She smiled, the shared memory of the night warm between them.

"I was just getting up," he said.

The smile widened into a grin as he got out of bed. On the way into the bathroom he noticed that he smelled like her and that it didn't bother him as much as he thought it ought to. It was hard to force himself into the shower.

Breakfast was coffee and the killer date-nut bread that Kate had baked the night before. "What have you got going on today?" he asked her around a mouthful. It was sweet and rich and heavy and nutty. Seemed appropriate.

"Bobby sent word by Johnny yesterday that Brendan wants to talk to me about a case, so I'm headed over to his house after I drop the kid at school."

"Can we pick up Vanessa on the way?" Johnny said. "And then pick us both up at Bernie's house after school?"

Jim refused to meet Kate's eye. "Sure."

Johnny read something unintended into Jim's neutral assent

and decided an explanation was called for. "We're working on a project together for science."

"Um," Jim said.

"Ms. Doogan's real tough about deadlines, so we wanted to get started on it before class this morning."

"Uh-huh," Jim said, totally absorbed in the precise width of the slice he was taking off the loaf of bread.

"It's a class thing," Johnny said. "Van and I, we're just lab partners. Along with Fitz."

Fitz was Bernie Koslowski's fourteen-year-old son. "Got it," Jim said, his mouth full. Behind Johnny's back Kate crossed her eyes. The bread went down the wrong pipe, and he choked.

"Are you all right, Jim?" Kate said, grave as Judge Singh in a hanging mood. "Are you able to speak? Can you say your name? I know CPR."

Bobby was on the air when Kate walked in. Katya, two and a half beautiful and precocious years old, spotted her godmother first. "Kate!" she said, waddling forward as fast as her pudgy little legs would carry her. "Kate! Kate! Kate!"

Kate scooped her up and blew big wet raspberries into her plump little neck. Katya dissolved into a bundle of giggles. It all went out on Park Air, of course, and Bobby was not loath to exploit the scene on his pirate radio station. "Yes, folks, that's the beautiful and deadly Kate Shugak walking in the door, so I'm going to wrap up this morning's broadcast of Park Air's weekly Rummage Sale with these last three ads.

"Billy Mike is looking for a chain saw, he doesn't care what size so long as it runs. That'd be Billy Mike, Lord High Everything Else down at the Niniltna Native Association, in case you've been living in a cave for the past two years. How's that new little baby of yours and Annie's doing, Billy? Cute as a kitten last time I saw her, and about as cuddly. Not as cuddly as Katya, though, sorry.

"Bernie out the Roadhouse says he's taking the Niniltna High men's and women's basketball teams to the Gold Medal Tournament in Juneau the end of March. This of course takes money, of which of course he doesn't have any, so the teams will be doing the usual bake sales and car washes and, he says, they'll be doing an exhibition game against a town team for which they will be charging admission."

Bobby dropped his already basso profundo voice to something approaching a sonic boom, what he thought of as a convincing murmur but which came across the airwaves as a clear and present danger to those who did not obey. "I don't know how many of you have been to the Gold Medal your own selves, so here's something for the history-impaired out there in radioland to chew on. Did you know that the Gold Medal tournament has been going on longer than the NBA championship? That's right, and what's more, there's a rock solid certainty that Bernie's kids'll get a chance to see some Edenshaws playing for Klawock, which as anyone who's ever seen one Edenshaw on a team let alone five will tell you is a learning experience all by itself. The teams are going, Bernie's taking 'em, you're paying for it. The exhibition game is at noon this Saturday at the Niniltna High School gym, and if you're not on the floor, I'll expect to see you in the bleachers.

"Last up, Auntie Vi is hosting her annual swap and shop the first Saturday in April, right after Bernie and the gang get back from Juneau, noon to six P.M. Bring by anything you want to sell, clean out those shops and sheds and crawl spaces to make room for mending gear this spring. Auntie Vi is donating ten percent of the proceeds to whatever expenses the team doesn't manage to cover, because you know there'll be some, and Bernie Koslowski tells me he's going to be anteing up a few choice items from his gold nugget hoard.

"I've got a heads-up for you cross-country travelers, too: Howie Katelnikof will have a booth there and you know how he's always got the good stuff priced to sell. He tells me he's featuring some like-new snow machine parts, everything from the track up, so be there! This is Park Air, and here's some music to get you in the mood for love. What'd I say? Of course I meant shopping."

Bobby sat back from the circular console that surrounded the central post of the A-frame as the strains of the Beatles' raunchy request for "Money" rocked out of the speakers. "Kate!" he bellowed. "How the hell are you?"

"Fine!" she yelled back, and reached around him to turn the volume down. Mutt galloped forward and elbowed Kate unceremoniously to one side so she could rear up and put both front paws on Bobby's shoulders.

His chair rolled back into the console with a sound thump. "Goddamn, Shugak!" Bobby roared, trying without success to fend off the tongue bath. "The house is fucking filled with fucking wolves again!"

"Goddamn!" Katya said, bouncing excitedly up and down in Kate's arms. "Goddamn!"

An ethereal blonde smiled at Kate from her seat in front of a computer on the other side of the console. "Hey, Kate."

"Hey, Dinah."

"How goes the battle?"

Kate's smile was slow and wicked. "I'm winning."

Dinah laughed. "Good to know."

"Be good to know what the hell you people are talking about even half the time," Bobby said. "Down!" he said to Mutt. She dropped down on all fours and laughed up at him, tongue lolling out the side of her mouth. He looked at Kate. "Unhand my child!"

"Daddy!" Without a moment's hesitation, Katya launched herself into space. In a well-practiced choreography, Mutt dodged out of the way so the latest aspirant to the Flying Wallendas could land neatly on Bobby's lap.

"One of these days you're going to miss," Kate said when her heart starting beating again.

Katya, a brown-faced, blue-eyed, curly-headed cherub, beamed at her. "Kate!"

"Yeah, that's me, kid, just several years older than when I walked in."

Kate gave Bobby a once-over, from his tightly curled cap of black hair, to the sharp angles of his cheekbones, his wide, firm-lipped mouth that seemed to be fixed in a permanently evil grin, to the broad shoulders and strong arms, to his muscular thighs that ended just below the knees.

He almost purred beneath her approving gaze, and she almost laughed out loud. "You are such a babe," she said.

"Why, thank you, Kate. You hear that, Dinah? About me being such a babe?"

"I heard. I'm considering the source."

Kate went for the coffeepot, poured mugs all around, and carried them to the living room.

Bobby Clark had acquired his land in a timely purchase just before d-2 had kicked in in 1980, forty acres on Squaw Candy Creek not far from where it flowed into the Kanuyaq and only a few miles from Niniltna. He'd built an A-frame with easy access for his wheelchair in mind (one big room, clockwise from upper left the bedroom, the bathroom, the kitchen, and the living room, floor clad in tongue-and-groove ash, and a central pillar up which snaked innumerable cables linking the electronics console that took up the center of the house to the 212-foot tower out back.

Bobby was the NOAA observer for the Park, reporting twice daily to NOAA and the National Weather Service and as needed on existing flying conditions to the FAA. This brought him in a very small amount of income, which led the curious to wonder how he financed his lifestyle. This included not only a wife and a daughter, but also a new truck every three years and a Piper Super Cub, as well as the stable of snow machines and four-wheelers required of any Park rat worthy of the name, all of them modified for use by a man who had left both his legs below the knee in Vietnam. The troopers out of Tok and Cordova had paid serious attention to Bobby when he had first appeared in the Park, but he had been scrupulous in giving them no reason whatsoever to continue this surveillance, and after a while they had gone away. After a while longer, the curiosity had gone away as well.

Attention resurfaced when Park Air went on the air, but Bobby was well able to afford the kind of devices that would deflect official notice from the FCC. Bobby had also from time to time been able to aid the troopers in their inquiries into various missing persons, as well as sundry personal property that had been, ah, misappropriated. Besides, the troopers enjoyed the broadcasts as much as the next Park rat, especially when Bobby, swallowing hard, put up a weekly two-hour show featuring the likes of Clint Black. Loretta Lynn he could stomach and he thought Patsy Cline divine, but he also thought the last decent country western singer had died with Hank Williams. Senior. "If they wanna be rock stars, let 'em sing goddamn rock and roll," he growled, but beneath his breath when the law showed up with the latest Tim McGraw CD.

Dinah had appeared in the Park almost four years before, a self-taught videographer with the declared intention of producing documentaries on life in Alaska. In spite of her being as white as he was black and twenty years his junior, they had married, and produced Katya minutes later. Kate had been in attendance front and center for both events, the memory of which she had been trying without success to erase from her cerebral cortex ever since.

As Kate watched, Katya wriggled free of her father's lenient grasp and scooted over to where Mutt was pawing through the wood box in search of the thighbone of a *T. rex* Bobby always kept there in case wolves got into the house. Bobby rolled his wheelchair around the console and picked Dinah up out of her chair and wrestled her into his lap. She protested but not too much, and he rolled them both over to the living room and shifted them to one of the couches that formed an open square.

Kate sipped coffee and waited for the giggling to die down, and then waited some more. "Perhaps the two of you would like to get a room."

Dinah, face flushed with laughter and perhaps something more, struggled free of her husband's grip and sat up straight. "Nonsense." She smoothed her hair back and reached for the mug of coffee Kate had placed on the coffee table. "We're an old married couple."

"Yeah," Bobby said, waggling his eyebrows, "and even if we weren't, we don't need no stinking room."

Kate rolled her eyes, but she and Bobby had had a thing back before Jack, before Jim, and way before Dinah, and she understood Bobby's talent for showing a woman the view from the mountaintop.

He bent a stern eye upon her, as if he knew what she was thinking. "You're looking awfully fucking smug there yourself, Shugak."

"I don't know why you would say that, Clark," she said with all the primness at her command, which wasn't much and which was pretty much ruined by the shit-eating grin that followed, but she forestalled further cross-examination. "What does Brendan want?"

Brendan was Brendan McCord of the Anchorage district attorney's office, a coconspirator of Kate's from her time served there, a longtime friend and an enthusiastic if erratic suitor.

Bobby waggled his eyebrows again, which given how thick and long they were were admirably suited to the purpose. "The reason they're called state secrets is because, you know, they're secret. ADA McCord doesn't think I need to know."

Kate waggled her own eyebrows back at him, which were less busy and altogether more elegant but did not fail of effect.

"The Smiths," Bobby said.

Dinah poked him in the side. "You're so easy."

He gave her a lascivious grin. "But not cheap."

Before they could get started again, Kate groaned. "I had a clue. What have they been up to lately?"

The Smiths had materialized in the Park the previous fall with the title to forty acres of land ten miles outside of the Niniltna city limits and five miles inside the Park boundary. Title to said land did not include a right of way between the road from Niniltna and the property. There was a dirt airstrip, but the Smiths, defying life as it was known in Alaska, did not number a pilot in their midst. Father Smith professed an aversion to civilization and all that came with it, which included aviation. Also electricity, running water, power tools, voting, jury duty, and public education. They also shunned birthdays and Christmas, but given their seventeen offspring this was generally seen to be more an act of fiscal survival than a faith-based initiative.

This aversion apparently did not include heavy-duty equipment, as their first act upon relocating to the Park was to rent a D6 Caterpillar tractor from Mac Devlin. Their second act was to bulldoze a track over fourteen miles of previously pristine Park land.

This had taken place the previous January. The Smiths woke up at least one bear by rolling over its den, felled a small forest of spruce that had managed to survive until that day the depredations of the spruce bark beetle epidemic, diverted the course of Salmon Creek, and wiped out Demetri Totemoff's duly permitted trapline along said creek. Demetri appealed to the Park's chief ranger, Dan O'Brien.

Upon inspection of the afflicted area, Dan went into orbit, not a great surprise to anybody watching. Everyone liked Dan, one of the few rangers in Alaska never to have been shot at in the line of duty. This was a real danger in the Park, first from cranky old farts who had homesteaded in territorial days only to see themselves after statehood slowly surrounded by the creation of federal and state parks, wildlife refuges and forests, and second from cranky Alaska Natives who had been hunting caribou and moose and bear in the area for ten thousand years and saw no need for either hunting licenses or hunting seasons.

But it had to be said that there was more than a little fellow feeling for the Smiths, who were only exercising their by-God given rights to access their own by-God land.

"Except it turns out," Bobby said, enjoying himself hugely, "that the title to said land may be in some question."

"You mean the Smiths didn't buy it after all?"

"Oh, they bought it, all right, but they bought it off some old guy who just got a divorce and hadn't waited for the property to be divided up between him and his ex-wife before he sold it off."

Kate paused with her coffee mug in midair. "Would that be Vinnie Huckabee?"

"And his lovely former wife, Rebecca, yes it would. God, what a bitch."

Dinah poked him in the side. "You used to think she was hot."

Bobby poked her back. "She was hot. Until I got to know her. Now she's just a bitch."

Rebecca and Vinnie Huckabee had split the sheets in spectacular fashion a year before. It hadn't been a Spenard divorce, exactly, but rumor had it there had been gunfire involved and later, and worse, a lot of lawyers who had distinguished themselves primarily by the speed with which they had serially decamped the case. Rebecca, an attorney prior to marrying Vinnie, in the end violated the cardinal rule of jurisprudence and represented herself, which didn't give her anything in the still-ongoing settlement hearings except continuity.

"The story goes that Vinnie hightailed it to town and hunkered down with his brother in Chugiak. His brother—"

"Walter."

"—his brother Walter put the word out about Vinnie having land for sale and along come the Smiths, new to the state and—" Bobby hesitated, "—and new to our ways."

Kate looked at Dinah. Dinah looked demure. "Let me guess," Kate said to Bobby, "they wanted to get back to nature."

Bobby clucked his tongue. "Don't be so cynical. They came to Alaska to reinvent themselves, as do all good cheechakos who hear the call of the wild." His grin flashed out again, partly righteous, all rogue. "They heard tell someone had some land for sale up back of beyond, and got in touch. Vinnie wasn't asking much, from what I hear, he just wanted enough cash to adios it. Last anybody heard he was on his way to Nome. Is Nome a good place to hide out from pissed-off soon-to-be ex-wives?"

"Beats the hell out of me."

"And she was pissed off, was the lovely Rebecca," Bobby said, dwelling upon what was evidently a fond memory. "Word is she went ballistic when she heard about the sale. Especially when she heard how much Willie sold it for. She figured it should have sold for a lot more. And she was right, was the lovely Rebecca."

"So," Kate said patiently, "the Smiths came here and rented a bulldozer."

"They have also begun to fell trees for a house and outbuildings. Some of them are Park trees."

Kate thought of Dan O'Brien and shuddered. "They must be pretty well financed if they can buy up that much land for cash and pay Mac Devlin enough to convince him to allow them to drive his beloved Cat. What does an Anchorage DA want me to do? This is a federal matter."

"Better ask him," Bobby said. "He said he'd be available all this afternoon."

Time was when Kate needed to talk to Anchorage, Bobby got on his ham radio, exchanged pleasantries with a ham in New Zealand and another in Iraq before raising KL7CC in Anchorage, who called Brendan at his office and patched him through over the air. Now Bobby went to his computer, got online via satellite, and bellied Kate up to the keyboard to do a little IM-ing. At least every Park rat with a radio wasn't listening in, but she missed eavesdropping on Bobby's conversations with the likes of King Juan Carlos, Jeana Yeager, and Barry Goldwater. Even if Barry was dead. She had a feeling most Park rats felt the same way.

In the meantime, she bellied. "Oh ha ha," she said when she saw the user name Bobby had assigned to her.

Bobby grinned his wide, nasty grin. "Thought you might like it."

"Very funny." Kate turned back to the keyboard before he could see her answering grin.

SHYSTERGUY: Hey, gorgeous, how you?

PARKDICK: Life is good, handsome. Whattup?

SHYSTERGUY: Right to business, that's what I love about you, Katie. The Smiths.

PARKDICK: I had a feeling. What about them?

SHYSTERGUY: They're driving the feds crazy.

PARKDICK: Great! Let's throw a party.

SHYSTERGUY: Spoken like a true Park rat. The feds are leaning on the state to exercise a little authority in this situation. Especially since they know Niniltna now has its own trooper in residence.

PARKDICK: How much authority?

SHYSTERGUY: Run them off, if you can. I'm told that their title to the land is in question.

PARKDICK: You want me to evict them?

SHYSTERGUY: Yeah.

PARKDICK: Kinda sorta need a court order for that.

SHYSTERGUY: Got one.

PARKDICK: Which judge?

SHYSTERGUY: Reitman.

PARKDICK: Figures.

SHYSTERGUY: Don't blame me, take it up with the Park Service.

PARKDICK: Why doesn't Jim's boss just order him to do it? Why me?

SHYSTERGUY: It may come to that. These folks seem ready to call out the National Guard.

"You miserable little shit," Kate said out loud.

"What'd I do?" Bobby said, injured.

"She means the other miserable little shit," Dinah said serenely, and went to the kitchen to open cans of salmon for sandwiches.

PARKDICK: You want me to be your process server.

SHYSTERGUY: Did I mention the National Guard? We were thinking—

PARKDICK: WE were thinking?

SHYSTERGUY: Okay, I, I was thinking. I was especially thinking when the Park Service started mobilizing for Iwo Jima here. If some mild-mannered, inoffensive little Park rat—

Kate snorted.

SHYSTERGUY: —I heard that—

"Sure you did," Kate said, toying with the mouse, running the cursor over the sign out option on the drop-down menu in a suggestive manner.

SHYSTERGUY: —I was thinking that if some rational person who knows everyone involved would go talk to these people and try to get them to back off before somebody brings out the assault weapons, it would be a good thing for all concerned.

Kate thought about it.

SHYSTERGUY: Kate? You still there?

PARKDICK: How much are you paying me?

SHYSTERGUY: The general thinking seems to be whatever you want to get the feds off our backs.

PARKDICK: Lots. It'll be lots.

SHYSTERGUY: Attagirl. I'll fast-track the court order and fly it in on George first available. And Kate?

PARKDICK: What?

SHYSTERGUY: You never heard me say this (you especially never heard me say this anywhere near Ranger Dan) but tell the Smiths to get themselves a smart lawyer. I've seen the paperwork the Park Service used to get this writ and it's totally based on technicalities. The current administration is coming down heavy on the side of the rights of the property owner, not to mention easier public access to parks and wildlife refuges in the public domain. Most Alaskan judges are already there, and it's a toss-up which Alaskan juries hate more, technicalities or the federal government. Barring an appeal to the 9th District, the Smiths will get a friendly hearing.

Brendan signed off.

"Yeah," Kate said, pushing back from the console, "but will you love me tomorrow?"

Sec. 11.41.100. Murder in the First Degree

(a) A person commits the crime of murder in the first degree if

(1) with intent to cause the death of another person, the person . . .

(B) compels or induces any person to commit suicide through duress or deception . . .

—Alaska statutes

She wasn't a weakling—she used to help her dad pull gear at the setnet site, and she could tote potatoes out of her mom's garden a bushel at a time—but the truck was so big, and she was so tired.

She paused to mop her face on her shirtsleeve. She cast a furtive glance over her shoulder at the house, scanning the windows overlooking the yard, worried that he would see her. Fear bent her over the jack handle again, working it up and down. The barely healed bone in her right arm ached with the motion, and she shifted her stance, but that just made the bruises on her back hurt. She shifted her stance a third time, so that she stood halfway under the enormous wheel well of the truck.

It wasn't a very good jack, and she'd get it up so far and it would slide down. Her movements became more frantic because time was running out and she knew he was coming, because he was always coming, and he wouldn't be pleased that she hadn't finished changing the tire. She knew by then that there was nothing he wouldn't do when he was displeased, from forcing her to have sex right there on the ground to locking her overnight in the woodshed. She was still cold from the last time. November was a harsh month to be out all night in nothing but a T-shirt and jeans and moccasins.

Maybe he would only beat her. It was the best she could hope for. And she healed up pretty fast so that no one knew.

She didn't want anyone to know, ever.

The tears were running down her face by the time she got the tire off. It weighed more than she did, and she had to let it fall. It rolled down the icy driveway to thump into the porch and fall over.

The door to the house opened, and she jerked in a panic, bumping into the jack. It wobbled. The truck leaned over on its unsupported side. She looked up and saw the wheel well coming down.

She had plenty of time to dodge out of the way.

She didn't.

FOUR

With what any Park rat would have considered true heroism, Kate tackled what she considered to be the most hazardous segment of Brendan's assignment first. Heroism notwithstanding, she took Mutt with her as insurance.

Her battered red pickup poked a cautious nose up over the edge of the Step and halted, engine idling, clutch thrown out, ready for a quick getaway. Kate poked an even more cautious nose up over the edge of the dashboard to peer through the windshield at the Park Service buildings clustered together at the side of an airstrip of snow so hard-packed it looked like an elongated hockey rink. The view was slightly altered by the canyon-sized crack that ran from side to side on her windshield, courtesy of a rock kicked up by Martin Shugak's truck when he passed her on the road into town last fall. She was going to have to speak to Martin about getting mud guards for his rear wheels.

Smoke was rising from the chimneys of the office buildings, mess hall, and bunkhouses. Neat paths had been cut through the snow, deeper here at two thousand feet than in Niniltna two miles down the valley.

At first viewing, no one had yet dug revetments for machine gun emplacements. Kate put the truck into gear and rolled discreetly up onto the small plateau that divided Park flatlander from Park mountain goat.

The light was on in Dan's office. She backed into a parking space, left the keys in the ignition with the engine idling, and went in.

He was hunched over his desk, scowling ferociously at a pile of paperwork, a man with orange-red hair the consistency of steel wool and bright blue eyes which on most days held a latent twinkle that invited everyone to laugh along with him at pretty much everything life had to offer. Kate opened her mouth to say hello, and his phone rang. Without looking up he reached over, picked up the receiver, and let it fall back in the cradle.

Kate closed her mouth again and gave some thought to a strategic retreat.

Mutt, suffering no such self-doubt, shouldered her way past Kate and bounded into the room and up on Dan's desk, scattering paper in every direction.

"What the—"

Mutt pounced, pushing him back in his chair with her front paws and giving him a tongue bath that would have wrung Bobby Clark's heart with envy.

"Jesus!" Dan said, trying and failing to twist out of reach. "Call her off before I drown, Kate!"

Mutt dropped back to all fours, scattering more paper, and grinned down at him.

He was not noticeably charmed. "Off!" he said, pointing at the floor. "Off the desk, right now!"

Before he could duck out of the way, she licked him again and then bounced off the desk, more paper flying, and headed for the mess hall where she knew there would be something edible and someone to either beguile or terrify into handing it over.

In a situation like this, Dan O'Brien could be relied upon to laugh loud and long. He opted this morning instead to curse, loud and long, while he picked up after Mutt. "Can't you control that fucking dog any better than that, Shugak?"

Kate said nothing.

Dan looked up at the extended silence, and he had the grace to look a little ashamed. It made him mad all over again. "What do you want, anyway?" He stood up suddenly, a sheaf of papers in one hand. "Oh. Oh, yeah, now I get the call I got this morning. You're here about those goddamn squatters, the Smiths, aren't you? Aren't you?"

"Yes," Kate said.

The mildness of her tone was a clear warning, but today it was like waving a red flag in front of an already enraged bull. "Jesus, Kate, do you know anything about these—these people?"

"No," she said. She sat down and smiled up at him. "Why don't you tell me."

He tossed the bundle of papers on his desk with no regard for in what order they landed and strode to the wall to pull down a map of the Park. Niniltna, Ahtna, and Cordova were small red urban enclaves in a huge sea of green, spotted with blue parcels indicating Native land, much of which followed the course of the Kanuyaq River and the coastline of Prince William Sound. Widely scattered and very tiny yellow polka dots indicated the less than 10 percent of the Park that was privately owned. There were a very few, very small, and very scattered brown parcels indicating areas of natural resources for which the Parks Department had with a show of great reluctance granted various exploration companies permission to look for natural resources, mostly timber, coal, and oil. Word was that someone had won a bid to explore for gold on a privately owned creek very near the land the Smiths had bought. She wondered how eager the Smiths would be to build when they heard a gold dredge would be starting up next door.

Dan stabbed a green portion north-northwest of Niniltna with an accusatory forefinger. "They rented a goddamn bulldozer from that well-known tree hugger, Mac Devlin—who has been laughing it up all over the goddamn Park ever since—and cleared four miles'—four fucking miles!—worth of road through a previously pristine section of a federally created, publicly funded national park. In the process they knocked down a section of spruce trees wasn't one of which was less than a hundred years old and crossed Salmon Creek a dozen times or more. I don't have to remind you that Salmon Creek is one of the main tributaries of that area, do I? Or that it's prime spawning ground for Kanuyaq River reds?"

"No," Kate said.

"Or that it's so healthy, the beaver population has finally come back enough that it's harvestable?" He flung himself into his chair, which rolled backward to crash into the wall. "I got notice of the sale, Kate, and I did my by-God duty, I hired a surveyor—at public expense—to run tape and set markers to show the new owners exactly and precisely where the boundaries of their land were. And they go and start building their goddamn house right on the western property line! They've got forty fucking acres, for crissake! They don't need to be hanging the ass end of their fucking cabin into the Park!"

He held up one hand and began to tick items off on his fingers. "I wrote to them when they first got here, and they refused any mail with a Park Service return address on it." Tick. "They could have filed a request for legal access with the service. They didn't bother, they just Catted right on through." Tick. "They've got an airstrip they won't use because none of them's a pilot and they say George is too expensive." Tick.

He clenched his hands and glared at Kate. "I won't be calmed down here, Kate."

"Okay," Kate said.

"I won't be soothed, placated, or mollified."

"Understood."

"I want to bust heads, is what I want to do, but I won't, because the federal government pays me not to."

"Good."

"But I'm pissed off and I see no reason not to be!"

"Me, either," she said devoutly.

"After they got done with their road, they started blading trails for their goddamn four-wheelers and their fucking snow machines! Jesus! There's such a thing as the public interest, Kate!"

"You betcha."

"They don't own the Park, we all do!"

"Yes indeedy."

"Supposing I took a Cat into Volcanoes National Park on the Big Island and started plowing up lava right, left, and center for the foundation of my new six-room ocean-view house?"

"Madame Pele would be seriously pissed."

"How about you and me, we take a rig out to Old Faithful and start drilling pipe to tap some of that geothermal energy just going to waste?"

"Hell of an idea."

Mutt wandered in, a length of pepperoni hanging out of her mouth, took in the situation, and wandered back out again.

"Or I'll tell you what, my grandmother's got a house on the downslope of the western side of Shenandoah. How about I push in a little right of way for her so she can hike up to the Appalachian

Trail whenever she wants? Be good for her, get her heart started in the morning, and hey, who's going to complain about a little old lady getting her exercise?"

"Hardly anyone," Kate said, and checked the clock.

"The public interest does not suffer at the hands of private convenience, Kate!"

"It shouldn't," Kate said. "Dan?"

"What?"

"I've got a court order evicting the Smiths from their property, until such time as it is determined that they have clear title to it."

He stared at her, uncomprehending, but at least she had stemmed the tide. "What?"

Patiently, she repeated herself.

Halfway through, he interrupted her. "They won't go."

"Dan—"

"They won't go, Kate," he said, his voice rising again. "Short of bringing in Smythe the Smoother Mover and a SWAT team, you're not going to get them to comply with a court order."

Kate looked at him. He stared back at her.

Mutt, attracted by the lowering of the decibel level, reappeared and looked at them hopefully, her tail sweeping the air in expectant arcs.

"Okay, fine." Dan reached for his jacket. "This I want to see for myself."

Dan rode with Kate, maintaining a righteously I-warned-you-and-you-refused-to-listen-upon-your-own-head-be-it attitude from Step to town. From Niniltna proper, it was a very few miles farther, past abandoned cabins with peeling log walls, asphalt roofs missing shingles and tar paper beginning to molt, doors hanging crookedly from the slash of grizzly claws. "These are on Park land, right?" Kate said.

Dan gave a curt nod.

"You ought to clean them up."

He glared at her. "We would have burned them down if the owners hadn't tied up the Park Service in court with the same litigation the Smiths are using to gum up the works right now."

As they passed the turnoff to Mac Devlin's Nabesna Mines, he actually growled out loud. Kate maintained a prudent silence. Mutt licked Dan's cheek. "Knock it off, Mutt," Dan said, giving her an irritable shove.

Mutt, unaccustomed to and offended by this kind of cavalier treatment, turned her back on him, not an easy thing to do even in the large cab of Kate's pickup.

Moments passed. "Oh hell," Dan said. "I'm sorry, Mutt."

She forgave him instantly, of course. Kate noticed that no such apology was forthcoming to herself.

At Dan's direction, Kate turned onto a trail not hardly wide enough for the pickup. Spruce limbs swept the cab clean of snow, and alder branches scraped at the windows. "There," Dan said, pointing.

Kate could hardly have missed it: a gaping wound in the trees exactly the width of the blade of a D-6 Caterpillar tractor. The drop-off from the track they were on to the beginning of the Cat trail was precipitous. The pickup bottomed out, and for a moment Kate was worried they were high-centered, but they crept forward. She had to yank on the wheel to avoid getting tangled up in the exposed roots of a toppled spruce. They lurched over a section of creek that was more mud than ice—Dan growled again—and then she swerved to avoid a bull moose quietly snacking on a diamond willow. He flicked one ear as they missed his rump by inches.

"Looks good, doesn't he," Kate said, who was never able to look at a moose without imagining it butchered and wrapped and stored in her cache. Or nowadays, her freezer. My freezer, she thought, my freezer, my freezer, my freezer, and then another downed spruce leapt out of the surrounding forest and she focused her attention on her driving.

It took an hour to drive the four miles, bumping over frost heaves and rudimentary creek crossings and averting collisions with three more moose who appeared to think the Smiths had cleared this path specifically to better their access to browse, and Kate was thinking that a mile every fifteen minutes was pretty good time. They emerged at last into a clearing, half natural and half Cat-made. The trail had risen steadily over the past half hour, and the clearing sat on a balding knoll with a spectacular view of the high, wide gravel moraine of the Suulutaq Glacier and the eastern horizon, where the Quilaks loitered with intent.

The sun played hide-and-seek behind large clumps of cumulus clouds, and a soft breeze kissed their cheeks as they got out of the pickup and walked forward to greet the group of people assembling on a ground-level deck that wrapped around the house on three sides. The deck looked comparatively finished next to the skeleton of the square cabin going up behind it. The canvas stretched over the frame was weighted down with ropes tied off to rocks. The foundation of the cabin looked solid and substantial, and all four walls were four logs up. The logs looked freshly felled and peeled. Kate heard Dan's teeth grinding together, and refrained from expressing any admiration of the unquestionable craftsmanship on display. They might be wearing rose-colored glasses, but the Smiths could see through them well enough to build, and build well. With or without power tools.

"Ranger O'Brien," the eldest man said in a voice that could lead cavalry charges.

Dan inclined his head and said stiffly, "Mr. Smith."

"Call me Father. Everyone does." He looked at Kate. "And who might this be?"

"This is Kate Shugak, Mr. Smith. Kate, Mr. Smith."

Kate's hand disappeared into an enormous sinewy fist and she was bowed over with a grace that would befit the court of Queen Elizabeth II. "How do you do, Kate. Do you live in the Park? A neighbor, perhaps?"

"I live in the Park, yes. I have a homestead about thirty-five miles away, as the crow flies."

He smiled benignly. "In the Park that's practically next door. Come, meet my family."

Father Smith was tall and burly, with a full beard and hair to match. Both reached past his waist in streams of pure and abundant white. His eyes were a bright, vivid blue. He wore jeans, a plaid shirt, red suspenders, and Sorels, topped by a leather fedora that looked halfway between an Australian bush hat and something Hoss Cartwright would wear. He had the tip of a peacock feather stuck in the hatband. Mother Smith was shorter and lacked the beard but was in every other way similar.

The children, boys and girls, looked like clones of their parents. They were brought forward to be introduced in order, alphabetical and as near as Kate could tell chronological, as Abigail, Benjamin, Chloe, David, Ezra, Felix, Gabriel, Hannah, Imrah, Janoah, Keren, Lod, Moses, Nathan, Obadiah, Phebe, and Quartus. Abigail looked to be in her early twenties, Quartus about kindergarten age, and Mother Smith not nearly so tired as she ought to be.

A movement caught the corner of her eye, and she turned her head to see what it was. Dan noticed her sudden stillness immediately. "Kate?" He followed her gaze to the man standing in the doorway of the framed-in cabin. "Oh. Oh holy shit." This last was said beneath his breath but earned a reproving glance from Father Smith nonetheless.

Kate moved forward. The crowd of milling children parted instinctively, something in the carriage of her head and shoulders parting them the way Moses had the Red Sea.

Louis Deem's smile was as lazy and charming as ever. "Kate." The gold incisor glinted as his lips pulled back.

Kate's voice cracked like a whip. "What are you doing here?"

The eldest girl—Allison? No, Abigail—Abigail came up to stand next to Louis, and before Kate's disbelieving and appalled eyes he draped an arm around her shoulders and pulled her next to him. Abigail, a slender brunette with melting brown eyes and creamy, translucent skin, looked up at him adoringly, and in reward he dropped a light kiss on her nose. "You've met my fiancée."

"Fiancée?" Kate tried to say, but the word came out in a high squeak.

Louis dropped his voice to a confidential murmur pitched to be heard all over the clearing. "It wouldn't have worked with us, Kate."

Kate gaped at him.

"I'm sorry," he said soberly, "but Abigail has shown me the way to the Lord. I'm home with her in a way that I never could have been with you."

He actually reached out and patted her shoulder, and she was so stunned, she actually let him. "You'll find someone else, Kate." He smiled down at Abigail. "You'll see."

Mutt suffered no such confusion and snapped at Louis's hand. He snatched it back and Kate, coming back to her senses, was pleased to hear a muttered oath, quickly stifled.

"That dog is dangerous," Abigail said in some alarm, and drew Louis back a step.

He pulled her against him. "It's all right." He smiled again at Kate, having regained his mask. "She didn't lay a glove on me."

Dan came trotting up behind Kate. She felt a hand grasp her arm, a voice say, "Kate, come on."

She shook her elbow free. "Do you know who this is?" she said to Abigail. "He eats little girls like you for breakfast. Also lunch and dinner. You don't want to marry this man." She wheeled and looked at Father Smith. "You do not want your daughter marrying this man." She heard her voice rising and could do nothing to stop it. "You do not want this man marrying into your family."

The family Smith was standing in a semicircle, watching, the children wide-eyed, Mother Smith serene, Father Smith avuncular. Two of the younger girls, Chloe and Hannah—or was it Phebe?—hunched their shoulders, drew together, and held tightly to each other's hands, fixing Kate with enormous eyes.

"Now, now," Father Smith said soothingly, "we know all about that business with that unfortunate young woman, but Louis was acquitted of any wrongdoing. He has been very frank about the mistakes he has made, but he has truly repented, and who are we to condemn what the law and the Lord have not? Louis wants to get on with his life, and he has chosen to begin again with Abigail." He hesitated, and said, "And forgive me, but . . . there seems to be some self-interest in your warnings toward my daughter, Kate. Louis is right, you know. I understand your disappointment, but there will be someone else for you."

"There has been," Kate said, "several times, and trust me, none of them was named Louis Deem."

But Louis had in a few choice words effectively destroyed any credibility Kate might have had with the Smiths. She looked at Abigail's mother. "Mrs. Smith? Surely you cannot accept this man into your family after everything he has done? I know you're new to the Park, but ask anyone, they'll tell you. This is not a man. This is a monster."

Abigail jerked beneath a suddenly tightened grip.

"It's Mother Smith," the woman said gently, and even went so far as to wag an admonitory finger. "Judge not, lest ye be judged."

"Judge me however the hell you want, feel free," Kate said. "Just know that if your daughter marries Louis Deem, you might as well start digging her grave. Louis's probably getting tired of digging them himself, seeing as how he's up to three now."

Louis's smile looked like it was taking a little more effort. "When he starts hitting you," Kate told Abigail, "and he will, leave him. He lands the first blow, you walk out the door." Kate looked back at Louis. "Because he won't stop with hitting. He never does."

She looked around at the circle of faces and couldn't bear to stay there another minute. She turned.

"Uh, Kate," Dan said, shifting from foot to foot. Like any other Park rat, he knew the long and bloody history of Louis Deem, but while Kate's priorities were all about the people, his were all about the land.

"What?" she said, biting off the word.

He jerked his head at Father Smith. "Aren't you going to serve him with the, you know, the thing?"

She stared at him, and then remembered. "Oh. Right." She pulled a document from her pocket and slapped it against Father Smith's chest. His hand came up automatically to catch it before it fell. "You are hereby notified by the state of Alaska that your title to this property is in question. You are ordered to vacate it until such time as clear title is established in a court of law. Have a nice day."

He'll kill her," Kate told Jim.

"Probably," Jim said.

His calm reply infuriated her. "He'll marry her, he'll steal everything of the Smiths' that isn't nailed down, and then she won't get the crease right when she irons his jeans, and he'll kill her for it."

"You really think Louis Deem irons his jeans?"

"This isn't funny, Jim!" Kate took a hasty turn around his office. Mutt, wisely, was keeping to her neutral corner. Mutt tended to stick with what worked.

"No." Jim shook his head. "It isn't funny, but I can't do anything, Kate, and you know it."

"Yeah, you have to let him kill her before you can do anything."

Jim opened his mouth to defend himself. Fortunately, Kate was on a tear, so it wasn't necessary.

"Let's take a walk down memory lane, shall we?" Kate ticked off on her fingers. "When Louis Deem is twenty-one, he gets hauled into court for the statutory rape of sixteen-year-old Jessie McComas."

"Who," Jim said, attempting to exercise a preemptive strike, "insists that it was not rape, that she and Louis are madly in love and are going to live happily ever after. She's half right. They do marry. They don't live happily ever after."

"Louis does," Kate said. "Jessie, on the other hand, dies six months later in a fall through the ice when she's fetching water from the creek out back of Louis's cabin. The inquest rules it death by misadventure, although they never could come up with an explanation for the lump on the back of her head. Particularly when she was found facedown in the creek."

"Who was the coroner on that case?"

"Magistrate Matthew Nelson."

"Oh yeah. I remember now. Meltdown Matt. He retired soon after."

"I'm pretty sure the state insisted on it," Kate said. "And then we have little Ruthie Moonin, Louis's second wife. She lasted longer than Jessie, almost a year, until Louis's truck fell on her when she was changing his tire. He never did explain why she was changing the tire and he wasn't, but the trooper—"

"Harry Milner."

"Trooper Milner couldn't find just cause and had to let it go. That's where our Louis got his homestead. It belonged to Ruthie's parents, and she was an only child."

"He kill them, too?"

"No," she said, reluctant to admit to even a negative virtue to Louis Deem. "Not that he wouldn't have, but they were dead by then. Ruthie was an orphan, and sole heir. Why do you think he married her?"

Again, the question was rhetorical.

"For crissake, Jim, this guy used to sneak up on Mandy's dog lot and use her dogs for target practice!"

"I didn't know that," Jim said. "What happened?"

"It took Chick three tries before he finally tracked Louis down."

"Chick turn him in?"

Kate snorted. "Chick beat the crap out of him. There were broken bones and internal injuries. For a while we were hoping Louis was going to die, but no such luck."

"What happened to Chick?"

"Nothing." At Jim's look, Kate added, "Harry Milner had his retirement locked in, and by then he knew how bent Louis Deem was. He was hoping Louis was going to die, too. He told Chick he was a bad, bad boy and refused to arrest him the next three times he caught Chick drunk driving."

"Did Louis bring charges?"

Kate's face hardened. "No. By the time he was up and walking around again, Mandy'd got Chick back on the wagon. Louis romanced one of Bernie's waitresses into supplying Chick with free drinks the next time he came in alone. Chick wound up in detox and he nearly died. Mandy kicked him out again and he wound up in the drunk tank again and I had to bail him out. Again."

"And the waitress—"

"Mary Waterbury. Pretty little thing. Almost married that asshole Lester Akiakchak. I wish she had. Lester's worthless, but at least he's not homicidal." She looked at him. "Jim, we taught this guy how to kill. Not only that, we taught him that he can get away with it."

"I know, Kate." They brooded together in silence for a moment, and then Jim said, "Louis only marries Natives."

"Of course he does," Kate said, "and only Natives with regular dividends from their Native corporations. And Ruthie had land and a house. And now Louis lives in it."

"And Howie."

"And Howie."

"And Willard."

Kate's lips tightened. "And Willard." She looked at him, her eyes glittering. "He'll kill Abigail. You know it, I know it, pretty much everyone in the Park knows it except for Abigail and her idiot family."

"Abigail isn't Native," Jim said.

"Abigail is the eldest child of parents who own forty acres of land that sit on the edge of the Park between the nearest town and an old gold mine, and gold at present is selling for over five hundred an ounce."

"You think that's what he has in mind?"

"No, I think that's what Father and Mother Smith have in mind." At Jim's look, Kate said, "You've heard the rumor that some outfit has been granted permission to do some exploration on Salmon Creek?"

"The one next to the Smiths' property?"

"That's the one. When I was up on the Step this morning, I was looking at Dan's map, you know the one?" Kate waited for Jim's nod. "I saw the flag on the area. Kanuyaq Mining and Minerals."

"Never heard of them."

"Me neither, but I bet if we did a search of the incorporation papers, we'd find somebody named Smith somewhere up the bread crumb trail."

It sounded as likely as anything else. "What are you going to do about it?"

"Nothing," Kate said. "It's Dan's job to worry about illegal mineral exploitation on Park land. I'm worried about Abigail."

"Me, too," Jim said heavily. "Me, too."

Mutt tested the tension in the air with an inquiring nose and ventured out of her corner, padding over to rest her head on Jim's knee. He scratched behind her ears, and she let out a heartfelt sigh that increased the air pressure in his office by at least ten millibars.

He looked over at Kate, who was staring out the window with a set expression. "Kate?"

"What?"

"What did Louis Deem do to earn him that gold tooth?"

Her eyes were flat and unreadable. "Come on, Mutt," she said, rising to her feet. "Let's head for the barn."

Jim listened to Mutt's toenails beat a retreating tattoo on the new linoleum floors.

But it wasn't Abigail's body they found a month later.

It was instead plump, perpetually unhappy Enid Esther Koslowski, sprawled head down on the staircase leading from her deck.

Two steps up from her lay her son, fourteen-year-old Fitz, in a broken, bleeding heap.

The two of them had been shot to death at point-blank range.

FIVE

THE FIRST SATURDAY IN APRIL

the Roadhouse

In the Roadhouse parking lot, people huddled together in small groups, holding on to each other like they'd fall over if they didn't. Jim opened up the back of the Blazer and pulled out the aluminum suitcase that held his crime scene kit. "Where's Bernie?"

The four Grosdidier brothers, the first string of Niniltna's emergency response team, gave a collective jerk of their heads. Jim squared his shoulders and threaded his way through the silent crowd, his mouth a grim line. Faces, pinched and pale and shocked, turned to watch, and one part of his brain began a list of potential witnesses.

In back of the Roadhouse were two rows of cabins which no matter what anyone said he knew from personal experience could not be rented by the hour. Bernie had put in a couple of covered picnic areas with fire pits and tables and benches for the occasional

RV that stuck out the road in from Ahtna in the summer. A thick stand of birch insulated the cabin area from the Koslowski house, two stories high with a large deck supporting wrought-iron outdoor furniture and a gas grill big enough to roast an entire bull moose that was the envy of every man in the Park. The deck was reached by a wide staircase with two landings, both landings laden with flower boxes that in summer overflowed with an artful riot of nasturtiums and pansies. French doors led from the deck into the house.

Kate was there before him. Naturally whoever called would have called her first. Jim had been working late at the post, so he got the news second. Another state trooper might have been annoyed by this assignment of second-class law enforcement status, but he was past protesting it.

Billy Mike, who would have been the third call anyone made, was standing behind Kate, who sat cross-legged on the ground a few feet away from the foot of the stairs. Like the shocked, staring crowd in back of them, no one was talking.

Even though he'd been told on the phone, years of on-the-job experience were all that kept Jim moving forward at a steady, deliberate pace. His hand was sweating on the handle of the suitcase. He halted beside Billy and set the suitcase down as quietly as possible before it slipped from his hand.

Bernie was sitting on the steps between his slain wife and son. Enid and Fitz were too far apart and the stairs too steep for Bernie to pull them both into his arms. His legs were braced against different steps and his arms were outspread, one fist knotted in his wife's shirt, the other in his son's, as if by main force he could pull them back from death. He was rocking slightly back and forth, his face turned up to an indifferent heaven, his mouth open in a soundless cry.

There was a sound from the doorway, and Jim looked up to see the outline of a kid crouched there. "Oh Christ," he said beneath his breath. "Kate," he said, and had to repeat her name before she would look around. He nodded at the French doors, one of them shattered, at the white face peering through them.

She drew in a sharp breath, shot to her feet, and started forward involuntarily.

"Not that way," Jim said. "Go around to the back door. Try not to go inside."

She halted as if she'd run into a wall.

"It's a crime scene," he said, as gently as he could. "Go around to the back door. Try not to go inside, but get him out."

She nodded, all her attention fixed on the face behind the French doors.

She went around the back almost at a run. A moment later, Jim could hear her voice. The face in the door wavered and then disappeared, and moments later Kate reappeared, a protective arm around Johnny Morgan's shoulders, a Johnny who was white as a sheet and very shaky on his feet.

Fitz. And Johnny. Lab partners.

Jim looked for Van and didn't see her.

Kate whispered something in Johnny's ear, and he nodded and whispered something back. Kate nodded and squeezed his shoulder and gave him a nudge toward Annie Mike, who welcomed him with open arms. He looked around and said something inaudible to Annie, and Jim heard Annie say, "She's all right, Johnny. She's at home, minding the baby for me."

He said something to Kate. She was clearly startled, and asked him a question. He nodded, white but resolute. She looked over at Jim and then back at Johnny and said something else. The boy nodded again, looking suddenly, infinitely weary. His face crumpled, and he leaned his forehead into Annie's plump shoulder so no one could see him crying.

Kate said something to Annie. Annie looked at Jim and pointed toward the parking lot of the Roadhouse before leading Johnny away. A minute later Jim heard the sound of a truck door opening and closing again. An engine started.

Kate came to stand next to Jim. "They'll wait for you in my truck."

"Where are the rest of the kids?" he said.

Bernie and Enid had three total. Fitz was, or had been, the eldest. "Annie's got them at her house."

"Good. Johnny okay?"

"Yeah. But he wants to talk to you." She looked up to meet Jim's eyes. "He says he saw who did it."

Jim took a deep breath and let it out slowly. "Shit."

"Not a name," she said. "A description."

"Shit," Jim said again, with even more feeling.

"First things first," Kate said. She walked steadily forward to stand behind Bernie. She let one hand settle gently on his shoulder. "Bernie."

His head had slumped forward, his chin on his chest. His hands were still knotted in the shirts of his wife and his son. He was still rocking, back and forth, back and forth.

"Bernie." Kate reached forward to loosen one of his hands. It took an effort, but at last he let go, and then his other hand was free, and Kate had him on his feet with an arm around his waist.

"He's half frozen," Kate said to Jim. "I'll take him to one of the cabins, get a fire going."

Jim nodded, avoiding looking at Bernie's face. Didn't seem right to be able to see that much on the face of someone he knew that well. Almost indecent, somehow, and intrusive, although any rookie knew that privacy was the first casualty of murder.

He looked at the bodies on the stairs.

After the victim.

He opened his kit to extract a camera and a ruler, and started taking pictures. When the first flash went off, there was a collective startled reaction behind him, and at last people began to speak, first in hushed tones and then with a steadily gathering volume. Jim paused and looked at Billy. Billy nodded, and Jim went back to taking photos. Behind him he heard Billy Mike's voice. "Okay, folks, let's let the man get on with the work, okay?"

Jim waited until the crowd had begun to disperse. "Billy?" He heard heavy footsteps come up behind him. "Make a list of everyone who is here, okay?"

"Okay." The footsteps receded.

Jim closed his mind to noises off and got on with the job.

Enid was sprawled head down with her legs on the deck and her back on the stairs. She had been shot at least four times and, if the powder around the bullet holes in the front of her prim, flowered blouse were any indication, at point-blank range. Her head lolled to one side, her eyes opened wide in what looked mostly like surprise.

One bullet had gone through the upper left shoulder, one through the sternum, one through the lower right abdomen, one was just a graze on the outside of the right thigh. From the position of the body, she'd probably caught the shoulder shot first, then the sternum, then the abdomen and thigh shots, the punch from the first spinning her around in a circle leading with her left shoulder and the shots from what had probably been an automatic stitching a line across her torso. The shooter was no marksman, which indicated an amateur who didn't know that an automatic kept firing if you parked on the trigger. Certainly he had been either frightened or determined enough to get the job done thoroughly.

But why had Enid been facing the house? If she'd been running away, she would have had her back to the shooter.

A glance at Fitz answered him. She'd been keeping herself between her son and the killer, trying to protect him.

He photographed Enid from every conceivable angle, taking his time, using up as much of the disk space on the digital camera as possible, consciously aware that he was delaying the inevitable.

Even for a seasoned law enforcement officer, murder was bad enough. Murder of a woman was harder.

But the murder of a child was almost too much to endure.

He knew without looking that Kate remained nearby, a sentinel at the extreme edge of his peripheral vision, vigilant and vengeful. He felt a corresponding kick of righteous rage, and it was enough to move him down the stairs, stepping carefully around Enid's body, to stand over Fitz.

Fitz had fallen facedown. The two bullet holes in his back were probably responsible for that. His hands were flung out as if he'd tried to catch himself when he fell. His cheek was pressed against the edge of the last step.

The way the bodies were lying, Fitz had most likely been shot in the same burst that had killed Enid, the shooter holding down the trigger of the automatic, the kick of the shots pressing back, the force of the kick pushing his hand away and causing the bullets to spray wide. It was entirely possible that, given enough caliber—nine millimeter, maybe?—one or both of the bullets that hit Fitz might have passed through Enid's body first.

He looked up. If the killer had spent the clip, there was a chance there would be bullets buried in tree trunks all around the front yard. He would look for them when there was enough light.

He photographed Fitz, also from every angle, and then took the camera back up the stairs and into the house, recording all the minutia that came with every crime scene, the debris field of toys that littered the deck, stuffed animals from Pooh Bears to Sebastian the calypso crab to gremlins, Lego dinosaurs and spaceships in various stages of construction, a nest of rubber snakes. At one end of the deck a Clue board looked as if it had been used to form part of a rebel base populated by Luke, Leia, Chewie, R2, Obi-Wan, Lando, and Vader action figures and bits and pieces thereof, a light saber, a helmeted head separated from its body, a tauntaun minus its saddle. A Barbie doll transformed into Dominatrix Barbie by an application of black electrician's tape had joined the cast.

Inside the door a table was overturned. On the floor next to it lay a telephone emitting the annoying off-the-hook beep. Beyond the phone was a broken vase scattering silken lilies across the doorstep.

He moved from the hallway into the living room, jammed with worn but comfortably overstuffed sofas and chairs, taking a photograph before every step. On the coffee table was a Monopoly game where it looked like someone had thrown down a handful of money in disgust.

In one corner of the living room stood a walnut shelf unit with glass doors. From beneath the top shelf a light shone down through the glass shelves inside.

Jim had been an infrequent dinner guest in this house, and he had had multiple occasions to admire Bernie's collection of gold nuggets and nugget jewelry and nugget objets d'art. Over the years Bernie had formed a habit common to Alaska bartenders going back to the Klondike gold rush of taking dust and nuggets in lieu of payment of bar tabs that had been running too long. He usually sold it off to a jeweler in Anchorage, but the more interesting ones he kept, like the biggest one, the size of a baby's fist, and the oddest one, the one that looked like Pamela Sue Anderson's chest. "An experienced miner can often tell what creek any particular nugget came out of," he'd told Jim, and showed him scribbled receipts in miners' hands attesting to the provenance of the nuggets in the case, some dating back thirty, fifty, even a hundred years that Enid had inherited from her stampeder grandfather.

The glass doors were fastened with a simple lock at the top, more to keep the kids from playing miner and madam with the nuggets than as a security measure, according to Bernie. Tonight, the lock was still fastened but both glass doors had been smashed and the shelves swept clean.

Jim trod on something and lifted his foot to see one of the smaller nuggets in Bernie's collection. He stepped back and his boot hit something and a second, larger nugget skittered across the floor. He sealed them into an evidence bag along with a third he found beneath one of the sofas, one he recognized as the largest in Bernie's collection, the one as big as a baby's fist.

The killer must have been in a hurry.

He looked toward the door.

In a hurry and on his way out the door when he'd been surprised by Enid and Fitz coming up the steps?

No. In a hurry because he'd heard something that had frightened him into smashing, grabbing, and running.

And shooting.

He took a few more photos, spent a blasphemous ten minutes bagging all the larger shards of glass from the broken display cupboard doors in what he knew was a very faint hope that some portion of the killer's fingerprints might be raised from one of them, and went back outside.

Kate had covered the bodies with army blankets and was standing guard over them. Just behind her Mutt prowled the perimeter, hackles raised at the scent of blood, showing her teeth to anyone who came too close.

"Who found them?" Jim said.

"Bernie," Kate said. "Pat Crowley's been hitting the sauce pretty hard since Karen split, and he's got no head for it. He blew chunks all over Bernie, right around nine o'clock near as I can piece it together. Bernie went to the house to change clothes. When he didn't come back after an hour and people were three deep at the bar waiting on their drinks, Amy went looking for him. She busted back in screaming and crying, and Old Sam went to see what had scared her. He sent for Billy, and Billy sent for me."

"Amy?"

"Amy Huth. Cindy Bingley's niece, came north last month from Minneapolis. Cindy asked Bernie if he'd take her on. She just started on Monday." Kate shook her head. "Welcome to the Park."

"Johnny?"

Kate nodded, her hackles looking every bit as stiff as Mutt's. "I'll get him."

Johnny looked everywhere but at the bodies. In the interest of getting the kid away from the crime scene as soon as possible, Jim dispensed with any attempt to put him at ease. "You were here when they were killed?"

Johnny nodded. "I was in the bathroom." He swallowed. "Or I'd be—"

Ruthlessly Jim cut him off. "Who was it?"

Johnny looked down. "I didn't get a clear look at his face."

Kate moved as if to say something, and Jim stopped her with a hard-eyed glance. "Back up a minute," Jim said. "What were you doing here? Why weren't you and Fitz at Auntie Vi's swap and shop along with everyone else?"

"We're behind on our science experiment for Ms. Doogan." Johnny's eyes slid away from the mounds beneath the blankets. "Fitz and me."

"Huh," Jim said. "So where's Van? Isn't she your lab partner, too?"

Johnny was silent. Again, Kate made as if to say something, and again Jim silenced her. "No one cares, Johnny, but I need to know exactly why you and Fitz came home."

Johnny ducked his head. He was shivering, and Jim realized

that they were standing outside in the middle of the night on the first Saturday in April. There was snow on the ground and their breath formed frost clouds in the air. "Come on," he said, "let's go inside."

"No!" Johnny's voice was loud and panicked.

"Inside the Roadhouse," Jim said.

En route he said to Kate, "Who's with Bernie?"

"Billy and the Grosdidiers."

"He tell you what happened?"

"No, he wasn't—he couldn't—no. I talked to Old Sam, though, and Amy, a little. He said everyone came here after the swap and shop and that there was a hell of a party going on, television and jukebox up as loud as they would go, people dancing and then the belly dancers came in, and a bunch of Big Bumpers right on their heels, and the scene was pretty much pandemonium city."

"And nobody heard the shots."

"No. Nobody in the cabins this time of year, either, and nobody walking from the parking lot to the door at the right time, apparently." She gave a tired shrug. "And come on, Jim, it's the Park. I don't think there's a ten-year-old within two hundred miles who doesn't carry. Who's going to notice shots fired as anything out of the ordinary?"

"This was a nine-millimeter automatic, Kate, judging from the wounds."

"Still," she said.

He knew what she meant. "Ask Billy if he'd come watch the scene while we're inside, would you?" He didn't waste his breath asking her to stay behind while he interrogated Johnny.

Inside the bar, the television was blaring from one corner and the jukebox from another. Jim reached up to punch the TV's OFF button and silenced Big and Rich's rap, rock and roll paean to country music by the simple expedient of pulling the jukebox's plug.

He tossed his cap on the bar and unzipped his coat. "Take a pew, kid."

This was the first time Johnny had been in a bar, and in spite of the circumstances he was curious. "Smells kind of sour in here."

"Years of people upchucking beer on the floor will do that to a room."

Kate came in, kicking the ice from her Sorels, followed by Mutt. She shed parka and mitts and went behind the bar. Johnny hitched his stool closer and accepted the Coke Kate poured, but shook his head at the bag of peanuts. She raised an eyebrow at Jim. He would have sold his soul for a beer, but he saw no sleep in his immediate future and alcohol wouldn't help. "Water'd be good."

She poured two tall with ice and wedges of lime, and hooked Bernie's usual behind-the-bar stool with one foot and hoisted herself up. Mutt came around to stand beside her, looking up with expectant ears, and Kate tore open a package of beef jerky. Mutt accepted it as no less than her due and retired to the end of the bar.

Jim let Johnny swallow his first pull before he said, "Okay, kid. You and Fitz left the swap and shop and came home. How come?"

Johnny ducked his head, and even in the dim light of the Roadhouse, Jim could see color creeping up his neck. He mumbled something into his Coke.

"What?"

Johnny glanced at Kate and then quickly away.

Kate looked resigned. "Were you watching the X-rated channels again?"

Johnny's head shot up and he stared at her, openmouthed.

"Oh, you thought it was some big secret?" To Jim she said, "Bernie got satellite television last year. He blocked the porn channels on the living room TV but not the bedroom TV, so the kids sneak up there to watch whenever the grown-ups are out of the house. I can't prove, it, but I think Fitz was charging admission." She gave Johnny a pointed look. "And I think Johnny sold the tickets." She looked back at Jim. "I asked Bernie to do something about it, but I guess he hasn't gotten around to it yet."

The painful red color had crept up to Johnny's hairline. He mumbled something else into his Coke.

"I'm sorry, what was that?" Kate said.

Johnny, face redder than ever, said in only a slightly louder voice, "I hate living with a detective."

In spite of the horrific circumstances, Jim had a hard time keeping his face straight. "Was that it, kid? Not the science experiment?" Not the one assigned by Ms. Doogan, at any rate.

Johnny nodded, studiously avoiding Kate's eye.

"And then Enid came home and caught you?"

Johnny nodded again. "She saw us sneak out of the swap and shop. She came home and caught us. She was mad. She yelled."

"And then what?"

"And then she turned off the television and talked to us." It was clear that Johnny had preferred the yelling.

But the talking would have been quieter. The master bedroom was on the second floor at the back of the house. Anyone coming in the front door, say someone there to relieve Bernie of his gold nugget collection, might have thought the house deserted, the residents up at Auntie Vi's along with the rest of the Park rats.

He could have come in the front door which, like most Park doors, was never locked, walked into the living room and directly to the display case. "What happened next?" Jim said.

"We heard something."

"Downstairs."

Johnny nodded.

"What? What did you hear?"

"It was something breaking, like glass. That's why Enid told us to be quiet. She said it didn't sound like it was someone who was supposed to be there."

Mistake, Jim thought. Enid should have screamed at the top of her lungs. Most intruders ran when detected. But then, most burglars didn't kill. Hell, most burglars weren't even armed. "Then what?"

"Then she made us sneak downstairs." Johnny's voice began to shake, and he shoved his glass away from him. "But he heard us."

"What did he look like?"

Johnny knotted his hands together and stared at them fixedly. "I don't know. I couldn't see much. The lights weren't on, except in that case with all the nuggets."

"Tell me what you did see."

"He was big."

"Tall?"

Johnny hesitated. "Not tall, exactly, but big around."

"Fat?"

Johnny shook his head. "Not fat." He appealed to Kate. "Burly?"

She nodded, and Johnny looked relieved. "And lots of hair. Messy."

"What color?"

"Dirty blond. Or maybe it just looked that way because it was dark and he had the light behind him."

"So, white."

"What?"

"Not Native."

"Oh. No. White." Johnny looked at Kate, uncertain. "Or mostly. I guess."

"You never saw him before?"

Wretchedly, Johnny said, "I don't know, Jim. I didn't know him well enough to call him by name, that's for sure. And everything happened so fast."

"So you were coming down the stairs."

Johnny nodded.

"Enid first?"

"And then Fitz, and then me. And then . . ." Johnny's voice failed him.

Kate was a motionless presence on the other side of the bar. Jim kept his tone matter-of-fact. "How far down the stairs were you all when he came out of the living room?"

Johnny gulped back a sob and said, steadily enough to be understood, "Enid was at the bottom. She was holding Fitz's hand. When the guy came out into the hallway, she shoved him in front of her and out the door."

"The door was open?"

Johnny nodded.

"What happened then?"

Johnny's voice lowered. "He—he didn't see me, he went after Enid and Fitz. I started backing up, all the way to the landing. I crawled into the bathroom and locked the door and laid down in the bathtub." His eyes filled. "I heard the shots. I should have done something, I should have—"

"You should have done exactly and precisely what you did," Jim said firmly. "You got away. You're alive. He would have killed you, too, Johnny, and what good would that have done?"

"But—"

"No buts," Kate said. "Jim's right. You did good."

Useless words. Johnny was already suffering from a bad case of survivor's guilt that would only get worse. He looked from Kate to Jim and back again, his face an agony of remembrance. "I keep thinking, if I'd just—"

"Let me put it this way," Kate said, leaning forward and placing a hand over his. "Thank you."

The awful beginnings of hysteria halted, Johnny stared at her. "Thank me? What for?"

"For staying alive." She squeezed his hands once and let him go. "Can I take him home?"

Jim nodded. "I'll need a formal statement tomorrow."

"Of course." Their eyes met in perfect understanding. To Johnny she said, "Take Mutt out to the truck, will you?"

When the door closed behind them, she said, "You thinking what I'm thinking?"

"Big and blond and an asshole," Jim said. "It has to be."

"You going to go get him tonight?"

Jim got to his feet and pulled his hat on. "You bet I am."

She followed him to the door. "I'll bring Johnny back into town in the morning. You want to do a lineup?"

"You bet I do," Jim said, holding the door for her. "This one goes by the book."

The Roadhouse door swung closed behind them with a solid thud, and Jim said with savage satisfaction, "No more acquittals or mistrials for Louis Deem."

SIX

Louis was amused when Jim insisted on taking him in, in handcuffs, no less.

He appeared even more amused when Johnny picked him out of the lineup the next morning.

The lineup was easy, given the common occurrence of Native-Scandinavian ancestry in the Park. Six other men resembling Deem's shape and size stood against one wall of the interview room at the trooper post. There had been no shortage of volunteers. Alex Mike had even flown in from Anchorage in his Cessna 172 when Billy called to tell him the news, but then some said he still carried a torch for Jessie McComas. There was one draftee, Willard Shugak. Jim had tracked him down to where he was ingesting massive quantities of sourdough pancakes at Auntie Balasha's and brought him in, too, and he'd brought Howie in with Louis because they were enough of a height and what the hell, if he was wrong about Louis, which he wasn't, maybe he could hang it on Howie.

Kate and Johnny stood against the back wall. Jim had dimmed

the lights to approximate the conditions at the Koslowski house at the time of the murders. He regarded the result with grim complacency. No, Judge Singh would have nothing to complain about.

Louis stood third in the lineup with a smirk on his face. If anything, the smirk increased when everyone was dismissed except him, and it increased further when four of the six managed to jostle, elbow, or shove him on their way out of the room. He said something to Willard, last in line, that Jim didn't catch. Willard, understanding enough to be frightened of the proceedings and sniveling into his shirtsleeve because of it, shrank back and made a wide circle around Louis to get to the door. Howie made some crack to Louis, and Louis's smirk broadened into a grin.

"Are you sure?" Kate said in a low voice.

Johnny nodded, his face pale, his expression resolute. "I'm sure."

She looked at his determined expression and said no more, but she had inner reservations. There was a crowd of Park rats outside the post, and as he'd walked through it from Kate's truck to the post's front door, those who hadn't been close enough to pat his shoulder in congratulation shouted "Way to go, kid!" and "We finally nailed the bastard!" and "Let him try to get away with this one!" Everyone wanted Louis for this one.

Well, so did she. But she wished Johnny had seen Louis's face.

Actually, what she really wished was that she'd taken Johnny to Disneyland.

Jim cuffed Louis and took his elbow to lead him back to his cell. Louis purposefully hung back. "I thought that was you back there in the dark, Kate. You got your boy with you?"

Jim shoved Louis forward. Nimble on his feet as always, Louis never lost his balance. "We haven't met, kid. But we will. Oh, yeah. We will."

"Hurry up, Louis," Jim said. "I need to get back to my office to look up the Alaska statute on threatening bodily harm. See if we can add some more time on that life sentence you've already got going for you."

He shoved Louis into the cell, slammed and locked the door behind him, and turned to go.

"Hey, Jim."

"What," Jim said without looking around.

"Not that this hasn't been fun, and not that I'd mind a free trip to Ahtna—I could do with a Costco run—but before you put Judge Singh to all the trouble of an evidentiary hearing, you might like to check out my alibi."

At that Jim did turn, to fix Louis with a bleak and unyielding eye. "Alibi?"

"Abigail Smith." The smirk was back in full force. "My fiancée."

"What about her?" Jim said.

"I was with her last night." Louis stretched and summoned up a yawn. "All night. I'd just barely gotten home when you showed up."

"And of course she'll swear to that."

"She's a religious person," Louis said piously. "They take that whole ninth commandment thing pretty seriously."

This time he let Jim get all the way to the door before he said, "Homely kid, that Johnny Morgan. Looks a lot like his dad."

I have to ask her," Jim said doggedly.

"She'll lie. God alone knows why, but women lie all the time for Louis Deem."

"I know, Kate. I still have to ask." Jim looked at Johnny. "Are you sure it was Deem, Johnny?"

Johnny nodded, chin resolute.

Jim met Kate's eyes, and she knew what he was thinking. After the lineup, Deem's face would be fixed in Johnny's memory, superimposed over the shadowy figure he had seen in the Koslowskis' house that night.

They both knew, too, that at a vengeful, visceral level every Park rat worthy of the name wanted it to be Deem, and that it was impossible for Johnny not to feel the weight of that expectation.

"Okay." Jim rubbed a hand over his face. "Sit down, both of you."

"Johnny's got school—"

"School can wait. Just a few minutes of your time, Kate. Please." When they were all seated, he spoke directly to Johnny, trying very hard to treat him as any other witness in any other case. "Johnny, you say it was Deem that you saw last night."

"It was." Johnny was becoming more positive with every iteration. Repetition breeds its own certainty.

"Are you willing to testify to that in court?"

Johnny, to whom Fitz's death was just beginning to feel real, with the subsequent and inevitable anger growing into the aftermath, said in a firm voice, "Yes."

Jim looked at Kate, and Kate leaned forward to be eye to eye with Johnny. "Louis Deem is a very bad guy, Johnny."

"I know."

"Juries like eyewitnesses, especially Alaskan juries, who always want to convict someone but who like to feel sure they're doing the right thing when they do. I don't know how much physical evidence there will be, that's all on the lab guys in Anchorage, but if this alibi of Deem's holds up, the case will rest on your testimony."

Johnny's face looked pinched. "I know."

He didn't, not really, but Kate let it pass. "I know we've said this like nine times already, but I want you to understand. Louis's—he's broken, Johnny. He's bad not because he doesn't know any different. He does. He's bad because he enjoys it. Hell, he revels in it. It's just more fun for him than being good. The people he's hurt, the people he's killed, that's just a Deem good time. Like you and me would go fishing with Old Sam, or those crazy-ass climbers summit Big Bump, or the four aunties building one of their quilts, or Bernie coaching basketball, or Jim here—"

"I get it, Kate," Johnny said, much to Jim's relief. He looked at the floor and said in a small voice, "Are you saying that Louis Deem will try to hurt me if I testify?"

Kate looked at Jim. "It wouldn't be the first time, Johnny."

Johnny looked at Jim. "But he'll be in jail."

It occurred to Jim that he was a little too close to the eyewitness in this case, but there wasn't a lot he could do about it now. "Yes."

He could see that Johnny was having a hard time dealing with the idea that sometimes the bad guys won. Jim wished with all his heart that he didn't have to be the one to introduce Johnny to the realities of American jurisprudence. For a moment he bitterly resented the role being thrust upon him, and then he looked into Johnny's face, the promise of strength in the strong bones and the honesty in the frank eyes, and he thought, Hell, if the kid can hitchhike from Arizona to Alaska at the age of twelve, he ought to know what he can and can't handle. He said, "Yeah, Deem is in jail, and I don't guess Judge Singh'll be throwing bail bones his way anytime soon. Or ever, if she can help it. But you should know, Johnny, that Louis Deem has a history of intimidating witnesses. And he's got a lot of money for a good attorney. Hell, I think he's got Rickard on retainer, and Rickard is never nice to witnesses against his client. If you were thinking anyone was going to be easy on you because you're only fourteen, think again."

Johnny's shoulders had stiffened. "I wasn't."

Jim looked at Kate. "What about you? Are you on board with this?"

Kate sat there, looking at Johnny, trying to sort out an answer to Jim's question. Was she? For the general well-being of the population of the Park, Louis Deem needed to be put away. A double homicide would make him a guest of the state for the lifetimes of most Park rats.

Correction. A conviction on a double homicide would. Louis Deem's almost preternatural ability to skate on the most heinous crimes had to be taken into account.

If he skated this time . . . well, Louis Deem always got even. He'd left Kate alone until now, but she was always wary of him, always aware of the malevolent interest directed her way. Because the six years following her return to the Park hadn't given him an opportunity for payback didn't mean he wouldn't take it when it was offered. Louis Deem had one thing most criminal types did not: patience. He was willing and able to wait for what he wanted.

Which led her to identify the niggling unease she had been feeling about the murders of Enid and Fitz Koslowski. The whole robbery was so . . . it was just so careless. Louis Deem was a lot of things, but clumsy wasn't one of them. The reason none of his arrests had stuck was because he was fastidious in choosing his targets, meticulous in making his plans, and shrewd in their execution. This rushed robbery, these hasty murders had amateur written all over them.

Amateur was also something Louis Deem most definitely was not.

They deposited Johnny with Bobby and Dinah, Kate deciding that Johnny needed family more than he needed school that day. Katya was as usual ecstatic to see him, and Kate could see visible signs of him relaxing in her exuberant two-year-old presence. Unqualified love was a great healer.

Back in the Blazer, Kate told Jim what she'd been thinking.

"'Clumsy'?" Jim said. "Maybe the word you're looking for is *arrogant.*"

Kate digested this. "You mean because he was acquitted of Mary Waterbury's murder."

"He's gotten away with so much, Kate. You said it yourself. We taught him he could get away with murder. This last acquittal may have put him over the edge, made him think he was invincible. Maybe he thought he could get away with a little smash-and-grab and—oh, oops!—eliminate some unexpected witnesses on his way out."

"Turn here," Kate said, pointing.

Jim gave a quiet but heartfelt curse at the condition of the Cat trail, which had not improved since Kate had driven it with Dan.

"Everyone in the Park knew about Bernie's gold collection," Kate said. "I've seen him haul total strangers out of the Roadhouse to go look at it."

Jim risked a glance away from the track to look at her. "What is this, Kate? You want Deem to be innocent?"

"No!" she said, loudly enough that Mutt, sitting in the backseat, put her ears back. "No," she said again, more calmly this time. "I just like things to fit, is all." She gave her head an angry shake. "No, you're right. It's hubris, pure and simple. Louis Deem always did think he was better than Superman. Why shouldn't he? Even kryptonite wouldn't kill this son of a bitch."

The Smiths must have heard the Blazer coming because they were all assembled on the deck when Jim and Kate pulled up. The deck now had a railing, and the four walls of the big cabin were eight logs high. A pile of trusses sat to one side, ready to start holding up the roof. They looked handmade, sturdy, and functional.

"Mr. Smith," Jim said, "I'm Sergeant Jim Chopin with the Alaska State Troopers. I believe you've met Kate Shugak."

"Of course." Smith effected a bow that reeked of noblesse oblige in Kate's direction. "Who could forget?"

"I see you're still here, Mr. Smith. Eviction notice notwithstanding."

"I am indeed, Kate." Smith bent a kindly eye on Jim. "How may I help you, Sergeant?"

"I understand you have a daughter named Abigail."

Smith's eye became less kindly. "Yes. My eldest." He did not indicate which of the seventeen assembled, but Kate saw her at the back of the crowd looking nervous. Near her were the next two oldest girls, Chloe and Hannah, holding hands so tightly, their knuckles were white even at this distance.

"I'd like to speak to Abigail in private, if I may."

"You may not." Smith was sounding very frosty.

Jim nodded as if that was what he had expected. "Then may I speak to her in the presence of you and her mother?"

Smith made a grandiloquent gesture with one hand. "You may speak freely in front of our entire family, Sergeant. We don't keep secrets from one another."

Kate had been watching Abigail during this conversation, and she had seen the girl turn white and then red and then white again. "Jim—"

"No help for it," he said in a low voice, and raised his voice again. "May I meet Abigail?"

"Abigail. Come forward."

Abigail threaded her way through the crowd of siblings with all the enthusiasm of one headed for the guillotine, which for all Kate knew about this family she might well be.

"Abigail, this is Sergeant Chopin. As a matter of curiosity, Sergeant, Chopin as in Frédéric?"

"He was a distant cousin a couple of generations back, yes, sir," Jim said.

"A brilliant composer. I've always been fond of his tribute to Mozart."

"I wouldn't know, sir. I'm a Bruce Springsteen fan myself." Jim looked at Abigail. "Hello, Abigail. I'm Sergeant Chopin."

Abigail looked steadfastly at her feet. "Hello."

"I understand you are engaged to be married to Louis Deem."

She nodded, sneaking a sidelong look at her father, and a second, more furtive one at Kate.

Jim hesitated, and Kate wondered if he was thinking of the putative guillotine himself. She watched him square his shoulders and plunge in. "Last night, there was—something happened at the Roadhouse last night, Abigail, something very bad. Two people are dead. They were murdered, shot at point-blank range by their killer. A mother and her fourteen-year-old son."

Jim was going into unnecessary detail, and Kate wondered if he was doing it deliberately, trying to shock her into telling the truth. He might also have been trying to poison the Abigail well for Louis Deem, if the case went into the toilet.

Abigail said nothing. Smith said, "And what has this to do with us, Sergeant?"

"We have an eyewitness who has identified the killer as Louis Deem."

Abigail's head shot up at this, eyes wide, face pale. "I don't believe you."

Kate closed her eyes and shook her head. How many more little girls? How many more?

She opened her eyes and looked at Abigail. Evidently one more.

"Come into Niniltna," Jim said, his voice hardening. "The Roadhouse was pretty full last night. Chances are the first person you'll meet saw the bodies."

"I don't believe Louis killed anyone!"

"Oh, for—"

"Kate." Jim's voice was quiet but firm.

"*Wuff.*" So was Mutt's. She leaned her shoulder against Kate's leg.

"Louis denies that he killed anyone," Jim said. "He says it would have been impossible, and, Abigail, he says you'll tell us why."

Abigail looked at her father. Smith looked back at her. "Abigail?"

She shook her head wildly, braid twitching back and forth like a short thick whip.

"In fact," Jim said, "Louis Deem says he was with Abigail all night, and that she will vouch for him."

"Abigail?" Mrs. Smith materialized out of the crowd. "Abigail, is this true?"

"No! No, I—"

"Abigail." Her father's voice boomed like the last trump. "Look at me."

Shrinking, Abigail risked a look. "Father, I—"

"Abigail." There was a world of patience and paternalism in the single word. It made Abigail flinch. It made Kate flinch too, albeit for different reasons. "Were you with Louis last night?"

"No, Father, I wasn't, I—"

"Chloe."

The older of the hand-clasped pair jumped.

"Come here."

Chloe exchanged an agonized glance with Hannah. Hannah wouldn't let go of Chloe's hand, and both girls came forward with faltering steps. "Yes, Father."

"Was Abigail in her own bed last night?"

Chloe looked at Abigail, and away again. "Yes, Father."

Inexorably, Smith said, "All night?"

There was a strained silence. Into it Smith said gently, "Abigail, will you really force your sister to lie for you?"

A tear slid down Abigail's cheek. She wiped it away with a furtive gesture. She raised her head and met her father's eyes straight on. "I went out last night after everyone was asleep."

"To meet Louis?"

"Yes, Father," Abigail said, her voice steadying. She stood a little straighter. "I waited until all the other girls were asleep and then I went down the trail to the outhouse. Louis was waiting for me."

"Where?"

She pointed. The outhouse looked as well made as the beginnings of the cabin, with carefully planed sides and a shingled roof. A well-worn track went past it from the building site to the Cat trail. "I met him up the track in his truck. He took me to his house."

There was a collective indrawing of breath among the other offspring. Mother Smith looked shocked and sorrowful. "Oh, Abigail," she said, shaking her head. "After all you have been taught. You were going to be married."

"I still am, Mother." It was the first sign of backbone Abigail had displayed, and Kate was insensibly cheered to see it.

Mother looked at Father. "That is for your father to say."

Abigail took a step forward and prepared to testify. She stared straight at Jim, willing him to believe her. "I spent the night with Louis Deem." She added, a little defiantly, "My fiancé."

"Was there any moment during which Louis was not with you?" Jim said. "When you fell asleep, maybe?"

Abigail blushed slightly and refused to look at either her parents or her brothers and sisters. "No. We—we didn't sleep a lot."

Ah, youth, Kate thought.

She couldn't make up her mind if Abigail was telling the truth. Later, negotiating the track back to the Park road, she said so to Jim. "She was pretty convincing there."

"She's in love," Jim said cynically. "And she's been trained in witnessing for the Lord. Question is, would a jury believe her?"

"Depends on the jury."

"Yeah. Jesus!" This as Jim coaxed the Blazer through a pothole that could be more accurately described as a lunar crater. Safely out of it again, he said, "We've got an eyewitness that places Deem at the scene, gun in hand."

"And about that gun."

"Yeah, and there are only fifty-two creeks he could have tossed it into on the way home from Bernie's house." Jim shrugged. "Don't necessarily need a weapon to convict. To continue. The suspect's alibi is his fiancée, young and head over heels in love, who could be relied upon to lie until she was blue in the face to protect him."

"Did you find Louis's fingerprints at Bernie's house?"

"The report isn't back yet."

"Did you find any of Bernie's gold at Louis's house?"

"No."

"Anything at all to—?"

"Kate." They came to the end of the track, and with relief Jim shifted into second for the first time since he'd turned onto the Cat trail to the Smiths' house. "I repeat, is there some reason you don't want Deem to be guilty? Of this particular crime, that is."

Kate shifted in her seat. In a lesser being, it might have been called squirming. Mutt panted at her, tongue lolling out of one side of her mouth, teeth bared in an enormous canine grin. "I guess I'm trying to think like Frank Rickard." She turned to look at Jim. "I don't want Louis to get off this time, Jim."

"Because of Johnny."

It wasn't a question, but she answered him anyway. "I look over my own shoulder enough already because of Louis Deem. If Louis hadn't been in jail waiting for trial at the time, he would have been the first person I talked to after my cabin was burned. I don't want to have to be looking over Johnny's shoulder, too."

"Abigail Smith would swear that she spent last night picking out place settings with Louis Deem if that was what it took to get him off the hook, Kate. Any DA worthy of the title is going to be able to break her. She's just a kid, don't forget. Not that much older than Johnny, if it comes to that. Don't worry. This time Louis's going down."

The memory of the two sprawled bodies on the front steps of Bernie Koslowski's house flashed into his mind, and his voice hardened. "The Waterbury acquittal made Deem feel like he was somehow immune from further prosecution, and he got arrogant, and it made him careless. He knew—hell, everyone in the Park knew about Auntie Vi's swap and shop, and he knew everyone would be there. And of course he knew about Bernie's gold stash because everyone knew about Bernie's gold stash. Everyone up at Auntie Vi's meant nobody home at Bernie's. Perfect time to rip it off. Deem didn't figure on a couple of hormonally challenged teenaged boys and a teenaged boy's suspicious mother acting like teenaged boys and suspicious mothers normally do."

Kate sat back with a sigh. "And he panicked."

"Happens to the best of us, Kate."

"And the worst," Kate said. "And the worst of us, too."

SEVEN

Days passed. Louis languished in Jim's cell, not quite so amused as he had been but not worried yet, either. Abigail visited him daily, throwing hate bombs at Jim by way of dirty looks and delivering meals of cold fried chicken and potato salad by the bucketload to the inmate, who didn't offer to share.

Sometimes the smells wafting out of the cells made Jim want to cry, and it wasn't like he was underfed, because Kate was baking bread like she was going to start a wholesale outlet. This week it was baguettes, in the French style, and she was on her fifth batch. The first batches hadn't survived the third proofing and the last had had the consistency of breadsticks. When he and Johnny had left this morning, Kate had been measuring out flour with the intensity of Alfred Nobel putting together the ingredients for dynamite, and Jim just bet he knew under whose house Kate was fantasizing setting off the explosion.

Bernie Koslowski had put Laurel Meganack in charge of the Roadhouse and remained at home. The aunties were making sure he and the two kids were fed, and intercepting and diverting the steady stream of Park rats who came knocking at the door out of compassion or curiosity.

It was a silent household, still too numb from shock to feel grief. When the grief abated, Jim knew from long experience with survivors of violent crimes, there would be rage, and a demand for someone to be held responsible. Jim made some excuse to drive out there daily to check in.

Bernie would recover first, before the children. Jim wanted to be there when he did, to reassure him that Alaska's finest was on the case. Bernie might not have been Alaskan born, but he had fully adapted to his adopted land. There was a gun rack above the French doors leading onto the deck, holding a Browning 12-gauge pump-action shotgun and a Winchester bolt-action 300. Jim had eaten enough ptarmigan and venison at Bernie's table to know that Bernie was proficient with both.

Four days later, the crime lab in Anchorage delivered the depressing news that no fingerprints other than the Koslowski family's had been found on the shards of glass or sections of doorframe on the display case that Jim had sent in. Jim hadn't really expected anything else.

There was a moment of excitement when Kate, scrutinizing the Roadhouse environs, found a tire track in the Roadhouse parking lot that she matched to the front right tire on Louis Deem's vehicle. Alas, Howie had driven it that day, which explanation Jim heard with an incredulity bordering on scorn until it was vouchsafed to by no less an upstanding citizen than Auntie Vi, to whose swap and shop Howie had delivered a load of sale items in the bed of said pickup. Auntie Vi remembered because Howie and Willard had needed a lot of room to display their goods, including a great many snow machine parts. And many witnesses had been the beneficiaries when Howie rang the bell at the Roadhouse later that evening on the strength of their sales.

"Trying to impress Amy Huth," Kate said.

"Is Howie smitten?"

She nodded. "I hear he left her a honking big tip."

"Did it work?"

"Reports are she remained unimpressed."

"Good."

It was the only good news that week. There was in fact no physical evidence to link Louis Deem to the murders of Enid and Fitz Koslowski. But there was Johnny Morgan and his steadfast determination to stand up for what he had seen.

"Gutsy kid," Jim said.

"Vanessa's been keeping close. Helps, I think. Good friends make all things bearable." Although Johnny had been quieter than usual lately, and Kate knew he was mourning Fitz's loss.

So was the Park. Auntie Vi organized a memorial potlatch and roped the other aunties and Kate in to help. It was held at the school gymnasium, where all such events were held, on the Saturday following the murders, and everyone in the Park turned out, more, it must be admitted, for Bernie and Fitz than for Enid.

Enid Esther Koslowski had been respected as a good wife and mother, but she hadn't had a lot of friends. Of course, Bernie hadn't made it easy for her, as she was always wondering which of them he'd been sleeping with lately. Bernie wasn't a rounder, per se, but there had been some serious inroads in infidelity on his side of the bed and while the Park was large in area, it was very small in population. It was impossible to hide those kinds of indiscretions for long. Especially in winter, when there was little to do except gossip about one's neighbors, and a familiar truck parked outside an unaccustomed cabin was fodder for intense speculation. Kate had always been glad her folks had had the good sense to homestead twenty-five miles out of town and another quarter of a mile down an access road.

Kate had filed Bernie's extracurricular activities under "none of my business," but she had often wondered what it was that made grown men act the fool in the spectacular way they all too often did. Laurel Meganack, the most recent light-o'-love, was seventeen years younger than Bernie. What was that about? Did Laurel even know who Jimmy Buffet was?

Men were definitely from Mars, and in spite of all the science fiction Kate had read she just wasn't big with aliens. It was still a source of astonishment that Jim had hung on for as long as he had. She still wondered every time he went out the door if that was the last time she'd see him in anything other than a professional capacity. Jim's relationships tended to last six months to a year. Apart from the fact that she didn't know when to start counting from (the time they had first slept together in Bering, sort of by accident? that day she'd assaulted him in Ruth Bauman's cabin and he'd assaulted her right back?), she did not delude herself into imagining that even the infinite mystery of Kate Shugak could lure Jim Chopin into digging in for the long run.

She halted in the act of dealing out paper plates and plastic cutlery on the folding tables set up at the side of the gym, dismayed to feel her heart sink at the prospect. Her heart had no business doing anything of the kind.

"*Aycheewah*, what you do there, Katya, fall asleep?" Auntie Vi bustled up, dealing out casseroles like so many cards.

It was the first civil word Auntie Vi had spoken to her since the scene in the Ahtna courthouse, and Kate was absurdly grateful. "Sorry, Auntie," she said, and went to work.

Half an hour later, the Kanuyaq River Band was blaring off the stage, or they were when they managed to wrest the sound system from the stream of Park rats who spoke in memoriam of Enid and Fitz Koslowski. More kids spoke of Fitz than adults spoke of Enid, and the kids who spoke of Fitz had more to say than the adults did who spoke of Enid. Kate recalled one of the few times she had seen Enid in a group of other women, the witches' coven in the woods following the death of Lisa Gette. An exorcism of the spirit of yet another of Bernie's lovers, however passing and passim. Poor Enid.

Bernie was there, with his remaining two children, Teddy and Kathleen.

A corn-fed Iowan from a traditional family, Bernie had followed a pretty girl to the Chicago Democratic Convention in 1968, where a beating by Chicago's finest got his attention. He attended Kent State, where he was further radicalized by the shootings in 1970. Later that same year he had burned his draft card on the steps of the Pentagon and spent the rest of the Vietnam War in Canada, where he remained until Carter pardoned everyone and he could come home. His father, who saw service in the Pacific in World War II, had never forgiven him. He and Bobby Clark had a lot in common, and he was first on the guest list to Bobby's vets-only annual uncelebration of the Tet Offensive.

He had migrated gradually westward, eventually to Alaska and finally the Park, where nobody cared what your personal history was before you crossed the border at Salmon Creek, and even if they did, they knew better than to ask what it was. Inquiries into the personal history of strangers were frowned on in Alaska, and could be fighting words in the Park.

Within a year, Bernie had married Enid, the daughter of a local entrepreneurial family with roots that went back to the gold rush, and proceeded to reincarnate the one president he believed could and would have kept the U.S. out of Vietnam in his children. John Fitzgerald Koslowski, Robert Edward Koslowski, and Kathleen

Rose Koslowski, the Kennedy clan was all present and accounted for at Bernie's house.

He built the existing Roadhouse first, then half a dozen cabins that he rented out by the week or day, and got the roof on the house out back just in time for Kathleen's arrival, Enid having made it known she would bear but not birth a third child in a tent, no matter how well insulated it was.

He had coached the high school basketball teams to, so far, three Class C state championships, and as a rule didn't repeat the stories he heard in inebriated spurts across his bar. He never served alcohol to minors, and he knew the birthdays of every kid born in Niniltna and, some believed, in the entire Park. Kate had watched him turn pregnant women away, too.

All in all, an exemplar of Park ratness, their Bernie. Except for that minor inability to keep his fly zipped. Although some and perhaps many would say it put the icing on the rat cake.

So to speak.

Billy and Annie Mike paused for a few words, Suzie in tow. Kate duly admired the baby girl they had recently adopted from Korea. She was a darling and it wasn't a stretch. Kate ladled punch into countless plastic cups, spooned endless portions of macaroni and cheese onto paper plates, and spread peanut butter and strawberry jam on hundreds of rounds of pilot bread. She helped Auntie Vi hand out the gifts, twenty-five sets of Tupperware bowls, another twenty-five sets of bath towels, both to the community's recognized elders, but everyone got at minimum a keychain or a shot glass with the Roadhouse logo on it. Billy and Annie Mike got round-trip tickets to Anchorage on George Perry's Chugach Air Taxi Service. The four aunties and Kate got beer boxes full of strips of smoked salmon, the real stuff, when your jaw hurt for a week and your house smelled for a month after eating it.

As the gifts were being handed out, Kate noticed a preponderance of Smiths about the gymnasium. Father and Mother along with all seventeen children stood in the gift line, and Kate further noticed that while no one was so impolite as to chase them off, the parents got shot glasses and the kids got key chains. No towels or Tupperware or squaw candy for Mother or Father Smith, elder status or no.

Abigail kept her head up but refused to look anyone directly in the eye. Chloe and Hannah stood joined at the fist as usual. Neither looked in good spirits. Chloe in particular seemed thin of face, and in some indefinable sense thin of spirit as well.

A while later Kate looked around for Auntie Vi and saw her leading Chloe out the back door. She wasn't surprised. Unhappy children had a way of seeking out Auntie Vi, the way a lodestone seeks out magnetic north.

Well, Auntie Vi had her own way of dealing with unhappy children, as Kate had cause to know. Chloe was in good hands.

Chloe's parents were busy offering condolences to Bernie on the death of his wife and child, and, from what Kate could hear, coming up fast from behind, extending the solace that Enid and Fitz now resided with their Maker. Bernie, who looked like hell, received these assurances with the anesthetized acceptance of someone who had tuned out presumption like this days ago.

Kate smiled sweetly at Smith and said, "I hear someone on the other side of the room calling your name." Her smile broadened to include Mrs. Smith and the progeny. "All your names."

Even Father Smith in all his oblivious arrogance was not proof against such steamroller tactics. The family moved on. "You okay?" Kate said to Bernie.

He shook his head. "No."

"Dumb thing to say," Kate said. "No way you can be."

A nascent gleam of awareness appeared in Bernie's eye. "There is one way. If someone stomps on that son of a bitch Louis Deem."

"Don't worry about Louis Deem," Kate said.

Something in her voice reached through Bernie's fog. He gave Kate the first aware look she'd seen on his face since the murders. "What? What's wrong? Kate?"

"Nothing's wrong, Bernie."

He was unconvinced. "There is no way he can get away with this, is there? Not this?"

"Chill, Bernie. Louis's going down." She touched his arm in reassurance. "Johnny's been over to your house a lot this week, I hear."

Momentarily diverted, Bernie nodded. "Yeah. Him and Vanessa both, hanging out with Teddy and Kathleen. They're good kids."

They both looked across the room at where Johnny and Vanessa stood in a circle of friends, cans of pop held in their hands, not saying much. Bernie didn't have to tell Kate that they reminded him of what he had lost. It was written all over his face.

Across the gym, Kate saw Chloe returned to the bosom of her family. Her face had a little more color, and she was able to summon a small smile for Hannah when her sister reached for her hand again. Fully assembled, the Smiths departed. Auntie Vi returned to the serving line, where Aunties Balasha, Edna, and Joy were scraping out what remained in the foil, tin, and Pyrex casserole dishes. Kate joined them in the cleanup.

Auntie Joy was looking at Bernie, her face sad. "Ay, that Bernie, he hurting bad."

"They're all hurting, Auntie."

"Yes," Auntie Balasha said, "but it hurt worse when you know you have wronged the dead. No way for Bernie to take it back now."

Kate looked at her, startled. It was so seldom Auntie Balasha said anything bad about anyone.

The other aunties gave sage nods. "Guilty," Auntie Edna said, not without a certain grim relish. "That boy be feeling guilty long time yet."

There was no way Bernie could have heard them all the way across the gymnasium over the sound of the band and the basketballs beginning to bounce off the rims at both ends of the court, but Kate looked around to see him watching them.

Auntie Vi had said nothing, but she slammed down a Pyrex casserole dish hard enough to make everything on the table jump and clatter. "Ay, Viola, you don't be breaking my favorite dish!" Auntie Edna said, snatching it up again. "I wash it myself, thank you."

Auntie Vi muttered something, gathered up a pile of dirty dishes, and steamed off for the kitchen. Kate looked after her, frowning. "What's wrong with her?"

"What isn't?" Auntie Joy said shortly. "I say not enough fry bread. She bite my head off."

Kate's brow cleared. The aunties had a decades-old running battle about fry bread, whose was best and who hadn't made their share for the last potlatch. She busied herself with the dirty dishes, and the next time she looked up Bernie was ushering his kids out the door.

"I'm out of here," a voice said, and she looked around to see Jim pulling on his cap. "See you later?"

Kate, wary of the previous odd behavior of her heart, shrugged, elaborately casual. "Sure. If you want."

"Your house?"

"Sure. If you feel like coming out."

He looked puzzled. "Are you okay, Kate?"

"Sure. Fine."

"Okay. Later, then."

"Later."

And she did not allow herself to watch him leave.

She raised her head to see the four aunties peering at her with owlish looks. "What?"

"Pathetic," Auntie Vi, attempting to make up for her previous bad humor, said to Auntie Edna.

"Trying to outsmart love," Auntie Edna said to Auntie Balasha.

"Trying to fix it so she don't get hurt," Auntie Balasha told Auntie Joy.

"Don't tell us how that don't work out," Auntie Joy said to Kate.

"I don't know what you're talking about," Kate said. She gathered up an armful of casserole dishes and made a dignified exit, spoiled somewhat when the top two dishes slid off the teetering pile and smashed down on the hardwood floor of the basketball court.

"Pitiful," the four aunties said in chorus.

Kate went for the broom.

The bulk of the work done, Auntie Vi and Kate remained behind to put away the dustpan and carry out the garbage. The cool air of evening was sweet after the overheated smells of deep-fried everything, and they both paused to enjoy it.

"Katya."

Kate steeled herself for more advice to the lovelorn. "Yes, Auntie."

"Louis Deem."

Kate's swing faltered, and the last bag of garbage hit the side of the Dumpster and broke. Kate said a bad word beneath her breath and stooped to pick up the detritus and pitch it over the side. "What about him, Auntie?"

"He going to jail this time?"

"Yes, Auntie." Without looking up, Kate started pitching things into the Dumpster. "Johnny saw him there, at Bernie's house. He's going to jail."

"You sure?"

What was this? Kate stood up and looked at Auntie Vi, and was surprised and alarmed to see the other woman's face drawn with strain, leeched of its usual life and color. "Yes, Auntie." She put any personal doubts she might or might not have had firmly to one side and infused her voice with confidence. "Louis Deem is going to jail. I'm sure."

"Good."

There was more than approval in her auntie's voice; there was something that sounded very much like relief. It was almost as if Auntie Vi had feared a different answer to her question.

Kate tried to remember the last time Auntie Vi had been afraid of anything.

She couldn't even remember the first time.

Enid Koslowski and Auntie Vi must have been better friends than Kate had thought. "Even better, Auntie, Jim Chopin is sure, and Judge Singh is expediting the trial."

"When?"

"Four weeks."

Auntie Vi grunted. "Good," she said again, "that good, Katya. Louis don't need to be out here with the people."

Kate couldn't agree more.

Auntie Vi poked her. "You think about what I said?"

Inches from a clean getaway, Kate thought. "I think, Auntie."

"We need you, Katya."

"I help where I can, Auntie."

"You could help more."

Kate wouldn't have agreed with that at gunpoint, so she didn't say anything. To her immense relief, Auntie Vi stretched and gave a yawn so huge, Kate could hear her jaw crack. "Long day. Tired now. Good night, Katya."

"Good night, Auntie."

Halfway across the parking lot, Auntie Vi turned and yelled, "And you give that boy a chance, Katya, you hear? Be safe when you dead."

Kate didn't think Auntie Vi was referring to Johnny, waiting for her in the pickup with his nose buried in F. M. Busby, his head pillowed on Mutt's side. She wasn't so foolhardy as to ask Auntie Vi to clarify whom she meant, though.

The sun had set and stars were creeping up the eastern horizon as they rolled through the village. The recent snowfall had been packed down enough by snow machine traffic that the winter ice on the gravel road was wearing thin, and the road's surface rattled every one of the pickup's million parts one against each other all at the same time. It took Johnny two tries to be heard above the racket. "Kate?"

"What?" The wheel vibrated beneath Kate's hands.

"What happens when you die?"

"What?"

"What happens when you die?"

She heard him the second time. She pulled off to the side of the road and killed the engine. Johnny said, "It's just—Fitz is dead. Where'd he go?"

Kate cleared her throat and was grateful for the warm presence of Mutt between them. She knotted a hand in the thick gray hair. "It's not that I haven't thought about it myself, Johnny. It's just that—I'm not religious."

"I know." Johnny sounded infuriatingly patient. "You've said that before. I just don't know what that means, exactly."

"I'm not big with organized religion, for starters. You know. Believe as we do or burn in hell. I don't think much of fear as a motivator to faith."

"Okay. So do you believe in God? Is there a heaven where we all go when we die?"

Her turn to hesitate, but she wouldn't lie to the kid. "No. I think this is it, Johnny. We're born, we live, we die."

Johnny sounded forlorn. "That's it?"

She looked over at the outline of his head against the window. "That's a lot, Johnny. That life exists, that we are here to show up and pay attention to it. We can laugh, we can cry. We can love. There is chocolate."

"Yeah, but what about Fitz?"

Kate let her head fall back against the headrest. "No easy questions today, huh?"

He was insistent. "What about Fitz, Kate?"

"I believe that the people we love live for as long as we remember them, Johnny," Kate said soberly. "Everything we learned from them we pass on to others. That way, they never die."

He sighed. "No big white light at the end of a tunnel?"

"Nope. One thing, though."

"What?"

"Live every moment of your life. Even if you're sitting around doing nothing, know you're doing it and why. Every time someone asks you a question beginning 'Do you want to go—?' say yes. Try everything once." She smiled into the darkness. "Once I chased a killer up a mountain. There was an earthquake and I lost her. So I climbed to the top of the mountain anyway, because it was there, and so was I, and I'd never been to the top before. The lights were out, and a full moon, and I swear you could see right out to the edge of the universe." She looked at him again. "You never know, Johnny."

"Never know what?"

She shrugged, and then remembered he couldn't see her. "You never know anything, really. I think a lot of people decide to believe in God because they want to feel like they're not alone, and that there are certainties, rules by which they can live their lives.

It gives them a sense of, I don't know. Order, I guess. Reason. Purpose."

"So you're a disorderly kind of person?"

She laughed. "I guess I am. I chose a disorderly profession, that's for sure."

He was silent for a moment. "So Fitz is really dead." Almost inaudibly he added, "And Dad."

"Yes. They're both dead. But not completely gone." She took a deep breath, trying to channel the air around the sharp but not entirely unexpected pain of the admission.

"I guess I was lucky," Johnny said.

"What? Why?"

"I had Dad for twelve years," Johnny said simply. "Much as Mom tried to mess it up, tried to keep me away from him, I had Dad for most all of that time. We were good friends. Best buds."

"That's more than a lot of sons can say about their fathers," she said cautiously.

"More than Fitz could say." He looked at her, but she couldn't make out his expression in the dim light. "Bernie's not a very good father, Kate. I think maybe he uses it all up on the kids on his basketball teams, and he just doesn't have enough left over for his own kids."

She couldn't deny it, so she started the truck instead. The rest of the journey was accomplished in silence. As she swung wide to pull into the narrow entrance to her access road, headlights flashed in the rearview. In spite of herself, her heart, that usually reliable organ, skipped a beat. She couldn't stop the smile from spreading across her face.

She stopped smiling when the lights, approaching swiftly, pulled even with her rear bumper and then pulled left to pass without waiting for her to get clear of the road.

She heard a loud crack, and for a split second thought the other vehicle had clipped her bumper, except that there was no corresponding lurch of her pickup. In that same moment, the driver's-side window disintegrated. Mutt was on her feet, barking wildly.

"Kate!"

"Get down!" She fought to hold on to the wheel with one hand as she reached around Mutt and caught the back of Johnny's neck with the other, catapulting him down in front of the bench seat. At the same time, she double-clutched into second gear and hit the gas. The rear wheels spun.

Another crack sounded, and the rear window splintered. Mutt barked, once, and then yipped, and then gave a soft whine, and then she slid off the edge of the seat and fell on top of Johnny.

Kate screamed something, she didn't know what, and forgot everything she knew about driving on winter roads. She slammed on the brakes with both feet. The engine jumped and bucked and died, and the pickup went into a skid that brought the end of the pickup bed around to the left. They slid off the road, bumped into the ditch, and nearly rolled, tipping up on the right wheels for a long, dangerous moment before the weight of the truck brought them back down with a hell of a bang.

And there they came to a rest, buried in snow in the ditch, headlights pointing at the sky.

EIGHT

Afterward, Jim could remember the night only as a series of stop-motion flashbacks, as if he'd lived through it through the lens of a camera, one shot at a time.

Looking up from his computer to see Kate standing in the doorway, face drained of color, her eyes fixed on him in a painful plea, blood smearing the front of her shirt and jeans, enough on the bottom of her right shoe to leave tracks.

Johnny, white-faced and mute, a retreat into the shocked little boy on the front stairs of Bernie's house.

The rubber track of her snow machine in shreds from traveling at full throttle over the twenty-five miles of near gravel between her place and town.

Helping her lift Mutt's inert body from the trailer hitched to her snow machine to the back of his Cessna.

Kate sitting next to him in the Cessna, leaning forward against the seat belt as if she could tow the plane through the air faster.

Kenny meeting them at the Ahtna airport, a comforting bulwark against the unreality of the moment.

The expression on Jennie Pappas's face when she saw who it

was coming through the front door of her clinic like a freight train.

Kate's dark head bent over the gray one in the harsh lights of the examining room, crooning something wordless into Mutt's ear.

Kate fighting him when at the vet's insistence he picked her up and carried her into the waiting room.

Johnny sitting across from them, hands dangling uselessly between his knees, staring vacantly into space.

The tick of the minute hand on the round plastic clock on the wall.

The scratched plastic of the bucket chairs.

For her part, Kate's world had narrowed to the square of linoleum between the tiny waiting room and the marginally larger recovery room, where Mutt lay on a stainless steel table, her left shoulder shaved and bandaged.

"I don't know," Jennie Pappas had said. "She's strong and healthy, but that bullet tore her up plenty inside. I've repaired the damage, but shock is a funny thing. It helped that you got her here as soon as you did." Jennie, a pudgy fifty-something with a short bob of dark hair streaked with gray, gave a tired shrug. "We'll have to wait and see. First twenty-four hours are critical."

"I'll wait."

Jennie nodded as if she hadn't expected anything else. "I'm going back home now, try to get a little sleep before I have to get back for regular hours."

Kate surfaced enough to say, "Thanks for coming in, Jennie."

Jennie gave a dismissive wave. "There's a coffeepot and some snacks in the back. Help yourself." Yawning again, she shuffled out the door.

Four o'clock became five o'clock, and five o'clock became six. Sometimes Kate paced. Sometimes she sat in the waiting room, hunched over her knees, hands clasped together, staring at the floor. Mostly she stayed with Mutt, finally levering herself up on the table and fitting herself against Mutt's spine. There wasn't any room for her. She did it anyway.

She didn't think about who had done this, or why. She didn't think about what she was going to do about it. She didn't think about what happened next. She merely endured, a careful but proprietary arm around her dog, willing her to keep breathing in and out, willing the torn muscles to repair themselves, willing death to keep its distance.

After a while she fell into an uneasy doze.

"Kate?"

A voice came at her from far away.

"Kate?"

She blinked and after a moment her eyes focused on Johnny's face. He was crying. It took a second to register. When it did, her heart simply stopped beating.

"No," he said, and now she saw that he was laughing, too. "It's okay. Look."

She pushed herself into a sitting position, muscles creaking in protest, and looked down at her dog.

Who was looking back, great yellow eyes blinking at her owlishly. One ear twitched and Mutt whined, a clear question.

Kate felt the tears she had as yet been unable to shed well up and spill down her cheeks in a warm, blinding flood. "Hey, girl," she said shakily.

She buried her face in Mutt's neck and let herself sob out her relief.

How long?"

Jennie compared Mutt's chart with the sound of the protest coming from the back of the building. Mutt had started howling the instant Kate left the room, and the other animals housed in the veterinary clinic started howling, meowing, clucking, snarling, grunting, and chirping in sympathy. The noise was deafening and there was a solid, substantial door between it and them. "I haven't got a cage big enough for her. Is she going to behave?"

"Probably not."

"Well, she can't leave yet. She's got to have a couple of days. I'm not going to sedate her, that'll play hell with her recovery."

"She won't howl if I'm with her."

"Then you stay," Jennie said firmly.

So Kate sent Johnny back to the Park with Jim, and she spent the next five days in Ahtna. It was impossible to keep Mutt on the table after the first day, so Kate checked into a room at the Ahtna Lodge, where Tony and Stanislav hovered around like anxious uncles, proffering bowls of fresh beef chopped with raw eggs every five minutes. At first Mutt displayed little appetite, terrifying all three of them, but on the third morning she deigned to nibble, and by the fifth day she was licking the bowls clean. They walked back and forth to the clinic every day, half a mile one way. At first Mutt was stiff and careful, thinking out each step before she took it. It hurt Kate to see this usually swift and graceful beast reduced to the plodding shuffle of a breakdown, but Mutt was moving better the next day, and better enough by the third day that Kate felt able to detour by way of the Bad Ass Coffee espresso stand in the Eagle parking lot on their way to the clinic. Jennie was appropriately grateful for the vente quadruple latte, three sugars.

The sixth morning they went for their daily checkup; Jennie shook her head at the end of it. "What?" Kate said, alarmed.

"Nothing to worry about," Jennie said, "I'm just amazed. And good," she added, handing Kate a staggering bill, "very, very good."

"Yes, you are," Kate said, and went to the bank and got cash for the full amount in a plain white envelope and had it at the clinic inside an hour. "Can I take her home?"

"Can I stop you?"

Kate held out a hand. "Thanks, Jennie."

Jennie took it in a warm clasp. "Glad to help. And you, you monster," she told Mutt, standing next to Kate's hip at her usual duty station, "stay the hell out of trouble, okay? Takes days for my regular patients, not to mention their owners, to get back to normal after you've been here."

Mutt flattened her ears and wagged a placating tail.

"Uh-huh," Jennie said, and gave her a rough scratch between her ears. "Get out of here, the both of you."

There was a parade waiting for them in Niniltna, or so it seemed. George circled the village at fifty feet three times, running up and back on the prop pitch to make a wah-wah sound that shook the fillings in everyone's teeth, and by the time they landed, a stream of villagers was on the way at quick march. Mutt was greeted like a conquering hero, everyone wanted a chance to pat her head and to congratulate Kate on Mutt's recovery, as if Kate had had anything to do with it. Billy Mike came down the hill, a smile lightening the care on his moon face. Bonnie Jeppsen closed the window in the post office and came out, followed by everyone who was checking their mail. Heather brought all the old farts up from the Riverside Café—Heather Meganack, that was. Laurel had brought her cousin in to run things while Laurel helped out at the Roadhouse. Old Sam toasted Kate and Mutt with a raised mug and winked. "Good to see you girls," he said, and there was a chorus of agreement. That day Kate and Mutt could do no wrong, and Kate understood why, but it was nevertheless very pleasant to be welcomed back so warmly.

The four aunties pushed forward last. Mutt ducked her head modestly—a four-auntie salute was not to be sneezed at—and was subjected to a minute inspection, ear to tail, which she endured patiently, after which the four aunties stood back and declared the work to be good and the dog to be well.

Auntie Joy underlined this benediction with a sharp nod. "I remember that puppy we give you, Katya, when you come home from town that time."

"Alakah," Auntie Balasha said with a sigh. "We don't know then if you going to make it."

"Either of you," Auntie Edna said.

Auntie Joy shook her head sadly. "Skinny little runt, abandoned, alone, sick, starving."

"And you not much better," Auntie Vi said, shaking her finger in Kate's face.

"You heal each other," Auntie Balasha said.

"Do it again," Auntie Joy said.

At which time Bobby mercifully pulled up and they were able to make a break for it. Auntie Vi shut the door behind them and then made a motion for Kate to roll down the window. Her face hadn't smoothed out from the strain Kate had noticed the week before at Enid's potlatch. "I be out soon."

Kate knew a sinking feeling in the region of her heart, which had already been given something of a workout over the past week, but she didn't have the energy to do anything but say meekly, "Okay, Auntie."

Auntie Vi gave a regal wave of her hand that came perilously close to the sign of the cross. Bobby took that as permission to put the truck in gear, which he did.

Bobby dropped them in the clearing. She saw the bed of her pickup poking out of the garage. "Thanks for rescuing the truck, Bobby."

"Jim did it. I just helped." He surveyed her. "Tough week."

Her laugh was a little shaky. "Yeah."

"You sure you don't need anything else, Shugak? Dinah told me to bring you home with me. She's ready to take you both on as permanent residents."

"I need to be home," she said. "So does Mutt." She opened the door and got out, followed by Mutt, who descended in stately fashion, a distinct and to Kate painful contrast to her usual gravity-defying bound. Kate closed the door and smiled through the window. "Thanks for salvaging the wrecks, Bobby."

He waggled his eyebrows. "Don't forget my finder's fee." He put the truck in gear.

"Tell Dinah and Katya hi."

"Tell 'em yourself!"

The tricked-out Ford Ranger roared off into the trees. The engine noise faded away, and Kate looked down at Mutt, who contrary to usual practice had remained at her side. "Aren't you hungry, girl?"

Mutt walked over to the stairs and limped up them to the deck, where she paused to look over her shoulder. "Okay," Kate said, and let them in. Mutt padded over to the rag rug in front of the fireplace, turned around three times, and curled up, burying her nose beneath her tail. Welcome homes were wearing on the invalid. Kate started a fire in the fireplace, let her hand rest on Mutt's head for a moment as Mutt slumbered on, oblivious, and went into the kitchen and got out the flour.

Baking bread was the only viable alternative to taking her .30-06 down to the trooper post and using it on Louis Deem.

She felt anger licking around the edges, threatening her composure. She recognized it, acknowledged it, and tamped it down with deliberation. For one thing, Mutt knew when she was upset, and she didn't want Mutt upset until Mutt was completely back on her game. For another, she wouldn't allow her personal inclination, no matter how strong it was, to in any way mess up the case against Louis Deem.

Howie Katelnikof had taken the shots at them, most likely at Louis Deem's instigation. She didn't need any evidence to prove it, she knew it in her bones, she'd known it almost from the moment she heard the first shot. Six years of an uneasy truce shattered with Mutt's shoulder.

She wondered if Howie'd been aiming for Mutt, or for Johnny. The rage began to rise up again, as it had every time she'd begun thinking about the attack over the past week.

But Howie was only a pawn in this war, a foot soldier, a red shirt. She could reach out and touch him any time she wanted to, and she would make it clear to him that she could at her first opportunity. Intimidating jurors at Louis Deem's behest was one thing. Pissing off Kate Shugak was something else altogether.

The grand jury went into session next week, and Judge Singh had promised to move the trial to the top of her docket. If all went well, Louis Deem would be a resident for life in the Spring Creek Correctional Center in Seward before the month was out. Rotting in jail was better than rotting in the ground.

She chanted it like a mantra, willing herself to believe it, while occupying her hands in measuring out flour, salt, yeast, and warm water. She stirred them together and turned the resulting dough out on a floured board to rest while she washed out the bowl. Ten minutes later, she began kneading flour into it, a handful at a time, until the dough was smooth and elastic and barely sticky. It was a strong dough and it took a full twenty-five minutes to do the job. She could feel it in her shoulders when she was done. She was still a little sore from the bruises she'd gotten when her truck was shot out from under her, when Mutt—

The gray lump on the hearth hadn't moved. Kate walked over and rested a hand on the warm flank, just to be sure, and was comforted by the steady rise and fall.

The baguette recipe didn't call for it, but she oiled the bowl anyway and turned the dough so that it was lightly coated, having learned from her first attempts that, left unoiled, the dough would grow a skin that would inhibit rising. She covered the bowl with a damp cloth and left it to rise while she puttered around the house, cleaning her bathroom, shuddering at Johnny's, pitching out those leftovers in the refrigerator that had been allowed to play host to foreign invaders, washing clothes. It kept her hands busy and her mind blank.

When the dough had doubled in size, she had a decision to make, and she gave it the attention Dwight Eisenhower might have given logistics for the D-day invasion. The recipe called for three risings. So far, the first two had been successful, whereas the third had failed every time, the yeast just wearing out before the loaves had reached baking size. She'd tried everything to effect a comprehensible translation from French *boulangerie* to Alaskan kitchen, adding more yeast, reducing the amount of flour, doubling the rising time. Nothing had worked. This time she decided to do away with the third rising altogether, to shape the loaves for baking after the first rising, the way she would ordinary white bread. She quartered the dough and shaped each piece into a tubular loaf. Air squeaked out of the dough in protest. She rolled the loaves from the center out until they were the length of her longest baking sheet, brushed on the lightest possible coat of oil, and left them to rise again beneath a loose layer of Saran Wrap.

She checked to see that Mutt was still breathing. She was. Kate filled a pan with water and set it next to Mutt in the event the dog ever woke again, put another log on the fire, and sat at the kitchen table to go through the pile of mail Johnny must have stacked there over the past week.

Johnny. She looked at the clock. Two in the afternoon. Allowing for Ms. Doogan's lab project, he'd be home in two hours. Good. The house was too quiet.

She pushed the mail away and went upstairs to get the book she'd been reading. Julian Barnes's essays on the art of cooking at home, including one where he proposed the assigning of hangmen's nooses, one to five, to each meal depending on how well it was going and how hungry the guests were getting while they waited. She curled up on the couch.

After three attempts to read the same page, she gave up. Barnes was worth a better effort than that, so she put the book down and went over to check on Mutt's breathing again. The warm gray pelt was still moving up and down in a reassuringly regular fashion. Kate knelt down and put her cheek against Mutt's side. One of Mutt's ears flickered, but otherwise Mutt slept on. Her heartbeat was a steady thump against Kate's ear. Kate lay down next to her, pillowing her head on one arm, the other draped across Mutt, careful to avoid the bandage on her shoulder.

The next thing she knew, she heard a soft woof, the scramble of nails on wood floor, tongue lapping up water. She opened her eyes to see Mutt standing by the door. The door handles were lever style, deliberately chosen so that Mutt could open them. She wasn't opening them today. Kate went over and opened it for her. Mutt gave her the evil eye, as if this tedious disability were all Kate's fault, and went across the deck and down the stairs with a cautious tread. Kate went around to the front of the house to watch her progress through the windows. Mutt watered a few plants, sniffed at a few more, and disappeared beneath the deck. Kate went out to check, and found Mutt lying beneath the deck. She gave Kate an annoyed look.

Kate went back inside and checked the bread, which had almost doubled in size. She turned on the oven and the burner beneath the water kettle. When the water boiled, she poured it into a pan and set it on the bottom of the oven. She brushed the loaves with more water, slashed their tops with a razor blade, put them in the oven, and set the timer. She might even have said a prayer.

She'd tried bread, bills, book. Nothing seemed to be able to hold her attention for long. And then, hallelujah, Johnny walked in.

She took one look at his face and thought, Or maybe not hallelujah. "What's wrong?"

"Where's Mutt?"

"Outside under the deck, last time I looked." She took his chin in one hand and said, "What's wrong, Johnny?"

He pulled free and let his daypack hit the floor with a thud.

"They're going to let Louis Deem go."

She stared at him. She could not possibly have heard right. "What?" she said.

"They're going to let Louis Deem go," Johnny said again.

For one inglorious moment all Kate could think of was, So that was why he didn't pick us up at the airport. Instantly ashamed, she shook the thought out of her head. "Jim Chopin turned Louis Deem loose?"

"Not yet, but he's going to have to," Johnny said, tired of playing the game. "Some lawyer or judge or something like that wouldn't charge him, and they can't keep him."

"Did Jim tell you this?"

"No. But everybody knows."

The school had been buzzing with nothing else, and there had been a lot of speculative looks cast Johnny's way. Did they think he'd been too afraid to testify to what he saw that awful night? Vanessa knew he wasn't. That was something, but a bunch of other people were looking like they thought that Johnny had weaseled out. Wouldn't be long before they'd be saying it, and then they'd say it to his face.

Maybe he hadn't always liked Jim Chopin. Maybe he had thought Jim wasn't necessarily the best choice Kate could have made after Johnny's dad died. Maybe he'd even been a little jealous, even if he did jump back from that thought like he was jerking his hand back from a hot fire.

But the more he'd got to know Jim, the better he had liked him, even if Johnny was a little worried about Jim's reputation with women. Anybody hurt Kate Shugak, they'd have Johnny Morgan to answer to. Maybe he was only fourteen, but that didn't mean he couldn't make someone's life a living hell if he put his mind to it. Just ask his mother. But so far Jim had behaved himself, earning Johnny's qualified approval.

And now this. Louis Deem was a bad guy. It was a cop's job to lock up bad guys. Instead, Jim was going to turn one loose. And not just any bad guy, but the one who killed Fitz, and Fitz's mom. The guy who would have killed Johnny if he'd known Johnny had been there.

Johnny wanted to be absolutely fair. He wanted to give Jim a chance to explain. He was sure Jim would have a reason for what he did. Cops were the good guys. Johnny's father had been a cop, or close enough. "Why would they let Louis go, Kate? Is my testimony not enough?"

"Not by itself," Jim said, "no."

They looked around to see him standing in the doorway. Mutt had followed him up the stairs, and she nosed his hand. It was the first time Kate had ever seen Mutt ask for his attention. Usually she simply demanded it.

Jim pulled off his cap, unbuckled his gun belt, and hung both from the rack next to the door. He walked to the table and slumped down into a chair as if all the bone had gone out of his spine. "I was hoping I'd get to tell you myself. I'm sorry, guys."

"What happened?"

Jim looked at Johnny. "I put all the evidence I had, which was your statement, in front of the district attorney. He won't even put it in front of the grand jury."

"But I saw him!"

"I know you did, kid."

Johnny looked at Kate. "What if I went to Ahtna and talked to them myself?"

Kate looked at Jim. Jim shook his head. "They don't want to go before thirty Park rats who are already pissed off that they have to look at pictures of dead people for three months instead of gearing up for salmon season with only the eyewitness testimony of a fourteen-year-old boy." He looked at Kate. "With whose guardian the arresting officer has a relationship."

Johnny flushed a dull red right up to the roots of his hair. "That doesn't have anything to do with what I saw!"

"You're right. It doesn't."

"It will at trial, though," Kate said. "Damn, damn, damn. I should have thought of this."

"I thought of it before I arrested the bastard, but that was also before we knew there was no forensic evidence to back up Johnny's testimony. Between that and Abigail Smith ready to get up on the stand and swear that Louis was with her all night that night, we don't have a case."

"I thought you said she was lying!"

"She is, Johnny, but I can't prove it. And if I can't prove it, Louis Deem will skate again. It's better to turn him loose now than he gets acquitted later. If Abigail's story ever changes, we can charge him. The statute of limitations never runs out on murder."

He rubbed his scalp with his fingers, leaving the thick blond mane in an unaccustomed disarray. "Hell." He looked at Kate. "I'll keep pushing Abigail for details. Amateur liars get caught because they forget what they said before and start contradicting themselves. I'm thinking Abigail Smith doesn't have a lot of experience lying. I'm also thinking her parents will be working on her, too."

"Or they'll marry her off to Louis that much faster," Kate said.

Jim rubbed both his hands over his face. "Jesus, I hope not. Wouldn't that just put the icing on Louis Deem's cake."

"He was standing as close to me as Mutt is right now." Mutt, back in front of the fireplace, looked and gave her tail a perfunctory wag. The corners of Johnny's mouth drooped. "He killed Fitz. He killed Fitz's mom. I wanted to say so. I wanted to say so in a court of law, looking right at him when I did."

Kate put a hand on his shoulder. "You may get the chance to yet, Johnny." But over Johnny's head, her eyes met Jim's, and she saw her own relief reflected there, relief that fate had delayed and probably denied Johnny's chance to testify against Louis Deem.

"I'll hang on to him as long as I can," Jim said. "Maybe another day, maybe two. Go out and talk to Abigail again. Go out and talk to Howie and Willard, see if I can shake something loose there."

"Why? What did they have to do with anything?"

"It was Howie that shot Mutt, Johnny," Jim said. "He was probably aiming at Kate. Or you."

Johnny went white at hearing said out loud what he had long suspected at heart to be true. "You don't know that," he said in an almost inaudible voice.

"Howie is Louis's go-to boy, Johnny," Jim said, his voice firm, maybe even a little harsh. "By now you've heard all the stories. I don't have a shred of evidence to back it up, but I know Howie Katelnikof. He took that shot at you, and he put you into the ditch, and if he'd tried a little harder, I'd be saying this over your grave."

"You're scaring him, Jim," Kate said.

"I want him scared," Jim said. "I want you scared. It's never a good thing to get into Louis Deem's sights, and you know it. He's got a notoriously twitchy trigger finger."

"Did you talk to Howie after?"

"Sure, I went out to Deem's place, right after I got back from Ahtna and dropped Johnny at Bobby's."

"What did he say?"

"He said what he always says, Kate, that he was watching television at the house at the time of the incident. By then of course he had the *TV Guide* memorized for the whole evening, and he was more than happy to recite it for me, chapter and verse and which episodes were reruns."

"And Willard backed him up," Kate said.

"Of course Willard backed him up."

"Well," Johnny said, "then maybe Howie didn't do it."

"Don't kid yourself," Jim said. "Willard's got the attention span of a first-grader. His one major skill in life is repeating the last thing he heard. Howie shot at you all right, Johnny."

"Enough," Kate said firmly. The boy was mute with misery. "Enough for tonight, anyway. Hungry?"

They nodded.

"I've got bread in the oven. I'll make spaghetti." She gave Johnny's shoulder a friendly tug. "Come on, chop me some garlic."

The baguettes came out of the oven, looking like four golden-brown torpedoes and smelling like heaven, and she set them aside to cool. For the rest, she was unaccustomedly clumsy that evening, dropping the frying pan, letting the bacon overcook, cutting herself on the bread knife, until finally Johnny threw her out of the kitchen and finished the meal himself. It wasn't as good as Kate's spaghetti, but Jim looked from Johnny's mild triumph at this small accomplishment to Kate's meaningful stare and filled his mouth with food before he could say so.

The bread was great.

Mutt spent the meal asleep on the hearth. "You sure she was ready to come home?"

"I'm sure," Kate said. "Hospitals are best for patching things up. Home is best for healing. You spending the night?"

She still asked, even though it had been weeks since he'd said no, or said no and made it stick. "That was my plan," he said cheerfully. It was in fact his plan to stick to her like glue, and Johnny, and Mutt for that matter. Once Louis was out, Howie's motive would vanish, but Louis wasn't out yet.

On that grim thought he took a shower, changed into a T-shirt and jeans, and pulled his boots on over bare feet and went to get the case file to see if he could find something he'd missed. It was part of an untidy heap in the passenger seat. He gathered the bits and pieces and forms and statements into the folder and was momentarily arrested by the golden glow streaming out of Kate's front windows. Johnny was helping Kate clean up in the kitchen. Mutt had resurfaced and was reaching up a paw to pull down the door handle. Before she could, Kate nudged Johnny and pointed, and he trotted over to open the door for her.

This time it was Mutt. Last time it had been Kate, laid out by the business end of a number 2 shovel. He had been terrified because for a few horrible moments he'd thought she was dead, and then he'd been angry because he'd been terrified. He had walked away from her afterward. Hell, he'd run.

They'd spent a winter at war, a war of attrition, during which by perseverance and not a little femme fatalism she'd worn down his resistance and pretty much vacated his autonomy. He was done trying to figure out how she'd done it, how he'd let her do it. Now he was just trying to deal with what was. In spite of a blameless life lived determinedly for himself and himself alone, he now had hostages to fortune. Three of them.

Previously, his family had consisted of his parents, who lived in southern California in a state of civil indifference that hadn't changed since his childhood. He'd let them define what a relationship was, calm, polite, bloodless. His relationship with Kate, by contrast, was turbulent, bawdy, challenging, exasperating, amusing, and passionate enough to melt his eyebrows, and infrequently not a little violent. He rubbed the scar on his forehead, a reminder of the file cabinet she'd heaved at him when she'd found out he'd slept with Ruth Bauman. That it had happened years before he'd become involved with Kate hadn't put her aim off any.

Not that it mattered, he told himself. He'd never told a woman he loved her. He was always scrupulously honest about the love thing. If it came to that, he was honest about everything. He raised no false hopes, he encouraged no long-term plans, he made it clear from the beginning that he was in it for the fun of it and when it was over no hard feelings, good-bye, and everybody's still friends. That was his plan and it had worked well for him.

Until now.

For the first time it occurred to him that if he spent as much time working on a relationship as he did in planning for its ending, it might last longer, and it might mean more.

If he had to boot Howie Katelnikof out of the Park, if he had to buy him a one-way ticket out of the state out of his own pocket, he was going to see to it that Louis Deem wasn't going to get any more free shots at Kate Shugak or Johnny Morgan. Or Mutt. The U.S. Constitution was a wonderful thing, no doubt about it, and he personally loved each and every one of the amendments, in particular the first ten. He'd meant every word of his oath when he took it. More, he believed absolutely in the law enforcement doctrine of "to protect and to serve."

But if the U.S. Constitution said he couldn't arrest Louis Deem for killing Kate Shugak unless and until Louis Deem actually did kill her, then fuck the goddamn U.S. Constitution and all who sailed in her.

In this patriotic mood, he carried the case file back into the house and sat down at the table to go through it piece by piece.

Sec. 11.41.110. Murder in the Second Degree

(a) A person commits the crime of murder in the second degree if

> (1) with intent to cause serious physical injury to another person or knowing that the conduct is substantially certain to cause death or serious physical injury to another person, the person causes the death of any person . . .

—Alaska statutes

He liked to have his hands around her throat during sex. She didn't like it, but he didn't give her much choice in the matter, and she had learned through experience that it was over quicker if she didn't fight him.

That damn Kate Shugak. She'd dropped in again today, oh so casually, looking at her with those eyes that saw everything whether you wanted them to or not. He was always angry after one of Kate's visits. She tried to tell him that it wasn't her fault, that she and Kate hadn't been that close in school, that they were hardly related at all, that Kate was just snooping around in what wasn't any of her business, but he wouldn't listen. He would be angry, and he would take it out on her.

Lately he'd been taking it out on her in public places, too, which she really didn't like, all the more reason for making no protest so it would be done and they could go home.

She shut her mind to the sound of other truck engines coming and going and let him bend her over the bench seat of the truck. Her head struck the steering wheel, and she made an involuntary sound and tried to jerk free.

"Louder," he said, and grabbed a fistful of her hair to push her down again.

Her head caught awkwardly between the wheel and the edge of the seat. The last thing she heard was a loud crack, and she had just enough time to wonder what it was before the broken edge of her axis vertebrae severed her spinal cord.

NINE

In that same patriotic mood, the next morning Jim drove to the post and strode back to the cells like Will Kane heading out to face down Sam Fuller.

Unlike Sam Fuller, however, Louis Deem was not holding a six-gun; he was reading a book. He looked up. "Hey there, Jim."

"Louis." It bothered Jim that Louis could read. It bothered him more that Louis was reading one of Jim's favorite authors, John D. MacDonald.

Louis smiled. "You seem upset about something, Jim. How can I help?"

Jim rallied. "I know why you wanted Bernie's gold, Louis."

"And I can see you're dying to tell me," Louis said. "Go ahead, serve it up."

"It wasn't the gold at all. Or not Bernie's. I couldn't understand why you left all those nuggets lying around. I figured at first you dropped them, but it's just not like you to get in a hurry when it comes to ripping somebody off.

"And then I remembered something Bernie told me once, and this morning I called the Alaska Miners Association and talked to a guy there. He told me an experienced miner can tell what mine a piece of gold comes from in a certain area. Emphasis on experienced, Louis. You aren't, of course. In a million years, you'd never dirty your hands on something as hardscrabble as mining gold. But you don't mind a controlling interest while somebody else pulls it out of the ground for you."

"So far I'm not seeing what this has to do with me," Louis said with determined boredom, "but it's a whale of a tale, and everybody likes gold rush stories, so by all means continue."

"That's why you shined up to Abigail, got her to say she'd marry you, and you'd have gone through with it, too, because hey, she's the eldest daughter, the one who's bound to have the most say over whatever her folks leave behind. Which brings me back to the gold." Jim produced a slip of paper from his breast pocket and waved it at Deem. "Bernie isn't an experienced miner, either, but he's a half-assed amateur historian and he likes to know about stuff. So whenever a miner brought in gold to settle up his tab, Bernie'd ask him to write down what creek it came out of, and anything else the miner could remember, any details that would spice up the tale."

Louis faked a yawn. "I'm sorry, Jim, was there a point to your story? A punch line? Any ending in sight at all?"

"Dan O'Brien's got a map up on the Step. It shows that someone has been granted subsurface mineral rights to a tract of land that sits partly on the land the Smiths say they own."

Louis's eyes narrowed, but his voice remained calm. "Really?"

"Really," Jim said. "Bernie showed me through his nugget collection a couple of times, Louis. I vividly remember the one that came out of Salmon Creek."

"Which Salmon Creek?" Louis said, displaying a mild interest. "There must be twenty of them in the Park, and a thousand of them in the state."

"But only one that rises in Suulutaq Glacier, Louis. You know what *suulutaq* means in Aleut, don't you? 'Gold,' Louis. It means 'gold.' "

"Really," Louis said, but he said it just a beat late. If Jim hadn't been watching him closely, he wouldn't have caught it. It was enough to confirm his suspicions, which was a good thing because it was very probably the only confirmation he was going to get in this whole sorry affair.

"You weren't stealing the nuggets when you broke into Bernie's house, Louis. You were stealing the little bits of paper with the nuggets' provenance on them. The one from the Suulutaq was more specific than general in directions, and it was going to show you and Father Smith the way to a gold strike, or so you thought. God forbid you get out there on your knees with a pan and try to find it for yourself. No, you wanted a shortcut. You always go for the shortcuts, Louis."

There was a brief silence. "Interesting story," Louis said, and smiled. "Needs an ending."

Jim turned on his heel and walked out.

Behind him, Louis started to laugh.

Jim was so angry, he didn't hear Maggie at first, and she had to repeat herself. "Boss!"

"What?"

Maggie recoiled, and Jim realized he was standing in the front office. "I'm sorry, Maggie. What is it?"

"Judge Singh on line one."

Jim swore beneath his breath and snatched up the phone from Maggie's desk. "Chopin here."

"Sergeant Chopin? Robbie Singh."

"Yes, Your Honor. What can I do for you?"

He heard a heavy sigh. "You have to let Louis Deem go, Sergeant. I'm sorry."

"Judge, I—do you know what this guy—?"

"I know all about him, but you haven't made your case, Sergeant. Mr. Rickard is quite prepared to sue you, me, the Department of Public Safety, the Department of Law, and the state of Alaska for wrongful imprisonment if we don't let his client go."

"Judge—"

"Let him go, Jim," she said. "Now."

She hung up, and he replaced the telephone in its cradle.

Maggie, who had heard too much of that phone call for her own peace of mind, hooked an unceremonious thumb over her shoulder. "Somebody to see you."

"Oh." Oh God. The very last person he wanted to see at this moment. "Hey, Bernie."

"Hey, Jim."

"Come on in." Jim walked into his office, trying to arrange his face into some semblance of sanity.

Bernie, receding hair pulled back in its usual ponytail from a drawn face and haunted eyes, sat in one of the chairs across from Jim's desk. Jim went around and sat in his chair.

"Do you mind?" Bernie got up again to close the door.

"No," Jim said, but he was wary. This was usually the part where the victims' relatives, suffering from survivor's guilt, sought out a target for their frustration and rage and grief. The easiest target was always the cop on the beat.

Bernie sat down again. He didn't say anything immediately. Jim, still mastering his fury at that smug, murdering son of a bitch in the cells, was happy to sit without speaking. Anything to delay the moment he'd have to actually turn the key in the lock and let him out.

"I was talking to Auntie Vi," Bernie said.

Great. Another country heard from. "Oh, yeah? About?"

"Auntie Vi says all you've got is the kid's testimony that it was Louis he saw at the house."

"That plus Abigail Smith says she was with him all night that night."

Bernie looked tired. "Come on, Jim, you know she's lying. Who knows why all these women lie for Louis Deem, but they do, over and over again, until it literally kills them. I've seen him pick up women at the Roadhouse and I want to go over the bar and grab them and nail them into a barrel and feed them through the bung-hole until they get over it."

There was an edge of bitterness to his voice that told Jim a great deal. "Bernie?"

Bernie sighed. "Yeah. Last summer."

"When you and Laurel Meganack—?"

"Yeah. Enid found out. She had a couple of revenge fucks and told me all about them. Len Dreyer was one."

Len Dreyer being the Park handyman who had been murdered the summer before. Jim already knew this, and Bernie knew he knew it. "And Louis?"

Bernie nodded. "Louis was another."

"What did you do?"

Bernie shrugged. "He scared her. She just wanted revenge, not to get killed. I think she only slept with him the once."

"Where?"

Bernie nodded, as if he'd known Jim would ask. "Our house. Our bed. She made sure I knew that, too."

There wasn't anything Jim could say that would help, so he kept quiet.

"I figure that's when he saw the collection, and he's been making plans to steal it ever since."

"Your nugget collection."

"But we can't prove it, can we?"

"No."

"You're sure, though, aren't you?"

"There is no physical evidence, Bernie. No fingerprints, no muddy footprints, no car tracks, no hairs or blood spatters to do a DNA analysis of, nothing like that."

"But you're sure."

Jim shrugged. "Doesn't matter if I'm sure. Matters only if I can prove it."

"Where's my gold? We find that, maybe . . ."

"The Park's a big place, Bernie. Louis's lived here all his life. It could be anywhere."

"It would help if you found some, though. Like maybe in his house."

Jim sat up straight. "We searched Louis's house and all the outbuildings the day after the crime, right after Johnny ID'd Louis as the guy he saw. We didn't find anything then, and it is highly unlikely that even the most credulous jury is going to think finding your stolen gold this long after the crime is convincing of anything other than that someone planted the evidence after the fact. Especially when Rickard gets done with them."

"Howie."

"And Willard."

Bernie shrugged. "Louis never calls Willard in any of his trials."

"Yeah. I know. The DA's stopped subpoenaing him, too. He's not the most convincing witness."

"So. It's all on Johnny."

"Yes." Bernie was getting at something, and Jim was curious enough to hold off telling Bernie the bad news. It was a minor miracle he didn't know it already, but then he'd been holding himself pretty incommunicado there at the house, and the aunties made a first-class defensive line.

"He's just a kid, Jim."

"He's fourteen."

"Still. Even if you by some miracle manage to get Louis to trial, I can hear his lawyer now. He'll say Johnny was terrified, confused, he didn't know what he was seeing." Bernie met Jim's eyes. "Then he'll talk about how you've persecuted poor Louis Deem all these years and how you've never managed to make anything stick. And you know what'll come next."

Jim was silent. Of course he knew.

"He'll drag Kate into it, and your relationship with her, and how through her you exerted undue influence on Johnny so you could finally nail Louis Deem."

There it was, Jim's nightmare given voice.

"It's the best kind of lie, Jim, and the most convincing because so many parts of it are true. You have been looking for a way to lock up Louis Deem practically since you were sworn in."

"I'm not exactly unique in that, Bernie. Everyone in Alaskan law enforcement has."

Bernie was relentless. "Yeah, but Rickard'll make it all about you. You have been sleeping with Kate Shugak. You do have a relationship with Johnny Morgan."

Jim thought of Frank Rickard and his rumpled JCPenney suits and his oxford shoes with the triple-knotted laces and that apologetic air that let jury after jury know how much he regretted having to point out the error of the state's ways, but that he was the sole custodian of the truth and he was bound by oath and by honor to share it with them. "Yeah," he said heavily. "I know."

"I figure you can stand up under it. Kate'll eat Rickard for breakfast and he knows it, so he won't do anything but hint, but some of that's bound to stick, too. Johnny, it'll go a little tougher on, but what I've seen of him tells me that, young as he is, he's a stand-up guy."

"But you're thinking—"

Bernie nodded. "Jury'll start wondering about your motive in charging Louis, instead of Louis's motive in killing Enid and Fitz."

"Thereby creating reasonable doubt."

"What I'm thinking," Bernie said. The longer he spoke, the calmer he got. He was matter-of-fact now, even dispassionate in his consideration of the possibilities. It was obvious he had given this a great deal of thought. "Of course, there's the photos you took. Be hard to overlook the bodies of a woman and child on their own doorstep. But we're also talking about the rest of a man's life here, and for that one guy on the jury who either just moved to the Park or who's been living in a cave the whole time he was here, he won't be thinking how Louis Deem's the new poster child for the Ted Bundy task force. And so they'll be looking at Johnny Morgan, and they'll listen to Rickard do that voodoo that he does so well, and they'll wonder."

Impeach the witness. Not like it hadn't worked before, and for Louis Deem, too.

"Or," Bernie said.

Jim couldn't remember when he felt more depressed. Or more impotent.

Or more terrified of losing something he wasn't even sure he had.

"Or what?" he said. "What is it you want me to do, Bernie?"

Bernie met his eyes straight on. "Your job."

Later that morning Jim opened the cell door and Louis Deem walked out a free man.

"Don't take it so hard, Jim," he said. "We'll see each other again soon, I'm sure."

He laughed all the way down the hall. Jim stared at the open, empty cell, and all that it meant, and he wanted to run down the hall and drag Deem back by the scruff of his neck. He did start after him and got to the office in time to see Deem bending over Maggie, saying something in a voice too low for Jim to hear.

A tear slid down Maggie's cheek.

"You son of a bitch," Jim said, and was on Deem like lightning. He grabbed him up by the collar and the seat of the pants, kicked the door open, and pitched Deem out.

Deem scrambled to his feet, his face for once black with fury.

Jim pointed a finger. "Start walking, Deem. Now."

Deem calmed, even managed to summon up his smile. "Whatever you say, Officer. I'll go peaceable."

He turned and almost walked into Kate. "Kate," he said, biting off her name.

"Louis," she said. "Oh look, you're all wet." She brushed a clump of mud from the front of his shirt. The breath whooshed out of him, and he bent over a little. She leaned forward and said something in his ear, patted his cheek hard enough that Jim could hear the crack of skin on skin, and walked past Deem to the post. Over her shoulder Jim watched Deem slowly straighten and start walking.

That was the scariest thing about Louis Deem, his ability to master his rage. To save it, to hoard it for use against a future day.

"So you let him go," Kate said.

"Got the call," Jim said. "Judge Singh was pretty firm."

"I'm going to talk to Abigail," Kate said.

Jim watched Deem as he disappeared down the road. He'd refused to get a message to Howie Katelnikof that Louis Deem needed a ride, and he only hoped the son of a bitch had to walk every one of the thirty miles to his place. "What's the point?" he said, suddenly very weary.

"She's his alibi. We have to start rebuilding this case somewhere. You want to come with?"

Jim shrugged. "I suppose. Might as well." He got his hat and coat. "Johnny's in school?"

"Surrounded by a hundred other kids and half a dozen teachers."

"Mutt?"

"Home under the deck."

"Weird to see you without her."

"She didn't like being left behind, either. Come on," she said, urging him toward the Blazer. "Let's go."

No new snow had fallen, and most of the last had worn away, so if anything, the track to the Smiths' property was even more rutted. Father Smith and the older kids were starting to lay the roof. Inside, the younger kids held up Sheetrock while Mother Smith screwed it into place.

Jim stepped onto the deck, Kate at his side. "Mr. Smith."

Smith stepped nimbly rafter to rafter to stand at the edge of the roof and look down at them with his usual benign air. "Sergeant Chopin."

"I wonder if I might speak with Abigail."

Smith sighed and said, courteous as ever, "You've already spoken with her."

"I'm afraid I have a few more questions. It'll only take a few minutes."

Smith looked at Abigail, up on the roof with him. Abigail crawled over the rafters less nimbly than her father and shinnied down the ladder.

"Abigail, wait," her father said, a foot on the top rung.

Abigail ignored him, marching up to Jim as if she were marching out to face a firing squad and said without preamble, "I lied."

Jim gaped at her. "I beg your pardon?"

Smith's feet hit the deck with a resounding thud, and Kate had the pleasure of seeing him shaken out of his customary sangfroid. "Abigail!"

Mrs. Smith emerged on the deck, squinting against the sun. "Father? What's wrong?" She saw Jim and Kate. "Oh, Oh, no. Abigail—"

"I lied," Abigail said stonily. "I wasn't with Louis the night those two people were shot."

"Abigail!" Mrs. Smith said.

"I'm sorry," Abigail said, and she actually held out her hands, wrists together. "If you have to arrest me, I'm ready to go."

Kate looked at her long and hard.

"I loved him, and I truly didn't think he did it," Abigail said in response to that look. It might have sounded more convincing if Abigail hadn't made it sound like she were reading, badly, from a script. "And we were engaged to be married. I thought it was my duty as his affianced wife. Wives submit ye unto your husbands as your husbands submit themselves unto God."

"What made you change your mind?"

"Abigail!" Smith said. Kate thought he looked more outraged than shocked, and the outrage struck her as bogus as the shock.

"It's a sin to lie," Abigail said, with more anger than piety in her voice. Kate wondered who she was so mad at. "I couldn't have that on my conscience. If Louis didn't do it then he won't need me to prove him innocent. It is in God's hands."

Automatically everyone except Kate and Jim made the sign of the cross. Chloe and Hannah were standing in the doorway, hands clasped. They were watching their sister with what Kate could only describe as awe, tears rolling down their cheeks. Poor little mites. Probably none of their siblings had gone against their parents before. Kate hoped she sniffed rebellion in the air.

Jim, she saw, was gloriously speechless. He'd been prepared to browbeat Abigail into telling the truth, bad cop all the way, and here she'd up and admitted it freely, of her own volition, without even being asked the direct question. "I, uh, you'll have to come to the post and retract your previous statement, and, uh, yeah, I'll have to take a new one."

"Let's go." Abigail marched around him, went down the steps, and climbed into the Blazer's backseat, where she folded her arms and sat, waiting.

The Smiths, *mère et père,* looked at each other. Kate, watching, saw dismay there, and something else, something she was unable to identify. She tucked the memory away for later, when she'd have time to puzzle it out.

In the meantime, Jim fell back a step. "Well, uh, thanks," he said. "I'll see that Abigail gets back home when we're done. With the statement. You know. At the post."

Mrs. Smith stretched out an impulsive hand. Her husband gripped her shoulder. She let the hand fall. Her question was forlorn, almost a wail. "Is she under arrest, Sergeant?"

Jim tugged his cap back on his head. "No, ma'am," he said, retiring in good order. Over his shoulder he added, "Not yet."

He drove as fast as he could back to Niniltna, ushered Abigail into the post, and lost no time in deposing her. He kept Kate and Maggie in the office with them the whole time so no one could say she was coerced or intimidated in any way. He had her swear to the truth of her statement in front of Maggie, Kate, and Billy Mike, dragooned from up the hill, and had Maggie make multiple copies, all of which he made Abigail sign individually.

Kate watched this frantic productivity a little quizzically. "Shouldn't you be going after Louis now? He can't have that much of a head start on you."

"Take Abigail home, would you, Billy?"

Billy looked less than thrilled, because like everyone else he'd heard about the condition of the Smiths' road, but he acquiesced. Kate, watching him usher Abigail out of the post, thought that he looked exhausted. His wife, Annie, had had that same look on her face at Fitz and Enid's potlatch, and they both looked like they were losing weight. Losing a son would do that to you.

Kate and Jim spent a good part of the afternoon searching Niniltna for Louis Deem, but it was as if he had vanished into thin air. He wasn't on the road home. He wasn't at the post office, the store, the Riverside Café, or the Roadhouse. They found Willard at Auntie Balasha's, chowing down on fresh bannocks as she watched with a fond smile. "Can't my boy eat? Can't he?"

He could. From what they were able to understand around the mouthfuls of bannocks, he hadn't seen Louis that day. He was sure he would have remembered, and if he had forgotten, Anakin would have reminded him, wouldn't he? He patted the action figure in his pocket and forked up more food.

Deem wasn't on his boat in the boatyard. George said he hadn't flown Deem out of the Park, but that didn't mean he couldn't have driven, Kate pointed out, so they called Kenny in Ahtna.

Kenny called back an hour later to say that he'd driven out to Deem's place. Nobody home. He'd driven back to Ahtna and checked the Seven Come Eleven. No dice.

By then it was getting on for four o'clock, and they drove back to Niniltna so Kate could pick up Johnny from the Mikes' house, where he'd had strict instructions to go after school.

Jim pulled up in front of the house. Kate stopped halfway out of the Blazer. "You okay, Jim?"

He stared straight ahead through the windshield. "Sure."

"You did what you had to do. No way you're going to get crosswise of Robbie Singh. You'd never get another conviction out of her court. So Louis's out again." She shrugged. "Maybe we were in too much of a rush. Maybe we should have taken a little more time before we hauled him in."

"Nice of you to say 'we,' " he said.

"We all wanted him locked up, Jim. Maybe me most of all.

Now we've got a chance to take our time, to gather the evidence, to put a real case together, one the judge won't throw out."

He put the Blazer in gear. "Meantime, he's on the loose."

"He is that," she said. "But we'll be careful. And we'll deal with what comes."

He attempted a smile, but it was a poor effort.

She stared at him, puzzled. "You sure you're okay?"

"I'm sure," he said, and went to meet Bernie Koslowski for coffee at the Riverside Café.

Sec. 11.41.115. Defenses to Murder

(b) In a prosecution under AS 11.41.110 (a) (3), it is an affirmative defense that the defendant

> (1) did not commit the homicidal act or in any way solicit or aid in its commission . . .

—Alaska statutes

TEN

Brendan McCord had been right. The Smiths' lawyer was better than the Park Service's lawyer, and the same day Robbie Singh made Jim Chopin spring Louis Deem, a superior court judge in Fairbanks stayed the execution of the Smiths' eviction notice. Not that the Smiths had taken any notice of it in the first place. That evening Dan O'Brien went down to the Roadhouse to drown his sorrows, and also because he had a mild flirtation going on with Laurel Meganack, of whom he had hopes of seducing.

It wasn't an entirely successful evening. Laurel brought him beer and smiled, but then she brought everyone beer and smiled. Half the Park was there, too, and most of the single men and some of the married ones were on the same mission he was. Bernie would do well to hire Laurel on full-time for all the custom she was generating.

"How's Bernie?" he said, pulling out his wallet.

Her smile dimmed. "Okay, I guess." She brought his change and lingered for a moment, momentarily dashing the hopes of

Dan's competition. "He was having coffee at the café this afternoon with Jim Chopin. They didn't look like they were having a good time, exactly."

He imagined the conversation. "No, I don't guess they would."

He finished his beer, which did nothing to ease his morose frame of mind, and headed back up to the Step.

It was late enough to be dark and, as he told Jim later, he was already feeling a little skittish. What with, in order beginning a mile up the Step road, first the pissed-off cow moose charging out of the brush with two twin calves on her heels who looked barely old enough to walk, second the grizzly in extra large who by the shine and length of his coat had just woken from a refreshing winter's nap and was probably feeling peckish, and third the porcupine that had for reasons best known to itself climbed into the back of Dan's pickup while it was parked outside the Roadhouse and frightened the living hell out of him a mile from home by scraping his quills along the metal bed loud enough to be heard over the engine, his nerves were shot to hell. "Jesus, Jim, what a sound. I thought the grizzly had somehow jumped into the back of the truck as I went by him and was trying to bite through the cab."

Breakup was the signal for every species in the Park to go stark raving mad. This did not exclude *Homo erectus*. Or judges.

Dan had climbed back into the cab after evicting the porcupine, waited for his heart to slow down to something approaching a normal beat, and started the engine. He put it in drive, rounded the next curve, and the headlights picked up the shine of two eyes. He braked hard. "Oh fuck. What now?"

He waited, the engine idling, for the eyes to blink. They didn't.

In fact, the longer he sat there, the more they looked like eyes in a face.

A human face.

After a while he steeled himself to climb out of the truck, his .30-30 in hand and a round in the chamber, and walked forward for a closer look. The headlights of his truck picked out the body of a man, arms and legs splayed in a grotesque starfish, his head twisted to the left, his eyes open and staring, his mouth open in a silent scream.

And Dan could have counted his vertebrae through the hole in his chest, if he hadn't been otherwise occupied barfing up three beers and a package of salt and vinegar potato chips by the side of the road.

When he had recovered enough to look again, he saw that it was Louis Deem.

I didn't know what to do, if I should load him up and bring him to you, or if I should leave him here and bring you to him."

"You did good, Dan."

Dan checked over his shoulder. "The bears are up, Jim." He checked over Jim's shoulder. "I told you about that one I almost hit on the way here, didn't I?"

"You did."

"Big bastard, big enough to make my truck feel pretty flimsy. He looked hungry. He could have come along and chewed on the body while I was getting you."

"Good thing he didn't."

Dan couldn't seem to stop talking. Nervous. Edgy. "I know how important it is to leave a crime scene intact. We do a little of that ourselves."

"I know you do."

"And, you know." Dan jerked his chin at the body. "Probably the guy who did this really was aiming at Deem, but you never know."

"No. You never do."

"I didn't want to hang around without backup. So I lit some flares and came for you as fast as I could."

The flares were still burning, two red glows in the darkness, one at the beginning of the curve below, one a hundred feet above the body. "You did good, Dan," Jim repeated.

"Have you got anything to drink, Jim?"

Jim walked to the Blazer and got out the pint of Scotch he kept there for medicinal purposes. Dan uncapped it and took a big swig. "Jesus. It's Louis Deem, isn't it."

"It sure is."

"He's really dead." Dan sounded awed, as if he, too, had subscribed to the Park mythos that Louis Deem was as unkillable as he was unconvictable.

"He really is."

"Are you okay, Jim?"

"Sure. Why?"

"I don't know. You sound a little out of it."

The trooper looked at the horizon. "Be light in another hour, be able to see more, take photos. Let's sit in the Blazer. Be warmer."

In spite of the alcohol burning its way down his esophagus, Dan was starting to shiver from reaction, and he welcomed the suggestion. They climbed in, and Jim started the engine and turned the heater fan on full.

Dan took another swig. "I gotta say, Jim, this doesn't break my heart." He passed Jim the bottle.

Jim took a drink and didn't say anything.

"Did I ever tell you about the time he hit on one of my rangers? New girl, fresh out of college, nice, smart kid. She'd been in the Park maybe five minutes before he zeroed in. Never mind kissing him on the first date, I told her, don't let him hit you on the first date. Two weeks later, she shows up for work one morning with a black eye. She wouldn't say he did it, wouldn't hear of calling you, but at least she stopped going out with him. Later on she told me she'd given him a bunch of money for some scam he was running." Dan toasted the corpse with Jim's bottle. "So long, you rat bastard. May you rot over a slow fire in hell."

Absentmindedly, he nudged Jim with the bottle. "Oh. Sorry. You're on duty."

"Right after I have another drink I am." Jim accepted the bottle, raised it in the body's direction in his own salute, and took another hit of the Scotch. He handed the bottle back to Dan.

"All right," Dan said, taking another swig. "My kinda trooper."

The sun came up an hour later. Jim photographed the scene as Dan, now feeling warm and cozy, directed. "Pretty neat," he said. "Not cool neat, I don't mean. Neat as in—in—"

"Tidy," Jim said.

Dan tried to snap his fingers, and then tried again with more success. "That's it. One shot?"

"Looks like."

Dan inspected the splash of blood and guts surrounding the body. "Got shot right here, you think?"

"I'd say so." Jim looked up from the camera. "Did any vehicles pass you on your way home?"

Dan shook his head. "No one. There aren't that many people living this far up, and besides, the Roadhouse was still open when I left."

Jim nodded as if that was what he had expected. "Pretty efficient killer. No crime scene, so no physical evidence except the body. No witnesses."

"Too bad you couldn't find him," Dan said. "We could give him a medal."

Jim eyed him. "You'd tell me if you had seen a vehicle, wouldn't you, Dan?"

"Sure! Absolutely. No question." Dan raised his right hand and with drunken solemnity he stared deeply into Jim's eyes. "Honest. I didn't see anyone, Jim. Well. Except for, you know." He turned and blew a messy raspberry in Louis Deem's direction. "Take that, you murdering bastard!"

Off balance he stumbled forward, and Jim caught him before he fell. "Okay, Dan. Why don't you wait in your truck?"

And it was on the way back to the truck that Jim saw the impression of the tire by the side of the road, a perfect imprint in what after yesterday's warm temperature had been mud when the tire drove into it, and had frozen into a perfect tread overnight.

He hoped he had enough plaster of paris in his crime kit to get an impression.

Jim rousted George Perry out of bed and had him fly the body to the crime lab in Anchorage. He walked into the post at eight A.M. sharp, and Maggie said, "Is it true?"

The Bush telegraph was operating at its usual light-speed efficiency, and Maggie, he remembered now, was a second cousin of Ruthie Moonin's, which went a long way toward explaining the scene in the front office yesterday morning, when he'd let Louis Deem go. He remembered, too, that he'd had to reprimand Maggie for "forgetting" to order meals in for Louis Deem when he was a resident of the post in the past. Verbally, of course, and behind the closed door of his office. No way was he going to put a written report in her personnel file that would haunt her state employment record for the rest of her professional life. Not for letting Louis Deem go hungry he wasn't.

"Is it true?" she said. "Is Louis Deem dead?"

"Yes."

"Murdered?"

"Yes," he said, and wondered if he should ask her where she'd spent the night. No, he decided, not unless he was prepared to ask the same question of every one of the Park's eight thousand residents.

Maggie didn't laugh. She didn't cry. She didn't leap up into the Snoopy happy dance. She was waiting, he realized, for the other shoe to drop. "Who did it?"

"I don't know yet."

She eyed him. "Why don't you not try too hard to find out?"

"Maggie."

Her laugh was entirely without humor. "Like I'm the only Park rat you're going to hear that from."

And of course she was right, he thought wearily, a couple of hours later. Billy Mike had been first in the door, and upon confirmation of the news, he'd shaken Jim's hand in warm congratulations, followed by the entire board and most of the 173 shareholders of the Niniltna Native Association, individually and in groups. In the middle of all this, Auntie Balasha appeared with a plateful of three different kinds of cookies and actually kissed him on the lips. "You good boy, Jim."

As soon as he could do so with any civility he shut the door of his office and called Kenny Hazen. Louis Deem's place was just the other side of Lost Chance Creek. He didn't want to drive out there a third time in a week. It would be quicker to fly to Ahtna and drive from there.

The Ahtna police chief was waiting for him on the tarmac. The road from Ahtna to Lost Chance Creek was in the same condition as it was the rest of the way to Niniltna, bare of snow with the thinnest veneer of ice. "I heart global warming," Kenny Hazen said.

Jim grunted agreement.

"Reason it's in such good shape is because people aren't used to the road being drivable at this time of year. Otherwise it'd be pothole city."

Jim grunted again.

"You'd think once the snow machines' treads started kicking up gravel, they'd get a clue."

No response this time.

Kenny gave up on light conversation. "How do you want to play this?"

"Bad cop, bad cop."

Kenny's grin was fierce. "Works for me."

Louis Deem's place was almost four miles down an expensively well-maintained gravel road. It was, to the best of Jim's recollection, the only road in the Park other than the main road wide enough for two cars. "Bastard puts all the money he steals into upkeep, I'll give him that," Kenny said.

"Yeah," Jim said, "I'm sure Ruthie Moonin would appreciate that no end."

The road ended in a driveway carefully laid with the same gravel that topped the road in, a driveway that circled a full-grown spruce tree thirty feet in height. The main house was built of logs and neatly roofed with asphalt shingles in a complimentary shade of brown. The trim around the windows and doors was painted red.

To the right stood a shop sided with gray tin and the same red trim. The shop shingles were dark gray.

"Looks like something out of *Better Homes and Gardens,*" Kenny said, pausing to take in the scene. "Where's the tar paper extension? The stack of fifty-five-gallon drums and Blazo tins? Where's the fucking pile of two-by-four ends?"

They parked at the end of the bull rail in front of the main house, each space with its own plug-in for those cold winter nights when a head bolt heater was needed to keep the engine warm. There were four parking spaces in front in all, one empty. The first hosted an orange Chevy Suburban with the left front fender missing and the right front fender next in line to go. In the second space an elder statesman of an International pickup resided with an air of matronly resignation to the depredations of time, a rusty black in color. It had probably rolled off the assembly line before Eisenhower was president.

It sat in direct contrast next to the Ford Expedition that looked as if it had rolled off the line in Detroit the day before.

Kenny killed the engine. "The International is Willard's, right?"

"Yeah."

"He's got a driver's license?"

"Yeah."

"How the hell did he pass?"

"He's good with mechanical things."

"Yeah, but how'd he pass the written? He can barely read." He climbed out, grumbling to himself.

Jim loosened his sidearm in its holster, just in case they got lucky and somebody tried to resist arrest. Through the windows on the shop doors he could see a wall hung with spare parts, doors, fenders, wheels, chrome fittings, and many other less identifiable parts. He had to admit it all looked very neat.

The closing of the doors on Kenny's pickup sounded like rifle shots. Still no one appeared. "Clear consciences?" Kenny said.

"The sleep of the just," Jim said. "I'll roust them, you do the thing?"

"Sure." Kenny took Jim's crime scene kit. Jim walked up the steps to pound on the door with his fist. "Howie! Willard! Police! Open up!"

He had to pound and yell a couple more times before lights came on and he heard a voice. Howie. "All right, all right, Jesus, I'm coming, I'm coming!"

The front door opened and Howie Katelnikof stood there, his

hair ruffled and a studied expression of injured innocence on his narrow face. He probably practiced it in the mirror every morning. "What the hell's going on, Jim? We were sleeping, for crissake!"

Jim stepped forward. After an abortive attempt to stand his ground, Howie fell back and Jim walked past him into the house.

Willard paused in the act of heading down the hall that led to the back door. "I have to use the outhouse," Willard said. He wouldn't look at Jim, and his hands kneaded each other.

"I have personal knowledge of at least one flush toilet in this house," Jim said, "and I refuse to believe that Louis Deem would live where he might have to wait to take a crap, so I'm guessing there's more than one." He looked at Howie. "When was the last time you saw Louis, Howie?"

"I don't know where he is," Howie said.

"That wasn't the question," Jim said. "I asked you when was the last time you saw him."

"When I brought him clean clothes on Saturday." All of Howie's answers had the sound of being rehearsed, but then they always did.

"You didn't see him yesterday after he got out?"

"He got out?" Howie's reply was quick and Jim thought lacking in surprise.

"Yeah, the judge sprung him," Jim said.

"Is everything okay, Howie?" Willard said timidly.

"Shut up, Willard."

Kenny came clattering up the stairs. He nodded at Jim, a smile of quiet joy on his face.

"Where were you yesterday, Howie?" Jim said.

"I was right here all day and all night," Howie said. "Right, Willard?"

"Right. So was Louis." Willard stared steadfastly at the floor.

"Louis was in jail last Saturday, Willard," Jim said, at the same time Howie said, "Willard, you fucking moron, shut up."

Willard flinched. He was wearing red, white, and blue polka-dot pajamas, and not little polka dots, either. They were too large, the sleeves hung off his hands and the legs draped over his feet. He looked like a mummy. A red, white, and blue polka-dotted mummy, with Anakin's head peeping out of his breast pocket.

There was something else, something that seemed a little off. Jim couldn't put his finger on it. But then there was always something about Willard that looked a little off. Howie and his rehearsed answers, Willard and his off-kilter attitude. Jim wondered what they would do now that Louis was dead. And then he wondered if Louis Deem had left a will.

"We were watching movies, weren't we, Willard?" Howie said. "Saturday night is movie night. We always watch movies on Saturday night."

"Movies," Willard said, looking hugely relieved. "Yeah, watching movies."

"What movie did you watch?" Kenny said.

"*Blade Trinity*," Howie said.

"*Buffy the Vampire Slayer*," Willard said at the same time.

"Both of them," Howie said immediately.

"A double feature," Kenny said to Jim.

"Gee," Jim said, "was there popcorn?"

"Yeah, popcorn," Willard said happily, and then his face clouded over again. "Howie made it because they won't let me use the stove after I almost burned down the house that time."

"I noticed you had a lot of parts for sale at the swap and shop, Howie," Jim said. "A bunch of like-new snow machine parts, right up front and priced to sell."

"Yeah?" Howie said. A veteran of the interrogatory process, he remained determinedly unfazed by the abrupt change of subject. "So?"

"So I was wondering where you got them," Jim said in deceptively mild tones.

"Pulled 'em off abandoned wrecks," Howie said promptly. "Where else?"

"Where indeed?" Kenny Hazen said.

"How about all those truck parts I see in your shop out there?" Jim said. "Where'd you get those?"

"Same place." Howie was feeling more sure of his ground every second. "People dump junkers all over the Park all the time. Trick is to find them before anyone else does, get the good parts first."

"Yuh-huh. You must be pretty good at breaking a vehicle down to the good parts, Howie."

"I do all right."

Jim did his best to look curious. "About how long does it take to break down a, gosh, I don't know—" He appealed to Kenny.

"Say a full-size pickup," Kenny said.

Fear of being led all unknowing into a trap warred with pride in a job well done. "A day, maybe. Depending on the tools I've got with me, and if I have any help."

"And probably if you've got a shop to work in," Kenny said. "Always good to work inside if you can."

Howie nodded. "Absolutely. Cold hands make for slow work."

Next to him Willard nodded enthusiastically. "Cold hands make me drop tools." He sniggered. "Don't they, Howie."

"You visited Louis the Saturday after the potluck for Edna and Fitz Koslowski, didn't you, Howie?" Jim said.

"The potluck? I guess so."

"Why, wasn't that the very day someone tried to put a bullet into Kate Shugak?" Jim said to Kenny.

"I'd have to check my calendar to be sure," Kenny said, "but I believe it was."

"Whoever it was was a lousy shot," Jim said dispassionately. "Missed her."

In spite of himself, Howie reddened.

"Hit the dog, I hear," Kenny said.

"Yeah, and you know how Kate feels about that dog."

Willard said, "Mutt got shot?"

"Shut up, Willard," Howie said.

On a rising note Willard said, "Mutt got shot?"

"Anyway, Kate's attention's been a little distracted lately, but the dog's gonna make it and now Kate's asking questions."

"Like who shot her dog?"

"Mutt got shot!" Willard cried.

"Exactly like that," Jim said. "She saw the truck the shooter was driving, too. An old pickup. Where's the truck, Howie?"

"What truck?" Howie was sweating but defiant. "My drive's the Chevy Suburban parked on the bull rail out front. It's orange, not white."

Jim frowned. "Did I mention the color of the truck that ran Kate off the road, Kenny?"

"I don't believe you did, Jim," Kenny said.

"I didn't think so." Jim's voice dropped to a growl. "So how did you know that the truck that ran Kate off the road was white, Howie?"

Howie looked trapped. "I heard someone say so at the Roadhouse."

"The Roadhouse. Really."

"Maybe it was the Riverside Café," Howie said.

"So, back to my original question, Howie. Where were you yesterday?"

"Here all day watching movies. Willard was here, he'll testify to that."

"Testify," Willard said, nodding his head vigorously. "We'll be there, Howie, just like I said we would, like Buffy and Blade. Wesley Snipes is so cool, I wish I could walk like that, I'd—"

Jim got into Howie's face and Willard shut up with a whimper. "You were here yesterday all day? That's your story?"

"I was here watching movies with Willard," Howie said obstinately. "Weren't we, Willard."

Willard gave this serious thought. "Saturday night is movie night. Wesley. I just love the way he walks." He patted the breast pocket of his polka-dotted pajamas. "He's almost as cool as Anakin."

"Anybody ever drive your truck but you, Howie?"

"Nobody better," Howie replied, and then looked as if he wished he hadn't. "Of course I never take the keys out," he added quickly, wiping his forehead with his sleeve.

"Of course not," Kenny said to Jim.

"Howie, you're going to have to come in with us," Jim said.

"Why? I was here all last night! Watching movies, with Willard!"

Willard started bawling, his eyes squeezed shut and his mouth wide open.

"Jesus Christ," Kenny Hazen said.

"Aren't you worried about Louis, Howie?" Jim said. "I turned him loose yesterday morning. I figured he'd come straight here. I know how much he likes that walk-in shower upstairs. We don't have anything like that down the post," he told Kenny.

Kenny had his arms folded and was scowling at the ceiling. Willard was still bawling. Kenny hated it when grown men cried all over him.

"I figured he went over to stay with his girl," Howie said.

"No shower out at the Smiths' place yet, not last time I was there," Jim said. "No, he'd come home first."

"He'll probably be home any minute now," Howie said. "If we leave, you'll miss him."

"No," Jim said. "No, I won't miss him, Howie. Louis is dead."

"What?" Howie said, over Willard's escalating wail.

"Yeah. Had a hole in his chest big enough to toss a salad in. And you know the only thing I found nearby?"

Howie wouldn't bite. He looked a little sick, and he swallowed, and then swallowed again.

"A tire track." Jim smiled at Howie. "It matches one of the tires on your Suburban, Howie."

"The right front tire, to be exact," Kenny said happily, which was the thing he'd been doing outside.

Howie was beginning to look a little panicked. "I didn't drive it up there!"

"Up where?" Jim said.

"Wherever!" Howie shouted. "I told you, I leave the keys in it all the time! Anybody could have taken it and driven it anywhere in the Park!"

ELEVEN

It was past six by the time they got back to Ahtna, having spent the day searching every square inch of Louis Deem's property. There was absolutely no paper trail to be found. From experience, Louis Deem knew that while oral testimony could always be contradicted or subverted, the written word could not.

They didn't find a will, either. Jim made a mental note to call Frank Rickard in the morning.

In Ahtna, Kenny put Willard and Howie in the Ahtna jail and Jim in his spare bedroom. The next morning Jim bought Kenny breakfast at the Ahtna Lodge. He had bacon and eggs, Kenny had a pancake sandwich, and Tony served them extra everything by way of congratulations on the death of Louis Deem.

Tony was so full of joie de vivre that Kenny said, "Louis act up a lot in here, did he?"

Stan, coming out of the kitchen, put an arm around Tony's shoulders. "Nothing Louis did could be as much fun as watching Tony watch him, waiting." He gave Tony an affectionate hug. "It was like watching *Friday the Thirteenth* at the Ahtna Lodge. You keep waiting for the coat hanger to come out. It never does, but it keeps you on the edge of your seat. Fun for Louis. Made him feel powerful. Not so much fun for my man, here."

"Oh, you," Tony said, giving Stanislav a halfhearted shove. "I suppose you never worried over what Louis Deem might do to our place."

"Not while I've got my cleaver close to hand." Stan laughed, kissed Tony, and went back to the kitchen.

"I would have liked to have seen Stan chasing Louis Deem with a meat cleaver," Kenny Hazen said wistfully.

Upon reflection, Jim had to agree.

Back in Niniltna, he stowed Howie and Willard in the cells, Willard still bawling, Howie still protesting his innocence. Of course, everyone in the Park heard the news a nanosecond after they landed, and he finally had to tell Maggie to stop putting calls through unless they were reporting breaking crime, and to stop all visitors at the door. She did it with her usual crisp efficiency, but he knew she wasn't happy. She didn't want Deem's killer found, not even if it was a loser like Howie Katelnikof.

Jim was fairly certain she could rest easy. A tire track wasn't enough to warrant much more than detaining for questioning. The state could hold Howie for twenty-four hours before habeas corpus kicked in, and Jim wouldn't have been doing his job if he didn't use any advantage granted by state law to use that time to the fullest extent, after which he'd turn them loose to find their own way back to Deem's place. Which reminded him to call Rickard's office and leave a message asking if Louis had left a will.

Louis was Howie and Willard's meal ticket, rent check, and to all intents and purposes their employer. Howie had no motive for killing Louis, and Willard lacked the ability, but operating under the dictates of Jack Morgan's First Law, Howie and Willard had been Louis Deem's closest confederates. In the unlikely event this investigation were ever reviewed—because, hey, who gave a shit who killed Louis Deem?—he wanted to be able to say he'd run the investigation by the book.

It would be just like Louis Deem to cause Jim more problems dead than alive.

So Jim interrogated Howie and Willard in turn. Howie had his teeth sunk into his story like a terrier and refused to let go. Willard had stopped bawling, but he was looking a little off-color, and Jim made a mental note to tell Auntie Balasha that she might like to take her grandson in for a checkup. As a rule, victims of fetal alcohol syndrome didn't live to be Willard's age, and everyone was always on the lookout for signs and symptoms. Especially Jim, as any time Willard was out of the Park and out of his hair was almost like a vacation.

Bobby, Dinah, and Katya pulled up to the post at five P.M., just as Howie and Willard were pulling out. Bobby made no bones about why he was there. "Gimme the straight skinny," he said, maneuvering out of the truck and into his wheelchair in a smooth series of well-practiced moves and wheeling briskly up the ramp to the post's front door. "I go on the air at two o'clock this afternoon."

Dinah was more compassionate. "You okay, Jim?"

"I'm fine," he said, surprised. "Why do you ask?"

"I don't know." She studied him with a worried expression. "You look a little depressed."

He smiled at her. "Just tired. Been a long two days."

"Does Kate know?"

His face closed up. "I don't know. I was working late when the body was found. Dan came here. I haven't seen her yet."

"Oh." She hesitated, as if she were about to say something else. Jim forestalled her by giving Bobby the short version, and reached for his cap. "I've got to go see a man about a horse. Good to see you all."

"Jim!" Katya ran to him as if she'd just seen him for the first time and tried to climb up his leg.

He hoisted her into the air and looked into her laughing face. Here at least was one girl child he would never have to worry about being preyed upon by Louis Deem. He looked at Bobby and saw the same thought reflected in her father's fierce eyes.

Not that Jim would ever have had to worry about Katya. Bobby had been a LRRP with the 101st Airborne in Vietnam. If an older Katya ever attracted the attention of a Louis Deem, said Louis Deem would simply vanish from the face of the earth, and no one would ever know how, and no one would ever know where, and only one would ever know why.

There was a great deal to be said for murder victims whose bodies vanished into thin air. It was a lot less labor intensive on him, for one thing.

It was the worst part of the job, any cop would agree, ranking right up there with responding to domestic disputes, although there was less potential for ITP, or injury to person. People in the first stages of grief were more apt to dissolve than attack.

Abigail took it a lot better than Jim thought she would. She stood between Chloe and Hannah, clutching their hands in hers. Her face was white and her lower lip trembled, but she shed no tears.

"I have to ask you this, Abigail. Where were you night before last?"

She looked uncomprehending. Chloe answered, her voice high and thin. "Here. We've all been here."

Hannah nodded vigorously. "Right here."

And of course the whole family chimed in with a similar chorus. They'd all been right here, building their cabin, and since they were already shingling the roof, there was considerable evidence to support their testimony.

At Jim's request, Abigail followed him to his car, and no one bothered to ask her parents' permission. Something in the balance of power in that family seemed to have shifted. He halted out of earshot. "Abigail, did you ever hear Louis say anything about the Koslowskis?"

"No."

"Any mention made of Mr. Koslowski's gold collection, how much Louis might have admired it?"

She looked straight at him then, the trace of an emotion he couldn't identify at the back of her eyes. "No." She looked over his shoulder again. "I'm sorry, Sergeant Chopin, but I have to go now."

He followed her gaze and saw that the Smiths had broken formation and that Father Smith was headed their way with a stride that had regained its purpose. "All right. If you think of anything else that Louis might have said, anything at all, please contact me at the state trooper post in Niniltna."

"Of course she will." Smith's voice boomed out as if it originated from a burning bush. He put an arm around Abigail's shoulders and ushered her away from Jim's contaminating presence. "Good day, Sergeant."

Who said *good day* anymore? Jim watched the way Abigail's shoulders shrank within her father's arm. Man, this story just kept getting better and better.

With a leaden heart, he took his leave of the Smith family and drove to the Roadhouse.

It wasn't even eight o'clock, and the parking lot was jammed. Jim had to park on the road, narrowly escaping being flattened by a truckload of Grosdidiers roaring up in their Dodge Ram Supercharger. They slid to a hockey stop eighteen inches off his starboard bow. Peter, driving, gave him a cheeky grin. "Hey, Jim! Here to celebrate?"

Without waiting for a reply, the four of them bailed out of the pickup and thundered across the parking lot and up the Roadhouse stairs like a herd of stampeding cattle. The Grosdidier brothers had been four of the starting five on the Kanuyaq Kings basketball team and were the proximate cause of two of the Class C state championship banners hanging from the ceiling of the Niniltna High School gym. Fishermen, hunters, trappers, mechanics, carpenters, and miners by day, they were also among the first batch of graduates of an emergency medical response team class held in the Park and coauthored by the state and the Niniltna Native Association, one among many of Ekaterina Shugak's best notions. Now in their early twenties, the Grosdidier brothers were still young enough to find the idea of riding to the rescue romantic, and they had always been brash enough to believe they could make a difference. It lightened Jim's load just to think of them, which was why he hadn't nailed their collective ass for reckless driving on the spot.

His steps up the front stairs of the Roadhouse were a heavy contrast to the joyous ones of the Grosdidier brothers.

When he opened the door, the noise nearly knocked him backward. The place was packed to the rafters. Literally, as one of the Kvasnikof boys—Grassim? Virgil?—was doing chin-ups on one of the rafters while assorted girls counted below. "Thirty-six! Fifty-eight! Seventy-four!" By which Jim deduced that the drinking had started early.

Bobby and Dinah must have come here straight from the post. No Katya, probably left her with Auntie Vi. Or no, because all four aunties, Vi, Joy, Edna, and Balasha, were seated at the round table in the back corner. They didn't look quite natural, because their laps were empty of whatever quilt they were currently working on.

They were facing the reassuringly usual mugs of Irish coffee, however. Balasha looked as if she had been crying. Trust softhearted Balasha Shugak to weep over the death of an asshole like Louis Deem.

Old Sam Dementieff sat at a table where the old farts were six deep, holding forth through an inhalation of Alaskan Amber on all the times Louis Deem had fucked everyone over, in the Park, in Ahtna, in Cordova, in the state of Alaska, and last Jim heard he'd moved Outside and was probably going for worldwide. At another table, Mac Devlin and Dan O'Brien were actually having a conversation without coming to blows, a sight that shocked Jim into momentary immobility. A congratulatory and painful punch on his arm from Demetri Totemoff got him started again. George Perry grinned at him from the crowd and said something.

Jim couldn't hear him. "What?"

"Best job I ever had!" George said in a near bellow. "Rather be hauling his sorry carcass to Anchorage than have to haul one of his girls to the Ahtna hospital again!"

Jim would never again have to take one of Louis Deem's victims to the morgue in Anchorage, either. Growing comfortable with the stain on his professional soul, he found the reminder comforting.

Multiple toasts were raised to the late, unlamented Louis Deem. Jim's presence was no sooner generally recognized than someone started cheering. He was slapped on the back, his reluctant hand wrung until it was numb, and by the time he got to the bar, he had four drinks waiting for him.

Bernie was in his accustomed place. "Jim," he said, unsmiling. "What can I do for you?"

Jim had to raise his voice over the hubbub. "A little conversation, if you don't mind, Bernie."

Those nearest him on his side of the bar overheard and stopped talking to hear more. It spread.

"What do you want to talk about?" Bernie said.

"Louis Deem."

Bernie shrugged and reached for a bar rag to polish an already spotless glass. "I hear he's dead. He killed my wife and my child. Don't expect me to cry any crocodile tears."

A muted but distinct murmur of approval rippled out over the growing silence.

"Maybe we could go over to your house to have this conversation," Jim said.

"Maybe we could have it right here," Bernie said pleasantly. "Say whatever you have to say, Jim." Bernie included his customers with a nod of his head. "I'm among friends here, and I've got nothing to hide."

Jim looked around the bar, which by now was dead silent. The jukebox was between songs, and someone had even turned off the huge television hanging from the roof. "Okay," he said. "Did you hear how Deem died?"

Bernie examined a minute speck on the glass. "I was told he took a shotgun blast to the chest."

There was a murmur of approval. Jim nodded. "You own a twelve-gauge, don't you?"

This time the murmur was less approving. Jim could almost smell the hostility gathering. "Yes, I do," Bernie said.

"Used it lately?"

"Not since duck-hunting season last fall," Bernie said.

"I'll need to take a look at it."

"Jesus H. Christ on a crutch," one of the old farts started to say. He was waved to silence by Old Sam, who had fixed Jim with a bright, keen eye.

Jim raised his voice to be heard. "Routine. You understand."

"Of course." Bernie waved a hand in the direction of his house. "You know where the gun rack is. Feel free."

"Thanks." Jim looked around and found an unfriendly eye everywhere he looked. It actually felt more comfortable to him than the hail-fellow-well-met cheer he'd been initially greeted with. "As I'm sure you already know, Louis Deem was found dead on the road up to the Step."

"I heard."

"Deem's roommate, Howie Katelnikof, says Deem never came home after I let him out day before yesterday. Everybody's best guess is that Deem went out to see Abigail Smith."

"What does Abigail say?"

"That he never got there."

Bernie nodded. "I assume by that that she's still living."

"Yes."

"Good for her."

Jim sighed and pulled at the bill of his cap. "Bernie, I hate like hell having to ask this, but I've got to know where you were night before last between the hours of five and eleven."

"Jesus Christ, Chopin!" someone said.

Bernie's voice overrode the protest. "That when Deem was killed?"

"From what I can guess by way of body temp and rigor, yeah. I'm hoping the ME can give us something more exact."

"Uh-huh." Bernie nodded. "Well now, let me see. I was home cooking dinner for my kids from seven o'clock on. We ate, I helped them with their homework, I put them to bed. Kathleen had a hard time getting to sleep, so I read to her until almost eleven. And then I went to bed myself."

"Where were you from five to seven?"

"From five to seven?" Bernie didn't have to raise his voice to be heard, because if someone had dropped a feather on the Roadhouse's stained floor at that moment, it would have sounded like a bomb going off. "Well, at five I stopped off here to talk to Laurel, see how she was handling things and to let her know I'd be back at work today. And from around five thirty to six thirty yesterday, I was having a cup of coffee at the Riverside Café, on Laurel. She's got that new espresso machine, and Heather likes to have someone to practice her lattes on."

Jim rolled his shoulders, trying to ease the tension that had been building there for what seemed like months. "Anybody you know see you there?"

A chuckle, quickly muffled, rippled around the room.

Bernie didn't smile. "Why, yes. If you will recall, I was having coffee with you. And as I also recall, you think Heather has the americano down."

Someone gasped. Someone else laughed out loud. He looked up and saw Old Sam. Old Sam wasn't laughing, just watching, and when he caught Jim's eye, he bent his head in acknowledgment and, Jim thought, approval.

There were no flies on Old Sam Dementieff.

"Yeah," Jim said sheepishly to Bernie, "I guess that was me." He produced a tired smile. "Sorry, Bernie. Been a long two days. I had to ask."

Bernie looked sympathetic. "I know you did, Jim. Have a beer?"

Jim gave his head a regretful shake. "Take a rain check."

They shook hands, and as Jim walked out, the crowd parted for him in silence. He rode the edge of a building wave of conversation and before the door closed fully behind him the party was back in full swing.

He stopped in the middle of the parking lot and pulled his cap off, wiping the sweat from his forehead on his sleeve.

"Hot in there?"

He knew that voice. He lowered his arm and looked into Kate's eyes.

Another truck pulled up; more merrymakers disgorged themselves and detoured around the silent couple to disappear into the Roadhouse.

"How did you hear?" he said. Mutt bounded over—well, maybe she didn't quite bound, but she flounced pretty good—and shoved her nose into his hand. Out of habit he scratched behind her ears and she wriggled with most of her old delight.

"Billy Mike came out and told me," she said. "Is it true? Deem was shot at close range with a shotgun?"

"Yes."

"When?"

"Sometime night before last between five and eleven, is my guess. I had George haul the body to the lab. I'm hoping the ME can get something a little less approximate, but you know how it is."

"Yeah," she said. "It was cold that night. That'll screw things up."

"Yeah."

"And let's face it, they probably won't try that hard. It's not like they hadn't had the opportunity to work on a Deem-related corpse before this."

"No."

She nodded at the Roadhouse. "What did Bernie say?"

"He's got a solid alibi. Lots of witnesses."

Some of the rigidity went out of her spine. "Good." She took a deep breath and let it out. "Good," she said again

"I had to talk to him," he said, driven to defend himself against an attack she hadn't made.

She raised her shoulders and let them fall again. "He would always be the obvious suspect."

"It was routine," he said.

"Practically in the handbook," she said.

Mutt trotted a couple of steps toward the Roadhouse and looked back, obviously puzzled. There was no point in driving all this way if they weren't going inside, where good things in shrink wrap waited for her.

"Did you think I was going to have to arrest Bernie?" he said.

"I knew you would if you had to."

Her words should have made him feel better. Instead, he felt worse. "Well, I don't have to."

One brow lifted. "I'm glad."

They stood in silence for a moment. "Any leads?" she said.

Glad to take refuge in shop talk, he shook his head. "Not a one. I talked to Howie first thing."

"You think Howie might have killed Deem?"

"Why would he? He's seriously lacking in motive. Louis was Howie's meal ticket. But it's the nearest and dearest—"

"—with the motive with the mostest," she finished.

He almost smiled. "Jack Morgan's First Law."

Neither one of them noticed how unselfconsciously they were able to speak the name of her dead lover out loud. Such would have not been the case a year ago. "What about Abigail?"

"Abigail." Without realizing it, Jim let out a sigh. "I went out there, told them what happened. They said none of them had left the homestead in the past week, and that they hadn't seen Louis since I locked him up."

She mulled it over. "I don't see Abigail killing Deem. But her father?"

"He's got eighteen eyewitnesses that put him ten miles away at the time of the murder."

"Too bad." She looked at the Roadhouse. "Well, at least you know for a fact Bernie didn't do it."

"At least."

"What?" She peered up at him. "Oh. You're worried about who did. Who you're going to have to arrest."

"At this point I don't have a single lead. I've got an imprint of

Howie's right front tire at the scene, but hell, he's just like the rest of us, he never takes his keys out of the ignition. Anyone could have taken off with his Suburban and driven it to Fairbanks. To Whitehorse, to goddamn New York City if they wanted." He pulled his cap off and scratched his head. "I could probably beat a confession out of Willard. Willard would tell me where Jimmy Hoffa was buried if I held off long enough on the Fig Newtons."

"Always supposing he knew who the hell Jimmy Hoffa was to begin with." She touched his arm. "You know, Jim, it's not going to break anyone's heart if you don't find out who killed Louis Deem. Not even mine."

This was a serious statement, coming as it did from Kate Shugak, that pillar of rectitude some called the conscience of the Park. And others called the enforcer.

"I know," he said, a little drearily.

"What's wrong?"

He nodded toward the Roadhouse. "You should see them in there, you'd think it was the Fourth of July. Any minute now they're going to be setting off fireworks. No one mourns the passing of Louis Deem."

"You weren't really expecting any *nil nisi bonum*, were you? Come on. I'll buy you a beer."

"Another time," he said, disengaging himself with an almost unobtrusive tug. "I've got some stuff to finish up at the post. I'll see you later."

With a slight frown on her face, she watched him drive off. It wasn't like Jim Chopin to take a case too much to heart, especially when the deceased so richly deserved his demise, and when said demise so richly rewarded his community. The Park would be a safer place without Louis Deem alive and practicing mayhem in it.

Kate looked at the Roadhouse, where Mutt was still waiting at the door. The Fourth of July, huh?

Suddenly she didn't feel much like celebrating, either. "Let's go, girl," she said.

Mutt, ears twitching at the steadily increasing decibel level from the other side of the door, gave this arbitrary decision her consent, and beat Kate to the truck.

"I let you win," Kate told her.

Mutt climbed sedately up on the seat without assistance, curled her tail around her paws, and fixed Kate with a smug yellow eye.

Sure you did.

TWELVE

He didn't go back to the post. Instead, he drove out to the scene.

There wasn't much left to see. Deem's body was in Anchorage. A moose had trampled the tire track. He'd already quartered the area looking for a crumpled shotgun shell, a cigarette butt. There was nothing else. This killer had been very neat.

What other questions could be asked that would need answering? Louis Deem had made himself unfit to live, and someone had taken vigilante action. All of the more recent suspects, Howie, Bernie, Abigail, Father Smith, had been questioned. All of them had alibis.

The only evidence Jim had from the scene implicated Howie, but as Howie's own statement showed, anyone could have taken off in Howie's truck, and Jim himself wouldn't have voted to convict on the evidence of the tire track alone, especially when he couldn't show motive.

Frank Rickard had gotten back to him finally. So far as Rickard knew, Louis Deem had died intestate. "Slippery son of a bitch probably thought he could get out of dying, too," the lawyer had said cheerfully. "Have to say I'll miss him. I never cross-examined better than I did when I was defending Louis Deem."

"My heart bleeds for you," Jim had said, and hung up.

So Howie had no expectation of inheriting. He frowned at the gravel road, hands tucked into his jacket pockets. What had he missed? He'd gathered all the evidence there was. He'd talked to anyone who'd had a motive.

Why was Louis Deem on this road?

He looked up, and in the lessening light saw the Quilaks hulking like the bullies they were against the eastern horizon. Halfway between earth and sky, from a flying wedge of rock, lights twinkled at him. Park headquarters.

Louis Deem's body had been found on the sole access road to Park headquarters. Beyond this point there was nothing else. From the blood he had been lying in, Deem had been shot at the scene, so he'd ridden out here with his killer. But what if he'd been on his way to the Step anyway?

Which prompted the question, What business would he have had there?

He was sitting in Dan's office, waiting, when Dan got back from the Roadhouse an hour later.

"Jim," Dan said, startled. "What are you doing here?"

Jim pointed at the wall. "Looking at your map."

Dan followed Jim's finger while he took off his jacket and hung it up. "Oh. Well." He went back behind his desk and sat down. "Whenever you need to." His grin looked a little stiff. "We serve at the pleasure of the taxpayer."

"Is it my imagination or are you granting a lot more exploratory leases on Park ground?"

Dan sat back. "I wouldn't say a lot more," he said warily. "Why?"

Jim shook his head. "I'm just seeing a lot more brown on that map than I did the last time I looked at it. Kate was mentioning it the other day, so I thought I'd come take a look for myself."

They contemplated the map together in silence. "The thing is, Dan, I keep wondering why Louis Deem was found on the road up to the Step."

Dan fiddled with a pencil. "It's a pretty lonely piece of road, Jim. We fly out of here a lot more than we drive, and not many people live much past the Gette place."

"So you think the killer drove him up here because he could be pretty sure he wouldn't be seen, booted Louis out of the truck, shot him, and drove back down to town?"

Dan shrugged. "I guess."

"You're probably right," Jim said.

Dan shrugged again.

"But I wonder if maybe Louis wasn't headed up here to begin with," Jim said. "Howie and Willard said he didn't go home the morning I turned him loose. He didn't go up to the Smiths'. Nobody else saw him. There just aren't that many roads out of Niniltna, Dan."

Dan said nothing.

Jim leaned forward, elbows on his knees, and looked down at his clasped hands. "I was wondering if maybe you saw something at the scene that you forgot to mention."

"Forgot what?"

Jim looked over at the map. "Kate thinks Louis Deem had something going on with Father Smith, something to do with gold mining on Salmon Creek. I haven't had time to run a title search, but I figured you'd know. Do the Smiths own the subsurface mineral rights to their property?"

There was a long silence. At the end of it, Dan sighed. He reached into a drawer and pulled out a manila envelope. He held it out to Jim.

Jim took it. A corner of the envelope had a dried brown stain on one corner. He removed the document and unfolded it. It was in fact the title to a piece of property whose legal description as near as he could figure it matched the location of the Smiths' forty acres, and they did in fact retain subsurface mineral rights, grandfathered back to the first owners of the property, circa 1896.

The most interesting thing on the document was the fact that it listed co-owners. Aloysius Conrad Smith and Louis James Deem. He looked up at Dan. "You figure Louis was bringing this up here to apply for permission to dig for gold?"

Dan nodded miserably.

"You take this off the body?"

"Yes."

"Ah hell, Dan."

"I'm sorry, Jim," and indeed, Dan looked wretched. "It was sticking out of his jacket pocket, ready to fall out. I was half in the bag already, and I wasn't thinking. I picked it up, and when I did, I knew what it was right away."

"What," Jim said, disgusted, "you were afraid I'd think you'd shot him for it?"

"No!" Dan said, stung. He got up and went to stand in front of the window. Over his shoulder he said, "You don't know what it's like nowadays, Jim. The Park Service is barely holding its own against an administration that wants public lands wide open for resource extraction. It's a battle every goddamn day." He turned. "I don't want them digging for gold on Salmon Creek, Jim. I figured if I took the title, it'd take the Smiths a while to get a new one." He tried to smile. "You know the federal government. You can't get shit if you don't have all the proper forms properly filled out. I figured if I lost their title, it might slow them down a little bit. Give me some more time to figure out how to stop them."

"So Kate was right."

Dan nodded again. "I think it's always been about the gold. I think it's why Smith bought the land in the first place, and I think Louis Deem bankrolled the purchase. I think it's why Louis Deem proposed to Abigail, and I think it's why Smith let him. I think they were both a couple of get-rich-quick schemers out for the easy money. Well. Smith probably still is."

"Anyone who's ever mined for gold knows that gold mining is anything but easy," Jim said dryly.

"Would have been for Louis," Dan said. "Seventeen kids to do all the work for him, and Papa Smith to run the show. All Louis had to do was get married, and he was good at that."

They sat in silence for a moment. "Now what?" Dan said.

Jim refolded the title and put it back in the envelope. "I'll take this with me." He stood up. "Anything else you forgot to tell me?"

"No. Jim, I—"

Jim headed for the door. "You shouldn't have lied to me, Dan."

"I know, Jim, and I—"

But Jim was already gone.

The next morning Jim's phone was ringing as he walked into the post. "ME on line one, Jim," Maggie said.

"Thanks." Jim went into his office and picked up the receiver. "Hey, Susan."

The voice in his ear was a low contralto and sexy as hell. In appearance, Dr. Susan Terry more than lived up to the advertising, a plump redhead with creamy skin and navy blue eyes. "You don't write, you don't call. . . ." She let her voice trail away suggestively.

His laugh was halfhearted and unconvincing. "How are you, Susan?"

"All the better for talking to you," she said, and waited some more.

"Yeah," he said, and for the life of him couldn't summon up any more enthusiasm than that.

Her voice changed. "You sound like hell. How are things in the Park?"

"I'm hoping they're about to get a little better," he said. "What have you got for me on Louis Deem?"

She and Jim had had a thing back when he was stationed in the Mat-Su Valley busting meth labs and pot grows and she was a newbie at the state crime lab. They had parted amicably, and Jim had never had any problems getting results early and often out of the lab, reason enough for him to keep up the phone flirtation. Besides, he enjoyed it, dammit.

"Death was caused by massive exsanguination and total cardiac failure caused by a single shotgun blast to the chest at point-blank range."

"Yeah, I kinda figured that when I saw the great big hole in his chest," Jim said. "What else?"

The sexy voice acquired a distinct frost around the edges. "There is no sign he was restrained. No rope burns, no duct tape residue. No evidence of drugs of any kind, not so much as an aspirin."

"Time of death?"

"Between four P.M. and six P.M. the afternoon before he was found."

"Can't narrow it down any more than that?"

"Temps were below freezing that night. This is as good as it gets. Jim?"

"What?"

"From what I've heard about Louis Deem, he wasn't the kind of a guy to let just anyone come up at him with a shotgun."

"No. He knew his killer. I've known that from the moment I saw the body. Any way we can tell what kind of shotgun?"

He could almost hear her shrug. "Kind, sure, twelve-gauge. No way of knowing if it was a single or a double, since the killer only used one shot. And unless you bring me the weapon with the blood still on it, no way of identifying the weapon from the wound."

"Great," Jim said with a sigh.

"You sound almost relieved."

"If I've got nowhere to go, I can't go anywhere," Jim said. "And I've got other cases. Anything new on Enid and Fitz Koslowski?"

"The boy and his mother from a couple weeks back? Did you find me a weapon?"

He and Kenny had done everything but rip up floorboards at Deem's place. There had been a locked gun cabinet in the living room with three rifles and two shotguns in it. No pistols, though. "No."

"Well, when you do, I've got a couple of nine-millimeter bullets we've got a better than even chance of matching to it."

"Okay. Thanks, Susan."

Her voice changed back into its customary purr. "Any time, Jim. Any time."

Meanwhile, back at the homestead, Kate was at the bread board again. Olive and rosemary bread, with garlic and onions. Garlic and bread dough. It was a partnership as natural and inevitable as peanut butter and jelly. Meat and potatoes. Kirk and Spock.

She set the timer for fifteen minutes and began kneading in earnest, balancing her weight between slightly spread feet and letting her shoulders and the heels of her hands do all the work.

Jack Morgan would have laid out the Deem murder in a precise chronology and would have asked, no, demanded her opinion. But Jim Chopin wasn't Jack Morgan. She was still getting used to that.

The dough felt good, smooth, resilient, giving up a sigh of escaping air often enough to ensure that its presence was felt.

Jim's workload was such that he was glad to put her on the payroll when he needed an extra pair of eyes, her investigative skills a welcome addition to the ongoing work of the Niniltna trooper post. Particularly in those cases that were specific to the Park, where Kate's relationships, by blood to half the Park rats and by history to the other half, had proved invaluable.

But Jim hadn't asked her to look into the death of Louis Deem.

She wondered what partnerships theirs could be compared to.

Holmes and Watson. Spade and Archer.

Wile E. Coyote and the Roadrunner.

After her remarks in the Roadhouse parking lot, Jim would think she didn't care who killed Louis Deem so long as Louis Deem was well and truly dead.

Well, that was true enough. Louis Deem deserved killing if anyone ever did, although she was uneasily aware this was specious reasoning in the extreme.

Kate had never felt what Matthew Arnold called that spark of faith. She didn't believe in God, or heaven, or hell, and what she'd seen of organized religion she didn't like. She had a rooted objection in being told what to think or how to act by anyone.

She did believe in the earth, in its generous, regenerative spirit, in its (so far) seemingly eternal capacity to take beating after beating and come back for more. She believed in life as something to be cherished, something made all the more precious by its brevity. She often thought that this belief was what had led her into law enforcement. There could be no more heinous crime than to deprive someone of their brief moment of walking with the sun on their face.

True, most people didn't seem to know how to walk, let alone turn up their faces to that sun. Some even seemed determined to squander it—every one of Louis Deem's wives, for example—but that was their call. Her job, as she saw it, was to make sure no one deprived them of that choice, to commit the grandest theft of all.

The timer pinged.

As someone had stolen Louis Deem's life.

She oiled a bowl, put the dough inside, and covered it with Saran Wrap.

As Louis Deem had stolen the lives of Enid and Fitz Koslowski.

On the face of it, it wasn't even close to a fair trade.

She set the bowl to one side, grabbed her parka, and went out to sit on the rock.

The rock in question sat on the edge of the bluff that fell to the creek below. Over the trees on the other side she could see dirty-white mountains hulking bad-temperedly beneath a sky going rapidly grayer. There was a front coming in out of the gulf, and the soft touch of the breeze on her cheek promised rain. Mutt sat at her feet, the solid, reassuring warmth both companionship and comfort. She put her hand on Mutt's head and Mutt looked up at her with inquiring eyes. Her coat had grown out to where Kate wouldn't have noticed the patch Jennie had shaved off. The stitches had been completely absorbed, and the scar was almost invisible. The mischief was back in Mutt's eye, the bounce back in her step, and she was hunting again.

Kate wondered if perhaps it might be time for the both of them to hunt up Howie Katelnikof and acquaint him with the error of his ways.

Just what punishment short of death was adequate for someone who had come so close to taking Mutt's life?

She did not dare go. She most especially did not dare go with a weapon. She looked down at Mutt's massive gray form, the dog's jaw open and panting slightly. It was hard to remember the tiny, emaciated, mistreated puppy, so unaccustomed to having a hand raised to her in anything but violence, painstakingly building trust until she would allow Kate to tip milk into her mouth from a spoon. For a while Kate was sure Mutt would lose her injured eye, and that her left hind leg would never heal.

Taking care of Mutt had taken all her waking hours and some of her sleeping ones, a welcome occurrence back then, when her nights were filled with dreams of children fleeing monsters but never quite escaping and her days with the reminder in the mirror of the last monster and his last victim.

She reached up and touched the scar on her neck, a ridge of thin white skin not so noticeable as it had once been.

The aunties had given her Mutt when she came home from Anchorage. For the first time, Kate wondered if it hadn't been Emaa's idea. Kate had been so angry back then, she'd lashed out at everyone. Ekaterina would have known that any gift from her would be unwelcome.

She decided not to ask Auntie Vi.

She took a deep breath and let it out.

Now that Louis Deem was dead, Howie would be a free agent. There was no chance he would take the opportunity to go straight, and he wasn't smart enough to stay out of trouble for long. Eventually he would slip, and she'd be there to catch him. One thing she had on her side was time.

Her hand tightened in Mutt's ruff. Glorious time. "We're immortal again, girl."

Mutt grinned up at her, yellow eyes glinting, tongue lolling out of the side of her mouth.

They sat there for some minutes, watching the dark clouds creep nearer, pregnant with moisture, rain or snow, probably both.

Kate was expecting it, hoping for it, but when it came, it still surprised her, still sent that not quite thrill, not quite chill down her spine and up again to raise the hair on the back of her neck. Three notes, each sustained, each descending, each equal in length and purity of tone. The call of the golden-crowned sparrow, the advance man of spring.

Her grandmother had died having made it clear that she wanted Kate to follow in her footsteps as leader of their tribe, the village, the entire Park, to step into her grandmother's shoes as the head of the Niniltna Native Association and one of the most influential leaders of the state of Alaska. She hadn't gone that far, but no matter what Auntie Vi said, in her own way Kate knew she had fulfilled Emaa's expectations. For whatever misguided reason, people seemed to follow where Kate led them, even if it was only by example in living a life where the definition of a good citizen was someone who minded their own business when times were good and was there to help when the times went bad.

She wondered suddenly if this, if the lingering weight of her grandmother's expectations, was what was stopping her from taking her rifle out to Deem's place and removing Howie Katelnikof from the Park once and for all. There was a time when she could have done that. There was a time when only Jack Morgan could have stopped her.

But murder, the taking of human life, willfully, with malice, no matter the provocation, was not minding one's own business.

What would Emaa have thought of Louis Deem's murder? Kate remembered, with an inward shiver, some of the draconian methods her grandmother had employed to skew events in the Park, like bringing the killer of Park ranger Mark Miller to justice with an almost Machiavellian calculation of what would be best for her tribe. Emaa would have thought the Park well rid of Louis Deem, and her people made safer by his absence.

Emaa, in fact, would have regarded the killing of Louis Deem as taking out the trash.

"But I'm not Emaa," Kate said out loud.

Mutt looked up at her.

The song came again, the three notes and no more, and then the forest was silent but for the rustle of the wind in the trees, the forerunner of the storm.

"I'm not," she said again.

A third time came the song, the same three clear piercing notes.

Though they sat there for another half an hour, it came no more that day.

Johnny still wasn't home when Kate went back to the house, but with Louis Deem dead, she was no longer worried. Mutt vanished into the underbrush in search of dinner, and Kate went into the house to start hers. She minced some garlic and sautéed it in olive oil over low heat until it turned gold. She chopped tomatoes, canned and fresh, and added them to the garlic with salt and pepper and fresh grated nutmeg and covered the pan to let it simmer. She sliced a baking sheet full of onions, tossed them in olive oil, and put them under the broiler. She started water for pasta.

The door opened. "Yum," Johnny said.

She looked up, smiling. "Fresh tomatoes at the store today. George Perry spread the word."

Johnny sniffed at them over her shoulder. He'd shot up almost six inches over the past year. It was starting to get alarming. "You're going to be as tall as your father before your next birthday."

He grinned at her. "Eat your heart out, shorty."

"Yeah, up yours, Morgan. I don't know why I keep surrounding myself with all these overgrown white men. I couldn't find a nice Aleut my own height?"

"Bitch, bitch, bitch," he said before he caught himself.

Much to his relief, she laughed. "Shut up and set the table."

Half an hour later they sat down to heaping plates of penne

pasta in a tomato sauce Johnny pronounced adequate, which nearly got him hit in the head with a slice of the fisherman's bread, butter-side impact. Things might have degenerated into a full-blown food fight if they hadn't both been so hungry.

He was mopping the juice up with another slice of bread when he said guiltily, "Oh. I guess we aren't waiting for Jim?"

"No."

He ladled up seconds with alacrity and sliced more bread. "Kate, has Jim said anything more to you about Fitz and his mom?"

"No," she said, pushing back her empty plate.

Jim hadn't been out to the house for three days running. She hated to admit it, even to herself, but she missed him when he was gone. And it wasn't only the sex. The sex was great, yeah, but this was more than that. She felt restless, a little cranky, like her day wasn't finished before she saw him in it. When something bad happened, or something funny or something exciting, he was the first call she wanted to make.

And how pathetic was that? There were probably only thirty-two other women out there who could say the same thing.

"Kate?"

"Huh? Oh. Sorry. What?"

"Are you guys still sure that Louis Deem was the one who killed them?"

She hesitated, and then nodded. "Yes."

He nodded. "So it's done."

"Pretty much," Kate said.

He frowned at his plate. "I keep wondering what Dad would have said about him."

"About Louis?"

"Yeah." He looked at her. "How hard would Dad look for Louis Deem's killer, do you think?"

Above all else, Jack Morgan had been a pragmatist. "He was a good cop, Johnny," Kate said. "One of the best I ever knew. Smart, skilled, and tenacious as hell."

"But?"

She smiled a little. "He was also very practical. He would put his effort where he thought it would produce the best result. Least effort, most effect. He wasn't going to waste the taxpayer's dollar and the court's time on a case that wouldn't stand up to a reasonable doubt."

"That's what I figured." He sat back. "I miss Fitz."

"I know," she said gently. "I hope you always do. Fitz should be remembered."

They cleared the table. She washed, he dried. As he was putting away the dishes he said, "Boy, I guess Bernie totally lucked out."

"Why?"

"Didn't Jim tell you? He's Bernie's alibi. Bernie and him were knocking back espresso at the Riverside Café at the exact time Louis Deem was shot." He looked over at her. "Kate? What's wrong?"

The need for an answer was interrupted when Auntie Vi's Eddie Bauer Ford Explorer nosed down the track and into the clearing.

"Oh man," Johnny said, and vanished into his bedroom.

THIRTEEN

Hey, Auntie," Kate said, opening the door as Auntie Vi mounted the steps to the deck.

Nobody knew how old Auntie Vi was, partly because she jealously guarded the information and partly because no one was issuing birth certificates to Native children in the Bush when Auntie Vi had been born. She had to be in her eighties by now, although her hair was still black and shiny as a raven's wing, which most certainly owed something to the ministrations of Auntie Balasha, her personal hairdresser, and her step was as light as a teenager's, which owed nothing to no one, unless she had a fountain of youth hidden in the back bedroom.

No, unlike Old Sam, she didn't show her age, but they each seemed ageless and indestructible in their own ways. And with a store of wisdom acquired over years of living, and the confidence that wisdom brought, they both shared an unshakable belief in the rightness of their opinions.

One of which was unleashed when Kate closed the door behind her. "So, Katya," Auntie Vi said without preamble, "you thinking about what I say?"

"I thinking plenty about what you say, Auntie."

"You don't mock, Katya," Auntie Vi said sharply. "This too important for making fun."

"I'm sorry, Auntie," Kate said. She put on hot water for tea and got out the cookies and her self-control.

Auntie Vi sat down at the table, very erect. It took an inordinately long time for the water to boil. Kate was sure there was a metaphor in there somewhere. She brought the tea and cookies to the table and sat down, grateful for silence. It gave her a brief space of time to gather her composure, on the ragged edge after Johnny's startling news.

Jim was Bernie's alibi? How convenient was that?

Auntie Vi took a sip of tea and a bite of a cookie and pushed both away. "There is board meeting next week, Katya. You should go."

"I got thrown out of the last board meeting I went to, Auntie."

A finger poked her shoulder, hard. "This time you be quiet. Listen. Learn." She gave a sharp nod.

"Auntie, I've never been an officer of a group. I've never joined a group I could be an officer of. I wasn't even on the student council in high school."

Auntie Vi was unyielding. "You learn."

Swish, two points, Auntie Vi.

They sipped more tea, munched more cookie. Johnny poked a cautious head out the door of his room, smelled the tension in the air, retreated noiselessly back behind his moat and pulled up the drawbridge. Mutt, after trotting over to greet Auntie Vi, had returned to the rag rug in front of the fireplace, and to all appearances was soundly asleep with her nose beneath her tail.

Kate cast about for a topic to divert Auntie Vi. "I was thinking about Emaa today, Auntie. I was wondering what she would think about Louis Deem."

"I tell you exactly what Ekaterina would say," Auntie Vi said, in the manner of one bringing the sermon down from the mount. "That Louis a bad boy, very bad, bad for his wives, bad for their families, bad for the village, for the tribe, for the Park. You think it bad that he dead? No! Good! Good for girl children! Good for families! Good for village!"

"I know, Auntie. But I was wondering if she would think the way he died was right."

Auntie Vi's face darkened. "You like this always, even little girl Katya poking her nose in everywhere, nobody's business is theirs it isn't hers, too. Good that you became police detective. Good, I say to Ekaterina, good all the aunties and uncles say. Nosy girl grow up into nosy woman, go to work at nosy job. Good. Maybe help peoples. That good, too. Maybe, Ekaterina say, maybe she come home and help her peoples. We all say, that be very good!"

Kate dropped her forehead into her hand.

Auntie Vi didn't notice. "But then you don't come home. No. You stay in Anchorage."

"I'm here now, Auntie," Kate said tiredly to the surface of the table. "I've been here for almost seven years. Don't you think you could maybe, oh, I don't know, let that go?"

"Anchorage!" Auntie Vi said, curling her lip. "Your people here, but you stay there. And then you come home!" Auntie Vi waved her mug in emphasis. Some of the tea splashed on the table. Auntie Vi took no notice. "Finally you come home. Because you hurt." An indignant forefinger stabbed in the direction of the scar on Kate's throat. "You hurt, almost you die, so you come home. You want healing. Good, we say. But you don't come home, you stay out here. Twenty-five miles from your family, your peoples, you stay. Alone, no one to help, no way we know if you well or if you die."

Auntie Vi seized another cookie. "So. We get you puppy." The finger stabbed at Mutt, who didn't so much as twitch an ear. Kate envied her deeply, and hoped Auntie Vi didn't notice that Mutt's bedding consisted of a quilt painstakingly handmade stitch by excruciatingly small stitch for their Katya by her aunties. "You get better. All right. We forgive. You work for your peoples. You do good for them. Mostly. Partly. Some of the time. Little bits anyway. But respected, you are. Honored, you are." Auntie Vi glared. "Loved, you are!"

When Auntie Vi got really wound up she started sounding like Yoda. Kate wondered if Willard, the *Star Wars* fanatic, had ever heard Auntie Vi on a roll. Probably not. He was such an aunties' pet. They'd never yell at him. She hid a sigh and stirred more sugar into her tea.

"When I ask you to do more for your peoples, Katya, this is what you do, this craziness, what is this, Katya. Louis bad man. Bad! He hurt many peoples. He would have hurt many more. Johnny, he threaten. You! That puppy! Good that he is dead. We all know this." Auntie Vi finished her cookie in one angry bite. "Except you!"

"I didn't say that, Auntie," Kate said, startled, but her words were swept under by the flood. "It's not like I'm going after his killer."

It's not like anyone is, she thought.

There was a brief silence. Auntie Vi studied the tea in her mug and seemed to come to a decision. "This Louis Deem a very bad man, Katya." Her voice had become very soft.

"I know that, Auntie. None better."

"A very bad man," Auntie Vi repeated. "The Smith girl. She come to me."

"Abigail? When? Oh God, don't tell me she's changing her story again?"

"Not Abigail. Chloe. At the potlatch for Bernie's boy." She added, as an afterthought, "And wife."

"Chloe?"

"You know how the girls always talk to me. If I know them, if I don't, they always talk to me."

"Yes." Kate thought back to the potluck, and vaguely remembered seeing Auntie Vi with Chloe. "Why would she need to—?" Kate stopped.

The silence hung heavy in the room. At last Kate said, almost imploringly, "No. No, Auntie."

Inexorable, Auntie Vi nodded once, up and down. "Yes. I see Chloe at potlatch for Enid and Fitz. She looking like she lost her last friend, so I bring her fry bread. She look at my fry bread and she start to cry. I take her out back. She tell me."

Kate remembered the Smiths turning out in force at the potlatch. She remembered how annoyed she had been that they had pushed themselves into the Park's social life without invitation.

"Not only Chloe," Auntie Vi said in a hard voice. "The little girl, Hannah, too."

Without knowing how she got there, Kate found herself on her feet, shouting. "What did this guy think he was doing, marrying into a fucking harem?"

Mutt scrambled up and shot like an arrow to Kate's side. She stood, four feet planted squarely, barking and growling in every direction. She even snapped at Auntie Vi.

"Shame on you, Mutt," Auntie Vi said sharply. "You don't know who are your friends?"

Mutt barked at her, ears flattened against her head. She had heard the pain and outrage in Kate's voice, and Auntie Vi was the only other person in the room.

Auntie Vi sat very still.

Kate looked up to see Johnny standing in the door of his bedroom, his face white. He swallowed, and said, his voice very small, "Is everything all right?"

Kate put a shaking hand on Mutt's head. Bit by bit she brought herself back under control. She sat down again and concentrated on breathing in and breathing out. Mutt had stopped growling, but she remained on guard, hackles raised. "Yes. We're fine, Johnny. Everything's all right."

He looked doubtful.

"Go back into your room," she said. "Please. Just for a few more minutes."

"I didn't know the boy is there," Auntie Vi said.

It was as much of an apology as Kate would get, and she knew it.

She remembered the last look she'd had at Chloe and Hannah, pinch-faced, shivering and crying, clutching to their elder sister's hands like it was their last hope of salvation. They had been terrified and brutalized, and a great part of their lives would be spent in learning that they had been victimized, that they bore no responsibility for what had happened to them no matter how guilty they felt. An even greater part of their lives would involve trying to regain some sense of confidence in their own authority, learning to say no with the certainty that they were in the right, that they could make it stick.

And the rest of it would be spent learning how to trust again.

From now on, their lives would be all about the rape, and the dice were weighted far more in favor of their failing to survive it emotionally. Kate had worked too long in the DA's office in Anchorage with hundreds of victims just like Chloe and Hannah to harbor any illusions. As they entered their teens, they'd start rebelling against what have you got. They'd become sexually promiscuous. There was a better than even chance they'd get into substance abuse, and if it turned into a habit, they'd rob and sell themselves and very possibly murder to support it. They'd be at risk for everything from herpes to AIDS. Statistically, they were destined to have children too young, and those children would inevitably repeat the cycle begun by their parents, a cycle that they would then hand down to their children, also born too soon, culminating in a downward, self-replicating spiral that seemed to have no end.

Maybe Kate was wrong. She hoped fervently that she was. But the damage of the kind that Louis Deem had inflicted almost never stopped with one generation.

When Kate could trust herself to speak in a reasonable tone, she said, "The other girls? The littlest ones?"

"Chloe and Hannah little enough, Katya."

At Auntie Vi's reproving tone, Mutt's ears twitched. She was the only one allowed to speak to Kate like that. Kate knotted a hand in her ruff, as much for her own comfort as to enforce Mutt's restraint. "Yes," she said. "But the others?"

"Chloe and Hannah say not. We hope."

We hope. Of course Auntie Vi would have told the other aunties. Kate thought back to that morning at the Smiths' house, with Chloe and Hannah holding fast to Abigail's hands, her determination not to let them go.

Not to let them down a second time, Kate realized now. To atone for the monster she had helped bring into the house. "That's why Abigail changed her story," Kate said. "Did you know that? That she said she wasn't with Louis Deem the night Enid and Fitz were killed after all? It's not generally known because Louis wound up dead shortly thereafter, but she repudiated her statement that she was with him that night."

"Ah." Auntie Vi sat back. "She know."

"She was lying," Kate said slowly, remembering the hard expression on Abigail's face. "She said she'd been with him other nights. When Jim and I went out to talk with her the day after Dan O'Brien found Louis Deem's body, Abigail said she just hadn't been with him that night. I didn't believe her." She looked at Auntie Vi. "I don't believe her now. Chloe and Hannah told her about Louis, and Abigail changed her story, said she lied about being with him so he wouldn't have an alibi for Enid and Fitz's murders." She paused, thinking. "Why wouldn't she just tell Jim the truth?"

She knew the answer before Auntie Vi gave it to her. "I swear to those girls no one else ever know."

Not counting aunties, who were well practiced in keeping their own counsel. "Their parents?"

Auntie Vi shook her head.

"They should know."

"Girls say no. No one know. Ever."

Someone would, though. One day the girls would weary of holding it all inside, of maintaining the façade. One or the other or all three of them would crack, and all the poison would spew out all over everyone within reach, and then there would be no hiding anything. "Better they tell their parents now. We could get them some counseling."

"They say no."

"They should be tested."

"Balasha's granddaughter Desiree a nurse practitioner at the school clinic. I will get girls to her somehow. She not talk."

Kate started to say something.

Auntie Vi overrode her ruthlessly. "Their choice, Katya. If you believe nothing else, you believe that." She rose to her feet and said with decision, "Board meeting next week, Katya. You be there."

Auntie Vi's SUV was barely out of sight when Kate said, "Johnny? I'm driving into town. I won't be long, okay?"

He reappeared in his doorway. "Is everything all right, Kate?"

"Everything's fine. You okay here on your own?"

His smile was wan. "I am now."

Her answering smile was grim. "Good. I'll be back as soon as I can. Stay," she told Mutt.

"Oh hey, Kate, you don't have to—"

Affronted, Mutt flounced back to the fireplace, pawed the quilt into a pile, and lay down with her back pointedly to Kate.

"Great," Kate said, "another country heard from." She grabbed her jacket and headed for the door.

FOURTEEN

Halfway to Niniltna, Kate rounded a corner and found Willard's rusty old International stalled in the middle of the road. He was changing the left rear tire. She stopped behind him so that her headlights would help him see what he was doing in the near dark, shut off the engine, and got out.

He looked up and saw her. "Hey, Kate!"

His hands were quick and deft on the lug wrench, and the nuts clattered into the hubcap like a pinball machine ringing up points. Kate stood by on the jack and the flat was off and the spare on in two swift, sure movements.

He locked down the last nut and hoisted the flat into the back, carefully wiped down the wrench and replaced it in the toolbox bolted to the back of the cab. He disconnected the jack, wiped it down just as carefully, disassembled it, and stowed it.

He beamed at Kate, who couldn't help but beam back. They were both happy she hadn't caught him doing anything she'd have to bust him for.

"Nice job," Kate said, and Willard beamed some more.

"I like working with my hands," he said, patting the tire fondly. "They aren't so dumb as the rest of me."

"Hey," she said, pointing. "Where's Darth?"

His smile faded a little, and he patted his shirt pocket, where Anakin Skywalker in Jedi robes peeped out. "It's Anakin, Kate."

"Yeah, but didn't it used to be Darth Vader? What happened to him? He was a permanent resident there for a while."

Willard's voice dropped to a confidential whisper. "You know, Kate, a lot of people make that mistake. Everybody thinks it's Darth, but it's always Anakin on the inside. Anakin's a good guy."

He was so earnest, so sincere, so totally Willard, and Kate understood perhaps for the first time why Auntie Balasha, how all four aunties could love him enough to forgive him almost anything.

"Anakin's a good guy, Kate," Willard said again. "That black mask is just a disguise. It makes people think bad things about him. But it's Anakin underneath. And Anakin's a good guy."

"Yes, Willard," Kate said gently. "Anakin's a good guy."

Jim looked down at his desk, where the Louis Deem case file was spread out. He'd been putting it into order before tucking it away. Almost a week old now, it was colder than Barrow in January. Barring a confession, no one was ever going to find out who killed Louis Deem. The killer could start bragging, of course, but Jim didn't see that happening, either.

No, Louis Deem's murderer had got away with it. What's more, he got away with it on Jim's watch, and Jim had already heard about it from his CO in Anchorage. "Two cold cases in one year, that's about your record, isn't it, Sergeant?"

"Yes, sir."

"I should think you'd want to see to it that this didn't happen again, wouldn't you?"

"Yes, sir."

"Makes the force look bad. I don't like having to go ask the legislature for funds for a service with a reputation of not getting its man."

"No, sir. I will continue investigating the case, sir."

The mellow tones of his superior's voice, so apt for film at ten, became a little testy. "Like hell you will, Chopin. You'll get on with the job at hand."

"Yes, sir."

"We're spread thin enough as it is, we don't need our officers wasting their time on crap like this. Louis Deem was an asshole and whoever shot him did us a favor." A pause. "No one says this in public, of course."

"Of course not, sir."

Another pause. "Well. Carry on, then."

"Yes, sir. Thank you."

He closed the Deem file and set it aside. The Koslowski file was much thicker. He spread the photographs out for a last look.

A sound at the door made him raise his head.

"Hey," Kate said. She hesitated in the doorway, as if she wasn't sure of her welcome. It wasn't a feeling she was accustomed to, and it showed.

She gathered her courage and took a chance. "Been missing you."

"Me, too."

It wasn't that she sensed a lack of sincerity, but there was something else going on here. In the best Kate fashion, she decided on a frontal attack. "Are we done?"

His first line of defense was bewilderment. "What? What do you mean?"

"Come on. You haven't been out to the house in three days."

His second line of defense was humor, beginning with an unconvincing laugh. "I don't know what you're talking about. I've been busy as hell, is all. You know what this time of year is like. Half the women in the Park toughed out the winter with men they've now learned even breakup can't make look good, and all the men in the Park have cabin fever because we're gaining daylight to the tune of six minutes a day and it's still too cold to be outside working on their boats or mending their gear. Stir some booze in, and I'm on call twenty-four–seven."

Her eyes narrowed. "That's not it, either."

His third line of defense was bluster. If she were being fanciful, she would have said that it was underlaid with fear. "What's the big deal? It's not like we're living together." Very unwisely, he gave a snort and added, "Jesus, anybody'd think we were married, the way you're carrying on."

By a fraction of an inch he got to her before she was out the door. He wrested it from her grasp and closed it with a bang and backed her against it, giving her no chance of escape. "I'm sorry. I'm sorry, Kate," he said, putting every ounce of sincerity into it he could summon into existence. "That was way out of line. It's on me. There's some stuff going on, I'm a little messed up, but we, you and me, we're okay. Nothing's done, nothing's over, you got that?" When she didn't answer, he said, even more anxiously, "Kate?"

She took in a deep breath and let it out again with deliberate, not to say ostentatious slowness. "I got it. Turn me loose."

Cautiously, he relaxed the death grip he had on her shoulders. She didn't hit him or kick him or otherwise retaliate, for which he was immensely grateful.

"Prick," she said.

"Absolutely," he said.

"Asshole."

"No question."

"You're not all that hot in bed."

"Wait a minute," he said. They laughed together. The tension in the room eased.

The hell with it. "It's good to see you." Quick, before she could jump on that and turn it to her advantage, he looked around and said, "Where's the beast?"

"Left her with the kid." She hooked a thumb over her shoulder. "You here all alone?"

He looked at the clock on the wall. Eight thirty. "Oh. I guess so. I didn't realize it was so late."

"Anybody in the cells?"

He shook his head, and sat down again. He watched her close and lock the door. She walked around his desk and smiled at him. "We wouldn't want any stray Park rats seeing the resident trooper reduced to a lump of quivering jelly."

He leaned back in his chair. "Am I about to be?"

She subsided gracefully into his lap. "We can only hope." She kissed him. He did not resist.

When she raised her head he examined her expression. She stared back, the corners of her mouth indented in a small smile.

"I'm sorry about the AWOL," he said, and then thought, Who said that?

What the hell. He let it stand.

She kissed him again.

"So we're okay?"

She kissed him a third time, and this time she put some body English into it.

Good enough. It had been a cold and lonely three days, and Kate's bed was infinitely more comfortable than any of Auntie Vi's rentals.

She nuzzled her face into his neck, her breath warm on his throat.

Yeah. It was all about the bed.

"Jim?"

"What?"

"Who invited whom for coffee that afternoon?"

He stiffened. "What?"

"And how specific was he on what time you should be there?"

He closed his eyes. He'd known this moment would come. He just hadn't thought it would come so soon. It was never a good idea to hook up with a smart woman.

Her raspy voice was even lower than usual. He had to strain to hear her. "When Louis Deem was killed, you and Bernie were having coffee at the Riverside Café. You're Bernie's alibi."

"We just ran into each other. Had a cup of coffee, shot the breeze. You know, like guys do."

"When was the last time you ran into Bernie at the Riverside Café?"

"You know how it is, Kate. Laurel's got the only espresso maker in town."

"Laurel was running the Roadhouse that day."

"She's got good help. That Heather's got the makings of a great little barista."

"So you just happened to run into Bernie on the exact day at the exact time that Louis Deem was murdered?"

"Give or take an hour," he said. "According to the ME."

"I stopped by Bobby's on my way here. He told me you questioned Bernie about it." She shifted a little. "I figure that would have been right before we bumped into each other in the Roadhouse parking lot."

"Yes."

"Logical," Kate said, complimentary. "Deem kills Bernie's wife and son, when Deem is murdered, Bernie's one of the first people to have to talk to."

"S-O-P," Jim said.

"At the Roadhouse," Kate said.

Jim shrugged. "Where Bernie works."

"In front of at least a hundred people."

Jim nodded. "At least that many."

"Pretty public interrogation."

"Pretty much."

"Almost like you wanted an audience."

"I did ask him if we could go back to his house."

"Almost like it was staged."

Jim paused almost imperceptibly. "But he refused," he said. "He insisted I talk to him right there in the bar."

Kate nodded, her face rubbing against his shoulder. "Yeah, I heard that, too."

"He wasn't under arrest, Kate. It wasn't like I could compel him or anything."

His hands slid around her waist, one coming to rest inside her T-shirt, warm and firm at the small of her back.

She sighed. "That feels good. Rub a little?"

He rubbed. Gradually her body relaxed, becoming a warm, solid weight. After a while he realized she'd dozed off. He looked down at the face resting on his shoulder, at the black lashes fanned across the cheekbones clad in golden skin. He shifted in his chair, pulling her more comfortably onto his lap, and she grumbled and wriggled and was still again.

Was that all she was going to say about it? Was it just that she wanted him to know that she knew?

He looked past her at the Koslowski case file spread out across his desk, at the photographs in all their stark black-and-white cruelty. Carefully, he reached past Kate with his free hand and returned them to the file folder, one by one.

Enid Koslowski sprawled on her back on the stairs, eyes surprised and staring. Fitz, the fourteen-year-old science whiz, face-down below her. The heavy wooden door with the stained glass panels standing wide open to the night. The broken glass of the curio cabinet, the shards scattered across the living room floor, intermingling with the litter of toys and tracked out into the hallway and onto the porch, half-built Lego spaceships, red Monopoly hotels, Clue cards and board that had been used to build a playpen for a blond and black-taped Barbie, action figures from every kids' movie made in the last thirty years, Shrek, Woody, Vader. Or rather Vader's head. The rest of him seemed to be missing in action. Or not, there was the body a couple of feet away. Willard Shugak would have been beside himself.

It took him a while to realize that it had been several minutes sinced he'd breathed. Or blinked. The photograph of the Koslowskis' front porch with the head of the Vader doll at the top of the stairs, one corner crumpled where his fist had clenched on it, blurred and then came back into sharp, almost painful focus.

He closed his eyes and thought back, willing the scene to come to him in its entirety. Willard at the Deem place, Willard in the red, white, and blue polka-dot pajamas that were three sizes too big for him, Willard corroborating everything that little weasel Howie Katelnikof said. Willard, a bigger, dumber version of Louis Deem, a guy just intelligent enough to grasp the storyline of a movie but not smart enough to tell fact from fiction or right from wrong, a guy—

The photograph he was holding swam back into focus, the head and body of the action figure of Darth Vader that Willard was never without, riding in his left front shirt pocket, an amulet, a talisman, a totem.

A coconspirator. "Anakin and me."

The last time he'd seen Willard had been at Deem's house. It was also, he realized now, the first time he'd ever seen Willard without Darth Vader riding shotgun in his left front shirt pocket.

It hadn't been Darth looking over the edge of Willard's pajama pocket that day. It had been Darth's alter ego, Anakin Skywalker, he of the no helmet and the brown robe instead of the black body armor.

He noticed that his hand had tightened on the photograph, crumpling it, and he made a conscious effort to relax.

Willard looked like Louis Deem. So did Howie. So did a lot of other Park rats their age, as the line of volunteers for the lineup had shown. But Willard was almost the same height, with the same coloring and the same general shape of head and shoulders. Johnny could easily have mistaken one for the other, in the dark, in fear of his life. They were all so used to regarding Willard as incapable of independent thought or action, no one had even considered him as a possible suspect. Jim least of all.

Kate had been right. The smash-and-grab had none of the usual Louis Deem characteristics.

Louis had bankrolled the Smiths' purchase of the forty acres. He'd affianced himself to the Smiths' oldest daughter to secure his interest.

Like everyone else in the Park, Louis knew about the gold nuggets in Bernie's case. He would also have known about the notes that accompanied them. One of the nuggets had come from Salmon Creek. He remembered the map in Dan O'Brien's office, the steady erosion of green, the steady encroachment of brown.

Louis would have been certain, though. And he could have deliberately speculated on the possibility of hitting Bernie's gold, in the comfort of his own home, a beer in his hand, feet in front of the fire.

An attentive audience at hand.

He could also have mentioned how important the little slips of paper that accompanied each nugget were. The papers that could give someone who knew how to read a map that little extra edge in finding where that nugget came from. Willard wouldn't have learned it from being told only once, but Louis had had months after his acquittal to tell the same story over and over again.

Jim had seen Willard frightened. The flight reflex was always ascendant at those times. He didn't think Willard even saw whoever was in front of him when he started to run, he just mowed them down like a bull moose running from a grizzly and kept on going.

Why the gun, though?

Again, Kate was right, Louis would never have taken a gun along with him on a simple burglary. You could walk on a burglary charge. Armed robbery guaranteed time, serious time.

Why would Willard take a gun with him?

Jim didn't have to think too long about that. Willard understood the criminal justice system only as a provider of a warm night inside, complete with Oreos, Fig Newtons, and on special occasions Nutter Butters. He lived and breathed *Star Wars*. Jim had seen the first movie a few times himself. *"Ancient weapons and hokey religions are no match for a good blaster at your side, kid."*

"Christ." It was a moment before he realized he'd said the word out loud.

Willard Shugak had made a clumsy attempt to do a job that his idol, Louis Deem, had only thought about out loud. Whether Louis had meant that to happen was anyone's guess. Maybe Howie knew. Maybe not.

Willard had bungled the job, as everyone but himself would have had every reason to expect.

And in his panic-stricken flight, he had dropped Darth Vader and had killed two people. He'd stepped on it and broken it on his way out, never noticing the loss.

Jim stared at the photograph, his mind going in circles. What the hell did he do now? He had no proof, only a *Star Wars* action figure in a house with three kids.

If Willard's fingerprints were on the head of the doll . . . He thought back. Had he bagged it? No. He had not, he hadn't thought of it as evidence, he had thought of it only as part of the detritus of Bernie's kids.

And what would it change? Willard would be inside and Louis Deem would be exonerated.

And Louis Deem would still be dead.

He looked down at Kate and found her eyes open, looking back at him. "What?" she said.

"What?" he said.

She pushed herself upright and ran her fingers through her hair. "My chair got awfully tense." She stretched and arched her back. "What's wrong?"

"Nothing," he said. He didn't know why he'd lied. He only knew he couldn't tell her the truth.

She caught sight of the photos. "Oh."

"I was putting the file in order before I put it away."

She looked at the photographs. "Ugly."

"Very."

"At least he's dead."

How could he tell her? How could he tell her that her simple cousin had committed a double murder? How could he tell Willard's grandmother, Auntie Balasha, that good woman, who saw only the best in everyone she met?

"Jim?"

He met her eyes and thought back to that moment of truth in this very office that bleak afternoon.

"What is it you want me to do, Bernie?"

"Your job."

And then the phone call the next day, and he had gone, knowing what it meant, practicing law enforcement professional that he was, sworn to protect and to defend, to fight for the right, to uphold the law, to enforce the Constitution of the United States of America. He had gone, knowing exactly what the invitation meant, and he had spent ninety minutes sitting there talking to Bernie, although he couldn't for the life of him remember what had been said.

If he was right, if Willard had killed the Koslowskis, then Louis Deem had been killed in error.

How could he tell Kate any of this?

And how could he not?

There was a knock at the door. Someone tried the handle. "Jim?" It was Auntie Vi. "You in there, Jim?"

Kate got up and unlocked the door. Auntie Vi stood behind it, her eyes stern, her mouth a white, strained line. She looked straight at Kate. "Come. Now."

"What is it, Auntie? What's happened?"

Jim got to his feet, only to be stayed by an unmistakably authoritative palm. She spoke to Kate and only to Kate. "Billy."

A tendril of dread slithered up Kate's spine. "What about him?"

"Dead." The word was a single-syllable dirge.

Jim moved out from behind his desk, and was again halted by Auntie Vi's hand. "Heart attack. Playing basketball with town team at the gym. Annie tell him and tell him he need to lose weight, need to stop eating salt, stop sneaking smokes. He not listen." She was still looking unblinkingly at Kate. "You come."

The dread spread into her gut. "Auntie—"

"You come now." Auntie Vi turned and left.

Kate stood staring at the door.

"Kate?" he said.

She turned her head, and what he saw on her face made him say, "Are you okay?"

She took her time answering, and when she did, her voice was devoid of feeling. "No," she said. "I'm not okay." She looked at him, mournful, miserable. Resigned.

"I'm an elder."

She looked again at the door. Her shoulders squared, and one foot moved out, followed by the other, slowly and very carefully gathering forward momentum.

It was like watching the march of the dead.

Which perhaps it was, and not only in honor of the death of the elder just passed.

Jim stared at the empty doorway until he heard Kate's pickup start and drive away.

FIFTEEN

The Roadhouse was packed to the rafters the next Saturday night. Billy Mike's potlatch at the gym had been the usual alcohol-free zone, and more than one Park rat felt the need for their anesthetic of choice after six hours of listening to everyone from the lieutenant governor to Senator Pete Heiman to Billy's wife, Annie, tell Billy stories. The food had been worth it, though, folding tables had literally groaned beneath the moose pot roasts and the salmon piroque and the hundred loaves of banana bread.

Kate resisted every effort made to push her to the microphone, and they were numerous, instead constituting herself an aide de camp to the four aunties, who were busy ladling out plates of food. But when the line eased off, she was dispatched forthwith to help Annie hand out gifts, beaded earrings Annie had made herself, boxes of food for elders, gift certificates to Costco for parents with children, gift certificates to Chugach Air Service for the young unmarried adults. Visiting dignitaries got soapstone carvings made by Tom Shugak, Niniltna's resident artist. The caliber of the gifts given at a potlatch indicated the status of the dead, and Annie appeared to be determined that no one would have cause to criticize her husband's standing in his tribe. Kate just hoped she wasn't going to bankrupt herself. She had one more child to raise, after all.

For her part, Annie was acting less like a bereaved widow and more like an auntie in training. With the giving of every gift, she drew Kate into the conversation, making her known where she wasn't, although that didn't happen often, and where she was known making it clear that Kate had all her confidence. Kate, about as uncomfortable as she'd ever been in her life, came very close to legging it out the back door, and was thwarted only by the collectively formidable glare of the aunties, a phalanx of woman warriors that would have put the Amazons to shame. Mutt, too, was never very far from her side, displaying a positive genius for being in the way whenever Kate even thought about making a move.

It was with heartfelt relief that Kate saw the last guest out the gym door, and she managed to time the last load of trash out to the Dumpster with the arrival of Jim in her truck, which she had left at the post that morning when the aunties en masse had picked her up. She swung the bag into the trash and vaulted into the driver's seat in one movement, Jim sliding over just in time, Mutt taking Kate and the steering wheel in one leap to land foursquare in his lap. He didn't scream out loud but it was a near thing.

Kate slammed the door and the truck into gear with one movement, and the tires spit gravel against the wall of the gym. "Where's Johnny?"

"With Van and the rest of the kids at the Mikes' house. He told me to tell you he was going to spend the night."

They bounced down the hill toward town. Kate made as if to take the turn for home when Jim shoved Mutt's head out of the way to say, "I passed Harvey Meganack on the way up. He took the turn for the Ahtna road."

She slammed on the brakes and they lurched to a halt. Even

Kate, no coward, quailed at the prospect of one of the four remaining members of the Niniltna Native Association camped out on her doorstep, lying in wait. She couldn't avoid them forever, she knew that perfectly well, but it had been a very long day. "I don't have any beer at the house."

This was something of a non sequitur. Kate never had liquor of any kind at the house unless Jim brought it in. "Shame," Jim said. "I could really use a beer. Why don't we go out to the Roadhouse?"

Kate put the truck in gear again. "Sounds like a plan."

On the other side of Niniltna, Jim said, "Did you get anything to eat?"

She hadn't, and her stomach took this opportunity to say so.

"I bet Dinah's got some of this winter's caribou left."

The bed of the pickup slid sideways as Kate took the turn down the road that led over Squaw Candy Creek.

We're getting awful goddamn good at potlatches," Bobby said glumly.

"I'll miss him," Dinah said. "Billy. You know how Alaskans are. If you weren't born here, there are people who will never remember your name, even if you've been introduced to them nine times already. Whenever there was something or someone I wanted to shoot, Billy was always ready to pave the way."

"Billy knew," Kate said, looking up from her plate. "Billy knew that there's a way of life going on in rural Alaska right now that isn't going to survive the people living it. He could never get the board to agree to hire someone to come in and start taping elder stories, and then you appeared. Billy thought you were an answer to a personal prayer."

"It's going to be tough for Annie," Jim said. "Raising that baby on her own."

"And what'll happen to the board?" Bobby said. "Who takes over as chairman?"

They all looked at Kate. She shrugged and looked back down at her plate.

"Don't you like the steaks, Kate?" Dinah said.

"No, they're great," Kate said, taking a bite to prove it.

Jim, watching her, said nothing.

He was still doing his best to forget about Louis Deem's murder and his part in it. Kate hadn't raised the subject again, for which he was profoundly thankful.

He still didn't know what to do about Willard. He could question him, try to find out if Willard knew what Louis had done with the gold and the slips of paper, but he knew from experience just how short-term Willard's memory was. And what would finding the gold prove if Willard didn't remember stealing it?

Jim could just imagine the expression on Judge Singh's face if he tried to get a warrant for Willard's arrest out of a second lineup, even if Johnny could persuade himself that it was Willard he'd seen in Bernie's house that night and not Louis Deem at all.

And then there was Kate. He cast a covert glance her way. She looked solemn, and remote, and a little sad. Probably thinking about Billy. Probably thinking about the vacancy his death had left on the Association's board of directors. One of the aunties had been out to the house every day since Billy's death. It was almost as if they were making sure Kate was still there, in the Park.

What would happen if he didn't tell her about Willard? Was he really prepared to keep that secret from Kate? For how long? It wasn't as if a state trooper didn't know how to keep his mouth shut—hell, any cop worthy of the name could medal in it.

Kate had a natural ability to ferret out secrets, one of the reasons she'd been such an asset to the DA's office. What if she found out on her own? Would she ever trust him again? He remembered the scene with Dan O'Brien and winced inwardly.

"Been out to see the Smiths lately?" Bobby said.

"Huh? Oh." Jim shook his head. "Not since Abigail recanted Deem's alibi. Not much point, now that he's dead."

"They've got the roof finished, and they're installing the windows and doors."

"Does anyone in that family have a job?" Dinah said. "How are they paying for all those building materials?"

"Dan O'Brien thinks they're panning gold out of Salmon Creek and selling it in Anchorage." Bobby saw Jim's expression. "What?"

"Nothing." He ate another bite. "Everybody lies," he said.

"What?"

"Everybody lies," he repeated. He looked at Kate and smiled. "Except you."

Kate had been watching Katya make snowballs out of her mashed potatoes and hook them into the kitchen sink with a consistent three-point precision that would have made Magic Johnson sit up. Her thoughts were far away.

Jim had asked about Louis Deem's tooth on the way home from Ahtna. She hadn't told him then, and she wasn't going to tell him now.

The first month after she'd come home from Anchorage, with the scar on her throat still red and her nerves still raw, Ekaterina had come to the homestead and asked her to talk to Evelyn, one of the Topkok girls, barely eighteen. Louis Deem was between wives at the time and Evelyn, a lovely young girl and the daughter of one of the most successful salmon fishermen in Cordova, had unfortunately wandered into range.

Her parents had tried to end the relationship by sending Evelyn to Ahtna to stay with her older sister. Louis had been visiting her there on the sly, but of course Ekaterina had learned of it five minutes after their first meeting.

Evelyn's sister was a very silly woman who appeared to view Louis and Evelyn as a modern-day Romeo and Juliet. Far from discouraging Louis, she gave him the run of her home. Her husband, the produce manager at the local Eagle store, was gone a lot.

Her two daughters weren't.

When Kate went to Ahtna to talk to Evelyn, she walked in on Louis Deem and one of the girls, the older one, barely fourteen. He wasn't molesting her, not yet. But he had her backed into a corner. Her face was full of dread.

Kate, who had earned her scar confronting another baby raper in another city not eight weeks before, could never remember with any clarity the next few moments. It had helped that she had taken Louis totally by surprise. She'd dropped to one hand and swept his legs out from beneath him with one foot, and the next thing she knew, Evelyn was pulling her away before she kicked him in the face again.

The daughter had for a miracle told her story to everyone who would sit still for it. While Louis hadn't done enough to get arrested, he was banished from the house and from Evelyn's life. Kate had returned to the Park, where her grandmother had—naturally—already heard the story. "Enough, Katya," she had said.

"It's not enough, Emaa," Kate had told her, "I've been working these cases for over five years. This kid won't have been his first victim. They never are. And he won't stop, because they never do."

And he hadn't.

Her heart ached for Chloe and Hannah. She wanted to tell Jim about them. She wanted him to understand why she didn't care what he had done or had not done in the case of Louis Deem.

Instead she kept silent, filling her mouth, chewing mechanically and swallowing without tasting anything.

If she wasn't lying outright, she was lying by omission. Jim was right.

Everybody lied.

Even her.

The Roadhouse parking lot was full when they got there, full of caribou roast and garlic mashed potatoes and both of them feeling a little more relaxed, at least outwardly.

It would not be fair to say that there was a moment of silence when Kate walked in the door, but she hadn't gone three steps into the room before she realized she'd made a mistake in coming here instead of going straight home, mostly because the horror waiting to pounce there was of a more manageable size. The burden of expectancy gathered weight every time someone caught her eye and smiled, or reached out to pat her arm, or made a point of saying hello. Mac Devlin inclined his head as she passed, which only enhanced her feeling of unreality. And when Old Sam, sitting between Ruth Bauman and Mary Kvasnikof, in from Alaganik Bay, raised his glass and the two women followed suit, there might actually have been a momentary lull in the din.

Mutt made a beeline for Bernie, who tossed her the requisite package of beef jerky. Jim grabbed a stool. He wasn't in uniform, so Bernie brought him a draft and looked across the bar at Kate and said, "So? What're you having?"

He looked calm but somehow hollowed out. He was missing Enid. Maybe he hadn't loved her, but they'd been partners in life for over two decades and they'd had three children together. Life would be changing big-time for Bernie, and it was obvious he was already feeling it.

Kate felt Jim looking at her, and turned to meet his gaze. "What?"

"Now you know how it feels."

She stared at him, uncomprehending.

He gestured at the room with his glass. "To stop a room dead in its tracks when you walk in."

Protest rose instinctively to her lips, and died there. He was right. Probably alone in this room Jim would know what it was like to make an entrance, to know beyond question that people saw the job, not the person. To be feared. To be respected. To be sucked up to.

To be hated.

Bernie brought her a glass of soda water poured over ice and garnished with a twist of lime. Kate clutched it without looking, her eyes locked with Jim's.

"It's okay," he said. His hand slid down her arm to clasp her own. "You'll get used to it."

The worst of it was, she believed him.

He turned back to the bar, to find Bernie facing him across it. The bartender's face was untroubled, and he met Jim's eyes without a hint of doubt or guilt.

"What is it you want me to do, Bernie?"

"Your job."

That was all Bernie had asked him to do, for Jim to meet Bernie for coffee at the Riverside Café when Bernie called, and for Jim to do his job.

But Jim had known what it meant when he agreed to Bernie's requests. And when the time came he had done his job. He had dotted every *i*, crossed every *t*. There was no avenue of the investigation of the murder of Louis Deem he had not traveled to its logical end. The forensic evidence, such as it was, had been tested and documented and filed safely away. The interviews with all the witnesses had been documented and saved. He had even compiled a list of people who had grievances against Louis Deem that amounted to two single-spaced typed pages, and had ascertained their whereabouts at the time of the murder.

No, Jim had left no loose ends, nothing that would ever make anyone suspicious, nothing that future investigators would see as something that required further examination, further interviews, nothing that might bring them stumbling to the real truth.

And Bernie would never know that they had conspired to kill the wrong man.

It was a fitting price for him to pay, Jim thought now. The decision to step outside of the law he had spent a lifetime upholding should cost him a great deal.

There was a heavy feeling in his gut that he was only just beginning to know how much.

He drained his glass.

"Refill?" Bernie said.

"Sure," Jim said.

"Coming right up."

In one corner of the room at the big round table sat the four aunties—Auntie Vi, Auntie Edna, Auntie Joy, and Auntie Balasha. They were working on one of their quilts.

Bernie waved off Amy Huth, who was working the tables for him that evening, and came out from behind the bar his own self, balancing a tray of mugs on his fingertips. He moved with a smoothness acquired from years of practice through the crowd, a nod here and a smile there, making everyone feel as if the bartender of this establishment was paying personal attention to each of them, and arrived at the aunties' table to lower the tray with a wide sweep of his arm. Presentation is all.

"Ladies," he said, placing a mug before each of them. "Four

Irish coffees, blisteringly hot, with half an inch of real cream floating on top. Just like you like them."

Casually, he let one hand settle on Auntie Vi's shoulder. She left her needle in the fabric to reach up and touch it, just as casually. "Thank you, Bernie."

His hand tightened on her shoulder, almost painfully. "No, Auntie," he said. "Thank you." He looked around the circle. "Thank you all."

Tears welled in Auntie Balasha's eyes. Auntie Edna was her usual taciturn self. Auntie Joy gave her customarily radiant smile. Auntie Vi cleared her throat and patted his hand. "*Aycheewah,* you interrupt our work," she said crossly. "We never finish. Away you go."

His answering grin was a reasonable facsimile of the real thing. "And awaa-aay I go. Give me a wave when you want a refill."

Auntie Joy waited until he was safely away before she clasped Auntie Balasha's hand in sympathy. Auntie Vi spoke, not unkindly. "You know it the right thing to do, Balasha."

Auntie Balasha made a valiant effort to stem the flood. "I know, Vi. He was such a nice little boy, though. So good."

Auntie Edna was made of sterner stuff. "He was never a good boy, Balasha, little or otherwise. It is good that he is gone. He will hurt no more of the people now." And then she added the clincher. "And you know Ekaterina would say we do right."

"I know." Auntie Balasha blew her nose. Auntie Joy took up her needle again.

"Auntie?"

Auntie Balasha looked around and her face lit. "Willard!"

He looked over her shoulder and his own face brightened. "Is that my quilt?"

"Yes," Auntie Vi said, a little testily. "We promise we make. We make."

A forefinger counted the nine squares and the illustrations that had been lasered onto fabric rectangles. "Luke, Leia, Han, R2, Threepio, Chewie, Obi-Wan, Jabba." His brow creased. "Where's Anakin? Where's—?"

Before his voice could rise any further, Auntie Vi interrupted him. "He go in the middle, Willard. We not put him in yet."

"Oh. Okay."

She patted his arm. "Go tell Bernie Auntie Vi buys you a beer. Then you come back and you watch us make your quilt."

He grinned hugely and lumbered off.

Four round dumplings perched on four straight-backed chairs, four mugs of Irish coffee on the table in front of them. The nine squares of the quilt assembled as if by magic beneath four needles flashing in and out. In the center square of the quilt, Anakin's face had broadened, his hair lightened, his eyes moved farther apart and the outer corners tilted up.

Howie Katelnikof came in, talked Willard into believing that Auntie Vi had meant to buy him two beers, took one for himself, and carried it back to the aunties' corner, carefully making a wide detour around that section of the bar where Kate and Jim were sitting. He leaned against the wall, one hand in his pocket, the other holding the bottle, from which he took the occasional sip. "Nice quilt," he said.

Auntie Vi looked at him, her mouth a straight line. He took that as an invitation and came to squat next to her chair.

"What you want, Howie?" she said in a low voice.

He sipped his beer. "I could use some money," he said, his voice equally low.

"We give you money already. You say you leave the Park with it but you still here."

"Yeah, well, Auntie, I like it here." He saluted her with the bottle. "I've got family and friends here. It's hard to leave home."

She scowled down at her stitches. The other aunties remained silent, but they were listening to every word.

"No more money, Howie."

He gave her a lazy smile. "You wouldn't want me to tell anybody what you paid me to do, now, would you, Auntie?"

"You not tell," Auntie Vi said with iron certainty. Clint Black and the Pointer Sisters were belting out "Chain of Fools" on the jukebox, in competition with an NCAA tournament game on the giant television. The dance floor resembled something between a forced march and a fertility rite, and Mac Devlin had been persuaded to mount a chair and give forth with a bellowed rendition of "The Shooting of Dan McGrew." There was a continuous cry for more beer, and the Grosdidier Gang were singing sea chanties, with "Barnacle Bill the Sailor" a frequent request. Nevertheless Auntie Vi had no difficulty making herself heard. "You kill a man. If you tell, you go to jail."

"So do you, Auntie," Howie said, and saluted the entire circle of women this time, a circle of heads bent over their work. "So do you all."

Willard came back with his beer and sat next to his grandmother, watching closely as the needles flashed in and out of the fabric, building his quilt.

"Hey," he said, squinting. A joyous smile spread slowly and delightedly across his face.

"Hey, Howie, do you see? Anakin looks just like me!"

Sec. 11.41.115. Defenses to Murder

(c) A person may not be convicted of murder in the second degree . . . if the only underlying crime is burglary . . .

—Alaska statutes